Nivalis

2017

Edited By
Anirban Ray Choudhury

Cover Art: Anisha Bhaduri
Cover Design: Anirban Ray Choudhury

Published by Fabula Press in November 2017

First Edition

This book is sold subject to the condition that it shall not, by way of trade or otherwise, be lent, resold, hired out, or otherwise circulated without the publisher's prior consent in any form of binding or cover other than that in which it is published and without a similar condition including this condition being imposed on the subsequent publisher.

www.fabulapress.com

ISBN-13: 978-1981187553

ISBN-10: 1981187553

CONTENTS

ACKNOWLEDGMENTS

As always, we thank the judges Brett, Clare, Sandra and Anisha for agreeing to read and evaluate the stories in these pages, and for their professional feedback. This book would not have been possible without their support. We remain in debt of the writing groups and writers' circles, large and small, both online and off, who helped spread the word about the contest in particular and about Fabula Press in general.

FOREWORD

So here it is – our second short story contest anthology of the year. Collected from our winter short story competition Nivalis, this batch of stories represents, as always, an experiment in cutting across the boundaries of genre, building upon a common theme of love.

We start off this edition with *Box 821*, a light hearted comedy about love, loss, and love yet again in post-war London. *Rachel Wants to Die* carries on in a similar vein, with hopelessness of purpose giving way to purposeless hope that leaves the protagonist exasperated and the reader in affectionate despair. In *Lessons* an art teacher's experience with a gifted student whose love for life is only visible in her silence leads us to question our own silences. *Snowball*, too, takes a questioning stance, asking if a cat should be painted pink; and in so doing it takes a satirical look at the mistaken priorities of the world today. *How it's Always Been* puts all such questions to rest though, with its teenage existentialist ask – is it wrong to have never cried at a movie?

We tackle bits of history in *Have a Nice Day...* and in *Bullets*. While the latter weaves a coming-of-age story in the backdrop of the Irish troubles, the former takes a trip down memory lane into the cold war era through the thoughts of Martyl Langsdorf, the artist behind the Doomsday Clock.

The Mimsy Borogove is a tale with a sense of foreboding, a very modern day adaptation of Lewis Carol's poem where a sinisterly interpretation of Alice's statement "however, somebody killed something: that's clear, at any rate" hits us with full force.

Scarecrows and *Stayin' Alive* are both tales of love in 25-year old casks; mellow, refined, and earthy, where neither the thoughts of death nor dementia can steal what was, and what is.

Love is back in *Ivan by the Sea,* but with a difference, as we see a trip to a faraway land bringing the protagonist closer to himself and his own identity. *She* carries on in much the same vein but in a different context, where we are taken through an emotional journey into one woman's acceptance of herself as independent of her difficult past. *Zag,* again, is about a difficult past, about losing someone dear, and about understanding what is not-so-understandable.

The Dark Dealer in Opposites is one of the three stories in this collection that deal with the paranormal. Exploring magic-realism, this deeply evocative tale is at once philosophical and scary, bringing to mind the foolishness of yearning, more so in the collective. *The Woman* is an equally complex narrative, a literary representation of Schrödinger's paradoxical cat through the lives of two women that are one and to whom love comes as a child, as a man. Love arrives in *The Post-Mortem Composer* too, although for an unearthly being, with a more earthly evocation of music.

As I had said at the beginning of my foreword, love remains the one theme that binds all these stories. Yes, the term is used loosely, but how does one go on to define the various hues of the word as they emerge in the tales to follow? Allow me to leave you here to read on and judge the merit of my words. As to the merit of the stories we hope that you will agree that each should have its own special place, but if you are inclined to compare your own favourites with the judges', please visit our website www.fabulapress.com for the Nivalis 2017 contest results. As always, bouquets/brickbats are welcome at editors@fabulapress.com, and we will certainly appreciate honest, fair feedback on Amazon/Goodreads and the like.

~ Anirban

Box 821
Judith Wilson

Judith Wilson is a London-based writer and an alumna for the Faber Academy Writing a Novel course. She writes short stories and is currently working on her first novel. She won first prize for the 2016 Retreat West Short Story Prize and second prize for the inaugural Colm Toibin International Short Story Award 2016. Judith is also the published non-fiction author of 14 books and writes about interior design.

For Judge Clare, Box 821's succeeds as an enchanting tale for it is "beautifully realised, utterly compelling with a distinctive, and very accomplished, style and voice."

'**FOR MY ONLY DAUGHTER**, 22, pretty girl, good figure, I should like to contact Gentleman with view of Marriage, Box 821.'

North London Gazette, December 1949

Eric Silver's eyes scan the Personal section in Classifieds, thoughtful. It's not much to go on. Enough. He folds the newspaper, puts it down. He pours a tumbler of whisky and takes a sip. Then, seating himself at the roll-top desk, he plucks his Mont Blanc pen and unscrews the cap. Meticulously draws forward a pile of headed notepaper.

Dear Sir or Madam

I write in reply to your advertisement, Personal, North London Gazette.

I am a bachelor with a steady income and my own home also, modest though it is. My jewellery shop, Silver & Sons, is located in Hatton Garden (though I do not have any sons). I would like to make your daughter's acquaintance. Might this be arranged? I await your response.

Yours,

Eric Silver

He folds the letter, addresses the envelope in neat script. Box 821.

Outside it is filthy cold, threatening snow. But there's no time like the present. He shrugs on his coat and hat, winds a muffler. He's into the freezing air in minutes. It's not far to the post box, and then - it's done.

Later, turning in, he twists the silk cord of the bedside lamp lightly in his palm, thinking. He pulls the cord; the room is plunged into darkness. But hope glows inside Eric like a personal nightlight.

It has been so long, *so* long.

3

He doesn't normally read the Classifieds. He's usually too busy: a concert, or the theatre, long walks on Hampstead Heath. Keeping active, it's a distraction, his salvation. He shuts his eyes, conjures those words again, knows them by heart '... *22, pretty girl, good figure* ...' He pictures a smiling face and flushed cheeks. Perhaps she has flaming eyes and dark hair, too. A good cook, hopefully. And '*with view of Marriage* ...' Matter-of-factly stated. It is a bold concept.

Still, one never knows.

A week later, lurking in the indigo shadows of a winter afternoon, Frieda Wolf stands at the drawing room window. Nose to lace curtain, she can see the tree-lined Belsize Park road but as yet, no gentleman. She narrows her eyes. She is hoping he's tall. He needn't be handsome, but strong and healthy. She is under no illusions. She doubts he will be young. There are few eligible males left; since the war, they are all dead, injured or returned sick.

Age is not an issue.

But she's after a man who can provide a comfortable house, prospects, and a steady income. And someone a 22-year-old daughter might love.

Even if true affection, that ephemeral layer of marriage, comes last.

She starts at the sharp rat-a-tat-tat, two floors down. The gentleman must be tucked beneath the porch; she guesses he arrived early. She raises her eyebrows. Surely that's a good sign? She tugs the hem of her serge navy dress and descends the communal stairs, the wispy steam of boiled cabbage clinging to her calves.

Mr Silver has grey hair. It's no surprise. He bows politely.

"Mrs Wolf?"

"We're expecting you." Frieda tinkles a laugh, snaps it off. Silly - of course he is expected.

He is not tall; but she can forgive that, too.

4

Her shady drawing room is crowded with carved mahogany furniture, a Turkish carpet. She sees it with his eyes and Oh! It seems so shabby. *What will he think?* She wonders about his home, why he's ... But no, she won't second-guess, not today, not yet.

"Please." She gestures to the best armchair. "I'll call Rachel. She's ..."

Frieda hesitates and retreats, already half concealed behind the drawing room door. "She's a little shy."

He gives a half smile. "I'm sure we'll get along."

She watches his dark eyes rake the room, alight upon the upright piano.

"Does she play?" he asks.

Frieda nods. "Yes. And you?"

She clucks her tongue when he nods, too.

"A shared activity – perfect start."

On the bare, timber landing she stands outside Rachel's bedroom and listens. There's no sound; it's the same every day.

"Our *guest* is here. Will you come out?" she whispers. "I've made rock buns."

Frieda doesn't wait. She swishes hastily into the back kitchen, assembles her grandmother's precious porcelain, lays it out on the enamel tray.

When she nudges open the drawing room door with a careful shoulder, Mr Silver is at the mantelpiece, his fingers on a frame. Frieda sees the photo with his eyes: a teenage girl, laughing, rolled up hair, tiny nipped-in waist. He turns, joyful.

"Rachel?"

"See for yourself! She'll be in shortly." Frieda's hand is on the teapot. "Milk?"

It's awkward, of course, when Rachel fails to make an appearance at the first meeting. Frieda and Mr Silver sustain the conversation for a full 30 minutes; the exchange isn't as stilted as Frieda had feared. Her guest, this stranger, is charming. His accent is impeccable but she suspects … 1933, that's her guess. He's had plenty of time to stitch himself into English ways; he'd speak the language, of course, but perfecting his intonation, that's the tricky bit.

She won't ask, not today.

Several times, she rises to coax Rachel. Whispers gently, so he won't hear. "Mr Silver won't come a second time. Rachel - darling?"

It is to no avail. Mr Silver eventually replaces his teacup.

"Should I encourage her myself?"

Frieda cannot have that. Instead, she retrieves the photo frame from the mantelpiece, places it directly on the tea table. They gaze at Rachel's image together.

"Perhaps I should have been frank." She hesitates. "The war's taken its toll. She's emotionally drained, a topsy-turvy way to grow up. My husband, her father …"

"I understand." Mr Silver bows his head momentarily. "We've all had our struggles."

She was right, then. She wonders how long it's been since he left Germany, fled like so many other Jews, whether he came alone or …

"But - would you try again?" Her voice lowers, hopeful. "I'll ask Rachel to write. She may find it easier, pen on paper."

Mr Silver stands in a trice. He's a neat man, late forties she guesses; his manners are impeccable. Not handsome. His gaze darts to the hall.

"Next time perhaps I'll meet Mr Wolf? He's at work?"

She stands and smoothes her skirt. He'll guess it is the signal to leave.

"Rachel will write," she repeats. *And anticipation doesn't hurt.*

Mr Silver draws a wrap of paper from his trouser pocket. Teases it open.

"I brought a trinket – for Rachel. From my jewellery shop."

Frieda peers down at the tiny brooch nestled in tissue. It's a bee: the body is carved in two-tone carnelian, delicate diamante wings.

"Oh, but we can't possibly …"

"Oh, but you can." Mr Silver has already pressed it deep into her palm. He's buttoning his overcoat. "I'll expect Rachel's letter."

Frieda watches from the window as Mr Silver walks the length of the street, heading north. She can tell so much from the way a man strides. That spring in his step; it's encouraging. When he turns the corner, she turns too. Silently, she places the bee on Rachel's bedside table. Says nothing, clicks shut the door.

These last two weeks, Eric has been alive to the world again; every morsel of food tastes fiercely fresh, the air is crystal sharp. He has received word:

Dear Mr Silver

Please accept my grateful thanks for the extremely generous gift of the brooch. It is the prettiest thing I've ever seen. I wear it every day.

I extend my sincere apologies for my absence at tea. It was kind of my mother to arrange, kind of you to attend. You must think me so rude. I have a nervous disposition that manifests itself as a severe headache. I was unable to rise from my bed. Please, do come again. I'll be quite well by then.

Yours,

Rachel Wolf

Eric holds the letter with careful fingertips and sits back in his leather armchair, whisky tumbler close. He conjures again the vivacious dark-eyed girl in the photo. He'll be able to charm her with the piano. Soon the age difference will disappear into thin air. He rises, sifts sheet music and selects Debussy. He places the tune on the walnut hall console, aware of the evening shadows shifting.

He likes a bit of light and shade. He'll take the music, next time.

For the second tea date and lacking precious eggs, Frieda makes scones. She splashes out with strawberry jam, a gift from Hampshire, saved for a special occasion. Tucked in the kitchen, Frieda licks the spoon, savouring her guilty pleasure. She has been firm with Rachel, spoken quietly but assertively. She has read out Eric Silver's reply, though her daughter refused to look. It's ridiculous behaviour. At 22, Rachel should know better. If Hector were here, there would *not* be a problem.

Still, when Frieda clip-clops again to the front door, she's hopeful. Today her daughter's bedroom door is wide open. Again, Frieda notes Eric Silver's hair, its strands shiny with oil. He follows Frieda upstairs, is already approaching the drawing room, hand outstretched. Frieda blanches.

"Oh! I thought she was here!" She clamps her mouth. "I can't believe it."

She levels her gaze to Eric Silver, sees a crease of frustration on his forehead. He's already standing beside the piano. In his fist, sheet music.

Frieda hesitates. "Please! I'll find out where she is. She was well today, quite well. I'll prepare our tea and then ..."

Somehow, they get through a second teatime. After the shock of Rachel's absence, Eric Silver is even more entertaining than before. He questions Frieda about Rachel, their life together. She describes Mr Wolf's demise; he appears suitably grave, bows his head. But after a discreet time lapse, he also makes Frieda laugh. And God knows, there's been little mirth these last years. Frieda keeps her joy restrained and suited to a woman her age. She'll be 49, next birthday. Her youthful flush is all gone.

The sheet music sits untouched. Now Eric Silver returns to the piano.

"Do you play?"

Frieda shakes her head. "Rachel, she's the musical one."

He seats himself at the stool, pats the space besides.

"Let's tempt her out - come, turn the pages. You can read music, no?"

The stool is thankfully wide; she can keep her distance. Frieda smells whisky and soap, it's lavender, she thinks. Deep inside her belly, there's burning warmth, spreading across her thighs. It's been so long since she sat close to a man. She has missed it. She's sure the strains of *Prelude a L'apres-midi d'u Faune* will coax Rachel out.

"My daughter loves music," she says. "*Loves* it."

When Eric Silver has finished, he settles the piece on the piano. Again, buttons his overcoat. He turns to Frieda. They both look at the Debussy. He gestures for her to keep it.

"Oh, but we can't possibly …"

"Oh, but you can. I'll write to Rachel. Two weeks - I'll come again."

Frieda stands beside her guest, her ruby silk dress rustles. She thanks him silently for one more golden chance. He glances sidelong at the photo frame; it sits atop the piano, a secret grotto for worshiping Rachel. Besides it, Frieda has placed an early hyacinth, its flowers newly forced.

"Rachel wears your brooch every day."

"So she said - in her letter. I'm flattered."

Frieda presses cold fingers to her temples as she watches Eric Silver depart, swaddled in winter dusk. His stride is even bouncier. She has a crucifying headache. It has been a delightful afternoon but a strain. She hopes she's doing the right thing for Rachel. The girl is so headstrong. A third meeting, that will set things on track.

Frieda hates being a widow. She wishes her Hector were here.

That dreadful evening, 1943; when Frieda was only doing her duty, as evacuation officer. The air raid siren, it came in time, but Hector's gammy leg … it had slowed him down. Rachel had dragged her father, as quickly as she could, but he didn't make it to the shelter. She doesn't know how Rachel survived the blast.

Mother and daughter, they're still in shock. *Darling Hector.* Frieda sees his face in her looking glass, as she brushes her hair. She misses him. She cannot bear the sorrow and the consequences

9

of the hideous war.

Dear Mr Silver

I owe you another apology.

I was awaiting you in the drawing room but was overcome with a terrible melancholy. Perhaps it was the sound of a manly voice on the stairs; it has been six years since my father died but I miss him. The Debussy was so sweet yet sad, I couldn't stop the tears.

I want to look my best when we meet. I hope you won't be disappointed.

Yours,

Rachel Wolf

Rachel writes well, Eric thinks, touching the single sheet of paper. Beneath the polite regrets, there's a youthful verve. He blushes. Sips the whisky at his elbow, a treat after a long day. His shop girl had the afternoon off, gone to see her fancy man. Momentarily Eric allows his imagination to wander, a little further than it should. He's hopeful Mrs Wolf will be discreet enough to leave he and Rachel alone next tea date. This correspondence, being made to wait, it has set him ablaze.

He hasn't felt like this in years.

He presses his forehead with clammy fingertips, trying to ignore the gentle bulge quickening in his trousers. He can't, shouldn't allow that. But the chance to start again, find a new love, it's tempting. *Rosa is not coming back.* He shuts his eyes. Rosa - his fiancée, with creamy skin and unforgettable dark eyes. Rosa, planning to join him in London, so close to catching the boat ... Rosa, her innocent temple smashed with a stray brick, crashing the shop window at Erik Silvermann & Sons, November 1938, Munich, the Night of the Broken Glass.

All hope gone. Eric judders out a sigh.

Is it too much to wish, that a new courtship might flourish?

He's not old yet. There's time; things can spool out slowly.

He's always wanted children.

He detects sadness in Mrs Wolf, Rachel too, it leaches from the flat. Together, they might make a new family. Don't they all deserve a little happiness?

Dear Rachel

I hope you'll forgive first name terms. I already feel I know you! I'm saddened to hear my presence at the flat caused you pain. I'd love to amuse you at our next tea. You're very beautiful in the photo, if I may make so bold.

Until then,

Yours,

Eric

He hesitates, taps the Mont Blanc to his teeth. Will she think his words too forward? But she's young; she'll forgive. For his third visit, he has selected another gift. He draws forth a black velvet pouch, inside a delicate string of pearls, creamy and expensive.

He likes to make a bit of a splash.

So much is riding on Eric's third visit that Frieda works herself into frenzy. She yanks her best tea dress, adjusts it in the looking glass. Hector's face smiles back. He understands she's doing this for the best. The dressmaker has done wonders 're-modelling' her tired pre-war clothes; the print glows with burnt orange and cinnamon flowers. Rachel's dresses have been re-stitched, too. Frieda likes to see them hanging on her daughter's wardrobe, nipped in, that tiny waist.

When Eric arrives, his happiness is palpable; he takes the stairs, two at a time, and Frieda feels joyful, too. The kettle sings and the scent of new-baked eggless ginger cake has spiced the air. Eric crosses his legs, relaxed – at home, one might say.

"So pretty," he remarks, as she rattles into the drawing room. "I mean, your engagement ring. Forgive me for looking. It's the jeweller in me."

Frieda blushes. She twists the modest diamond on her finger. It is a daily reminder that Hector is no more. And it's too loose now; she's a pale shadow of her former self.

"Mr Wolf bought it in Paris, long before the war."

"How very romantic," Eric says, eyes twinkling.

"It was. Very." She whispers it. Her green eyes, flecked with hazel, swim with tears. But she mustn't be self-indulgent. She needs to find a new love – for Rachel.

"Never tempted to marry, Mr Silver?" She stops. "I mean - before now?"

She thinks they have an understanding. He responded to her advert, after all.

He shakes his head, looks away. "I was engaged. She died."

She mustn't ask more. Now Frieda wills Rachel to burst in at this perfect moment, the stage is set, the emotion high. Eric lays out a black velvet pouch.

"Would you like to see my gift - for Rachel?"

Frieda leans forward, a queer feeling in her stomach. It is something like excitement. Today's tea is going better than she had hoped. The string of pearls glows softly.

"She'll love them," she breathes. Downstairs, the mansion flat front door bangs.

They stand swiftly together. Eric almost topples the tray.

"Let me take her coat," Frieda announces. "Then I'll bring her in."

After Rachel's third and final absence, Frieda has been unable to persuade her guest to return again. If she had hoped for another bout of piano playing, it was not to be. He had departed, muttering excuses in a clipped tone. She had watched him disappear, rain striking bleakly at the road, his stride long and forthright. He was angry. She knew that much about a man.

He has forgotten the pouch. She's been tearful in Rachel's room. There's the tiniest hope, though. She has wrung out one more letter to send.

Dear Eric

What can I say? I am a silly 22-year-old without a sensible bone in my body. I had indeed been for a walk, but on my return I lost all my confidence.

I suppose there's no hope you will return?

Yours,

Rachel

Tonight, after Eric has finished his supper of cod and fried tomato, he pushes away his plate. He reads the letter again. He is disappointed, bitterly so. Perhaps the daughter is mentally unstable, a real-life 'Mrs Rochester' hidden from common view? That would explain Mrs Wolf's need to write an anonymous advertisement. If Rachel is so pretty, why hasn't she met a *beau* in the usual way?

Now he considers, it's all so obvious! He's been blinded by anticipation. Tonight there's no hopeful swelling in his trousers. He's been a fool. He is almost 50, too old for matrimony or a love affair, too smart for matriarchal scheming.

Well, no more.

He crumples up the letter, throws it into the kitchen fire.

Orange flames shoot up the chimney.

Eric wishes he could have left the matter right there. He is bruised, but hurt pride, after a while - it fades. Try as he might, he can't forget Rachel. Those tender feelings, so carefully packed away after Rosa's horrific death, have been roused. He's enjoyed the warmth returned, the excitement of a new future. And Mrs Wolf hasn't put a foot wrong. He has seen the care she has poured into sparking the yet-to-be romance, an eager light in her eyes.

A mother's hopes for her youthful daughter; it's quite admirable.

And Mrs Wolf makes wonderful teatime fancies.

Two weeks later, Eric rings the bell again.

"Mr Silver, I didn't expect … oh, did I make a mistake?"

Mrs Wolf is clearly shocked. She covers her mouth, her complexion pale beneath the carefully waved dark hair, with a streak of grey. She's not so unattractive.

"I'd like to apologize for my abrupt departure. You must have thought me so rude. Might I – come in?"

Mrs Wolf uncovers her mouth. Eric sees she has pretty lips, her teeth crossing over slightly. The effect is rather charming. She's wearing a scarlet cardigan buttoned tight; the garment nips the waist. Like mother, like daughter.

Hope fires inside him all over again.

"Is Rachel here today?"

Mrs Wolf's hand returns to her mouth. "I'm afraid she is out. If I'd known … why not call?"

Eric wanted to surprise her.

Eric is afraid Frieda won't invite him in. His excuse has dissolved. But he's already picturing the cosy sitting room, the roaring fire. He imagines playing the piano, Mrs Wolf sitting close, turning the pages.

"I'm a little tired after my walk. Might I …"

Mrs Wolf tips her head on one side. For a moment she's girlish, as he imagines Rachel to be. The door opens wide.

"Come in."

The flat is cold today, no scent of baking. For the first time, Eric notices the Turkish carpet is worn and the velvet curtains faded. But it's not a problem. They will discuss Rachel and then – some music. Mrs Wolf unbuttons her cardigan, carefree. It's only then that Eric notices three things, in quick succession.

The bee brooch pinned to her dress. Around her neck: the pearls. And on the piano, open, the Debussy …

Mrs Wolf puts her hand to her pale throat. Stricken.

Eric says nothing. It would be rude to draw attention.

He moves to the piano, pats the stool.

"Are you ready? While we wait for Rachel - shall I play?"

Three months have passed, and Frieda couldn't have imagined how their friendship has flourished. It feels like a gift. Every week she and Eric go for a walk, to the cinema or a theatre matinee. Eric's shop girl holds the fort. Frieda hasn't shared the burgeoning relationship with Rachel. Her daughter has no taste for the mature gentleman. There's been no more perching in Rachel's bedroom, persuading and cajoling. Her daughter need not guess until the time comes.

Frieda holds hope like a precious egg, fragile and intact - full of goodness.

After spring and early summer stepping out, Eric had been surprised, then delighted, When Frieda suggested he come to tea at the flat, 'just like old times'. Frieda has pooled her rations, made a Genoese sponge. Eric can't wait. So much has changed since his winter visits. As he canters up the stairs, he is full of hope.

Once the tea is drunk, a litter of sweet crumbs scattering plates, he takes Frieda's hands. He holds them tight. He fancies he feels the blood pumping beneath her skin. Outside, the chestnut trees are full and swishing green. For all their burgeoning friendship, they've been proper at each meeting, only recently on first-name terms.

"My dear Frieda." He keeps his voice low. He strokes her skin and she doesn't draw away. His heart is cantering.

"I've admired your rings before, may I look? Would you remove them, dear Frieda? Indulge a curious jeweller?"

He hopes she'll agree. He's so happy when she slips them off with a tiny chink.

"Thank you."

It is only now that Eric notices the tray is laid with two cups and two plates, not three as was customary before. And that is as it should be, he thinks. Rachel, once so clear, has faded. He and Frieda speak of her less and less. Eric has even begun to wonder whether Frieda invented her? She's a lonely widow; it wouldn't be such a crime. Eric is lonely too, so perhaps ... he glances at the piano. The photo frame has disappeared.

Eric can admit now that he's grown to love Frieda. He'd never thought he'd find another *beau*. He'd never considered marrying an *older* woman, but they suit one another. Frieda is beautiful. This mature, sweet woman is what he needs.

She's staring at him steadily, her expression expectant.

"Close your eyes."

Inside his pocket, he squeezes a ring. Eric pictures the circle of gold, feels the weight of the diamond. He'll draw out this moment a little longer. He's sure of what he wants, but needs to be certain Frieda is, too.

"Open your eyes." He stops, starts again. "Have you enjoyed my company, dear Frieda?"

Eric sees her lips start to move but no words come. She nods. A single tear slides down her powdered cheeks.

"So I wanted to ask you ..."

Bang!

Two flights down, the entrance door slams hard. Eric and Frieda jump. There's the sharp rattle of quick feet, a key turning, a low voice muttering. Eric's gaze snaps towards the hallway. He's dropped Frieda's hands. He half rises; she sits, frozen. He sees the drawing room door pushed open.

"I decided on an afternoon off, Mummy, I thought ..."

"Rachel!" Frieda stumbles up.

Eric sees her face, creased with surprise. He looks from Frieda to Rachel; he's rooted to the chesterfield, its buttons sharp against his back. He watches as Rachel – she's not a figment but real and breathing, so *gorgeous* - steps forwards with an elegant smile. She's taller than Frieda, and oh, that nipped-in waist. In a tailored suit, the skirt contours her hips like butter. Not the shy girl who wrote to Eric. *Oh no.*

Eric is enthralled, his blood pumping. He takes a step, clutches Rachel's cool hands in his and musters an intimate smile.

"I'm so pleased to see you at last. Such a wonderful surprise!"

Rachel stares blankly, draws away. Her glorious face and those sparkling eyes shut down in glacial retreat.

"I'm sorry. I don't know you. You are?"

"I'm Eric ... I'm ..."

"He's a jeweller." Frieda steps in; she's swift and standing already. "He's valuing my rings. It was a business appointment."

Eric looks back at Frieda. And in that moment, he understands twin certainties. One: Rachel doesn't know of his existence – she's never known, she's in no need of a husband. And two: given a choice between these women, one so vital, one so much older, he'd pick ...

Frieda clears her throat.

"We're almost done. Leave us, Rachel; go to your room."

But Rachel has already turned on her heel, left with a pout. In seconds, it is just the two of them. Eric sees Frieda's sadness, and he can't bear it.

"But she didn't recognize ..."

"She didn't know ..."

Their words clash. The air between them, it's cool as ice.

"After all this time," he says. "She's more beautiful than I thought." He can't stop the words tumbling from his traitor mouth, knows already he's severed something precious.

Frieda doesn't reply. There's nothing more to be said, Eric understands. In his pocket, the engagement ring hangs heavy as sand.

He makes his excuses and leaves.

Frieda sits on in the quiet drawing room, suffused with emerald light, the leaves swishing on the trees. She is like a statue, hands in lap, for seconds, minutes, then one hour. It is a high-summer day, but she is shivering.

"I'm going to have a sleep, mother!"

Rachel's voice echoes and the door slams.

Frieda's disappointment is like ash in her mouth. Since the war ended, Rachel has never once returned home by day. Frieda had thought it safe: last winter, to attempt her epistolary experiment, and now, to escalate a love match. She's only ever wanted a man, a comfortable home, a steady income, for Rachel. She'd needed to use a little subterfuge at first, but she was certain that, after an introduction, good humour and sexual interest would have done the rest. Eric is handsome. Rachel, she's beautiful, fresh.

They'd have fallen in love. Frieda would have been looked after in her old age.

Rachel has loved her post-war clerical job; she's so fiercely independent. "I'm a modern woman, mother." She has no intention of marrying. But Frieda knows her daughter has no clue about money. And there are debts. Hector's death has left them compromised. Frieda has only wanted security. She's found the right candidate. It had almost worked, except ... *Oh, Hector.*

She hadn't bargained on falling in love herself.

Eric pushes back into his leather armchair, whisky tumbler at one elbow. He's on his third drink; this afternoon has been a shock. He has always wanted a younger woman, that's the nub of it, he repeats. He thinks of Rachel's tempting hourglass figure. How could he have stayed with Frieda? He wants children! A love union! He wants someone to caress! He sips, he thinks. He'll write to Rachel, perhaps a sandwich lunch, a quiet cocktail one evening? He'll enjoy the thrill of the chase.

Frieda will understand.

She was the one who advertised on behalf of her daughter, after all.

She won't mind.

He gets up, draws out the three letters from Rachel (one, slightly singed) stacked on his desk; now he knows who wrote them, and why.

Yet Eric doesn't receive a reply. He has written, six times, with Miss Rachel Wolf, carefully lettered and marked 'Private' top left. Night after night he frets and muses, a double whisky at his elbow. He should be celebrating; he's met Rachel, after all. He wants the young girl, not the faded woman. Inside his trousers, he waits for the gentle bulge, expects it. But it does not come. Each time he thinks of Rachel, it is Frieda's face that swims into view.

But he had his precious moment. She won't entertain him again.

A month on, Eric sits at his roll-top desk. Rachel has bundled up his notes, unopened, and posted them back. He's resisted temptation but finally today his hands stray to the *North London Gazette*. He picks it up, turns to Personal, Classified ads. He scans the page through half-closed eyes, then catches his breath:

'**WIDOW** (49), good appearance, efficient housewife, wishes to meet Gentleman in good position between 50-60. Object Matrimony. Box 821.'

North London Gazette, August 1950

He stares, thoughtful, reads it again. He taps the Mont Blanc against his teeth.

Dear Madam ...

No, that won't do. He crosses out the words, scratches hard. He puffs a breath and waits for a moment. The envelope, already addressed to Box 821, sits at his elbow. Outside, the sun is high in the evening sky and he takes a sip of whisky.

Dear Frieda …

He falters and comes to a halt; stills his pen.

Love. Isn't that what they both want? Yes, of course.

My darling Frieda …

He writes slowly at first and then very fast. There is no time to waste.

***

Rachel Wants to Die

Kerry Craven

Kerry Craven is an English and creative writing teacher at O'Neill C.V.I., the arts high school in Oshawa, Ontario. She is also a member of the Writer's Community of Durham Region. Her story "Rachel Wants to Die" was inspired by the indomitable spirit of her now 98 year old grandmother, Margaret Grant of Straffordville, Ontario.

Judge Sandra says of the story *"Rachel Wants to Die* is a quiet, contemplative piece, both warm and moving. It could have easily crossed the line and become melodramatic, but the final twist made it a clever, thought-provoking read."

A little girl sits on the beach. It's the first time she has ever been out to watch the stars. When she slipped out the door, she was afraid she would be caught, but her father was shut up in his room alone, thinking of a wife he would never see again, turning himself into the father that someday Rachel would never see again. As her father went through the slow, painful process of giving up, Rachel discovered the wonders of the universe in a sky full of stars: a universe open, expanding and full of promise.

But this morning, a Wednesday, Rachel woke up and decided this would be the day she was going to die.

After ninety-seven years, she saw no reason to start her day any differently than the thousands of others that had come before. A piece of toast, cut in diagonals with raspberry jam. A small etched glass full of orange juice. It was the same glass she'd been drinking orange juice from since she was two. Perhaps that's why her mind was still so sharp: 97 years old, minus two, times 365 glasses of orange juice.

Rachel did take special care of her appearance that morning. She wanted to be a presentable corpse. Her hair had been set yesterday, just like every Tuesday, so a quick brush and spray once the curlers were out would do it: pink curlers, made of Velcro. She had good skin for her age, so a little cream, a little blush were all she needed. Were it not for her hands and her wispy legs, people would still mistake her for 80.

She wore the smart new pantsuit that she'd ordered from the catalogue two weeks ago. It was a soft, smooth grey, tailored to give her some semblance of a figure again. She fastened the matching pin. Rachel had mocked herself a little when she bought the outfit, but she liked to stay current, or people might think she was old. She set a simple blue dress with a white collar on the bed. It was important that they find it. . . for later.

The walker rested by the door, a little dusty. She rarely went out of the house for fear of people seeing her use it. Today she

23

would make an exception, since the beach was only two blocks away from her tiny home, the home she'd lived in her whole life. Yes, the beach was the right place to go. Beaches are good for starting a journey. But the beach was downhill, a gentle but treacherous slope. To die on the beach would be glamorous. To die like a turtle on a sidewalk would be humiliating; her whole life had been spent sidestepping humiliation, so she wasn't about to let that happen.

One last glance behind her as she opened the door, and she could see the whole house: the chenille bedspread, her mother's wicker chair, the cross stitch of the Blue Boy, her teaspoon collection. It was not much, her life, but it was enough. A life in teaspoons was not such a bad thing.

She only had one memory of her mother, in the rocking chair. Rachel sat in her lap as her mother slowly swayed and hummed, a tuneless, seesawing song. Rachel thought she must have been about two. She remembered long brown hair, braided for bed: a soft dressing gown with blue flowers that Rachel had pressed her face against to wipe her tears. No matter how hard she tried, she could never remember the nightmare that had awakened her: just the soft hand stroking her little, yellow curls. When her mother was gone, she would sometimes think she felt that hand pressed against her, a humming in her ear. In her whole life, no matter what she lost, Rachel was never entirely afraid.

But for now, the hardest part would be getting the walker down the three concrete steps. In her childhood, the house had been red brick, but now it was clad in smart, white aluminium siding. It was nearly noon. Everything took longer when you were old, a frustrating slowness, made worse by stiffening hands. She took a moment to rest at the bottom as the lake-smells drifted up the street on the breeze, mostly the smell of dead fish. The day was warm, but it was comfortable. She could feel the first of fall creeping inside of her bones.

When she finally arose, she dropped a small bag of garbage at the curb. She didn't want to leave any work for anyone, or leave anything unfinished. When the delivery service came to bring her meals, they'd find no garbage, no mess to tidy. Rachel hated to leave a mess.

Carefully, with small steps, she allowed the walker to let her drift slowly down the street. She gingerly put the fixed back legs down with a 'thunk' each time she took a step.

The street was empty, quiet, so everyone must be at work by now. Most people worked in town, and wouldn't be back until late. Not much had changed in the small village over the years. The world had expanded, grown and gorged itself, but here, things had grown more quiet, more still. There was no ferry anymore to take you to the U.S. No pavilion by the lake where Guy Lombardo would come to play, and where boys would take her to the dances. No cruising past her house in beaten up cars. No more trains through town to carry young soldiers away.

At the halfway point, she turned back one last time and saw the pine tree her young husband had planted when he had come home from the war: when a part of him had come home from the war. He tended his lawn like it was something precious, planted her some rose bushes. The garden teemed with small creatures and he never put out traps. Life mattered now, every life. The two of them had never had children, but sitting out on their front porch together, Rachel had never minded, not really - not until the first time she had to sit out there alone.

He'd planted an elm too, but it had been a long time since she'd seen an elm around these parts. Soon all the ash trees that lined the road would be gone as well: the borers tore away, killing from the inside - like the pain in her ribs.

There was not much beach left now that they no longer dredged the lake, but she could not get close; the walker dragged too much in the sand - became heavy. She'd wanted to dip her toe into the cool water one last time, but instead she settled herself for a wait. She had no idea how long it would take to die. In life you were taught to time your moments, time your dinners, time a soft-boiled egg, but there was no way to practice timing for death. She'd had the sense to pack a lunch, and pulled out half a mac n' cheese sandwich. Normally, she'd not even be able to finish that, but today she was famished, though she still nibbled at the edges, politely. She nursed the tea in the plaid thermos for hours, slowly sipping as she watched the sun sink down, a rippling orange echo appearing in the water below.

Finally, she closed her eyes, thought peaceful thoughts. She gave one last relieved sigh. It had been a good life and it had been a good day and now it was done.

So Rachel waited. And the stars winked on, and she waited. And the moon whispered through the lake, like laughter, and she waited. And all over the world, lives flickered out, thousands of them, as they always do, every moment of every day. Some died in bed. Some died in loving arms. Some died in tears, and horror, and blood.

But Rachel didn't die. A stillness overcame her. This was the time and she knew it was right; there was nothing left to give - but still, it would not come.

She tried again, but she didn't know how to try to die. Did you breathe more slowly? Did you cross your arms? Did you have to pray? Did you just relax? Maybe she shouldn't have eaten that sandwich? But the moment passed, and her world persisted.

So Rachel sighed, and opened her eyes to the miracles of the universe that she had seen a thousand times before, since that lonely, wonderful night on the beach; the night her mother had died; the night she had seen her future. It was now so terribly disappointing, so senselessly splendid. She dusted the sand off her shoes, and stood up.

"Damn," she thought to herself with a shiver, looking at the streetlights which led up to her house. "Now how in hell am I going to get back up that hill?"

***

Lessons
KF Lee

KF Lee grew up on the coast of Northumberland, England, and has since worked in Australia, Europe, Hong Kong, Singapore, America, Mexico and Canada. Currently living in the USA, he actively supports a number of humanitarian organisations, has been a volunteer literacy tutor in a high-security jail and is a frequent decoder on Amnesty International's Somalia/Darfur project.

An avid student of modern history, human rights and Middle East/South Asia affairs, Lee writes short stories in between crafting two full length books towards publication. His work recently earned an Honourable Mention in Glimmer Train Magazine's 2017 Short Story Award for New Writers.

Of *Lessons* Judge Brett says 'A terrible and heartbreaking beauty in this story. Brilliant characterisation, and the merciless critique of our popular media's shallowness, as well as of the entertainment-saturated global culture that enables it, is spot-on and devastating."

$\mathbf{I}$'d never sketched bruises before and hadn't understood how intricate they are: myriad striations of red, brown, blue - even green - blend into each other and into the surrounding flesh in a seemingly uncoordinated manifestation of the encounter that must have taken place between fragile skin and a solid object.

An artist's nemesis? Possibly, but I don't really feel qualified to describe myself as a true artist. More honestly, I'm a retired commercial illustrator who supplements a meagre pension with a stipend from giving drawing lessons two nights a week in the basement of the public library. Yes, the basement; visual arts classes in a windowless room aptly illustrates the importance given to the programme by the town. A handful of tree huggers and hippies, a male-male couple - searching to find, through drawing, *the inner meaning of their relationship* -, several middle-aged returnees-to-art (some with reasonable talent), more than enough fellow retirees seeking any activity to occupy their new-found surplus time…and her…the girl with the bruises.

Artists, real or aspiring, are supposed to be observers, keen eyes noticing the important detail which can be transposed onto paper or canvas, conveying to the viewer, in a powerful or meaningful way, the essence of an object, a situation or a scene. At least that's what I tell the class at the start of each exercise. In my case, *do as a I say, not as I do* might have been an appropriate rejoinder as it was not until, sitting in my usual coffee shop, I found myself sketching the girl's bruises and realising how often she had come to the class with quite livid marks on her body.

I like that coffee shop. I feel comfortable there - despite the annoying television above the counter, tuned, as ever, to a local TV news channel broadcasting intensely important reports on some vital issue like a perceived increase in the number of cyclists running red lights, or the old civic fountain which has started splashing water on pedestrians trying to get to their work places. I can make a latte last hours, sitting at the end of one of the three long benches which provide rough, but ample, space for customers. The benches are just the right height to place a sketch pad securely between my knees and the lip of the wooden surface, so I can trace harried business people chugging back quick espressos or earnest looking students, heads buried in dog-eared text books, pens poised expectantly over fresh notebooks.

These lazy latte mornings are a way of treating myself: an indulgence which costs very little and yet allows me to play at being the artist I had always intended to be. But the day, on which I was aware I was drawing the girl's bruises, brought a concern I didn't really want to face. Stirring the then tepid latte with a pencil and afterwards licking it dry – a habit which often drew disapproving looks from my fellow customers – I became coldly conscious that those bruises were something to which I should, perhaps, have paid more attention.

When I first saw her at the opening class where the students introduce themselves, she reminded me of Jean Butler, the tall, dignified, very Irish-looking and superbly modest lead dancer of the highly successful *Riverdance* stage show. The reality, however, was different. This riverdancer was dressed in old jeans and a faded thin cotton shirt – which, likely as not, had been part of her wardrobe for many, many years and, even then, had probably not been bought new. While the other students assuredly flicked the corners of their Strathmore sketch pads and ranged boxes of various grade lead and coloured pencils on the desk in front of them, she had one HB pencil and a school notebook which she clutched in arms folded across her chest. When it was her turn to give us her name and tell us why she was here, she simply raised one hand in a limp greeting, smiling weakly at the room. She said nothing.

Students that desperately shy often don't turn up again after the first lesson, so I had made a point of talking with her at various times during the class. Well, not exactly talking with her; more accurately, I made the odd encouraging comment and received in reply a simple nod of her head or another weak smile. But she did turn up again – at the second lesson that week, and again at both lessons in each of the following weeks.

I don't mind admitting I was intrigued by her. Teaching is not my natural talent…at least, if I actually had a natural talent, I'm not sure teaching would be it. Mostly I find the students and the lessons a little tedious, but I want the job and do my limited best to make each class interesting. Having a student who I could not understand and who I found fascinating was, therefore, quite a welcome change - even if some of her mannerisms were disconcerting.

For example, if, at the start of a lesson, I was demonstrating the difference between using outlines, bold outlines, stippling, scumbling or hatching, all the other students would start pulling out their Prismacolors or Faber-Castells to replicate my pencil strokes on their pads at the same time as I was doing them. She, on the other hand, would sit perfectly still and stare directly forward for the entire briefing – not a flicker of an eye or even a glance at her pencil.

After my abstract, the students would clatter and bang as they moved their chairs into position to reach their pads, which were usually propped on easels or resting on a crossed knee. Her notebook would lie on the desk immediately in front of her and would not be opened until she had leaned forward with one arm circling the pad and her head and body blocking sight of her work from all other angles. It was not even possible to see how she was holding the pencil – her hand was hidden at the centre of her little personal fortress.

It wasn't until the third lesson that I felt confident enough to ask her to show me what she was drawing. The class that day was on light and shadow, which I had demonstrated by using a small lamp shining on a pile of books. Most of the other students' drawings were simply some basic object in a bland setting, illuminated by an obvious light source. When I asked to see hers, she turned her head sideways towards me and grimaced awkwardly. I smiled as reassuringly as I could, and asked again. Slowly she moved her body back to reveal the pad on which she had sketched the perfect shadows of what were clearly a mother and young son running away from something, their heads turned back over their shoulders towards the direction from which they ran. The action of the shadows was well captured, but there were no figures from which the shadows would have emanated. I asked her if she intended to draw them.

31

"No," she replied in almost a whisper. "You said light and shadow. Can't have no shadow without light…so I've done light and shadow."

She grimaced again at my raised eyebrows. "Ain't no-one who don't understand there *has* to be people there," she added quickly. "Don't need to draw them in if you know they're there."

As soon as I see students responding to what I am trying to teach, I ask them to start cataloguing their work by putting their name and the date on each piece and adding a title or a lesson reference. Seeing her *Shadows*, I decided it was time to start that practice with this group. It amused me how often students see these simple details as the real beginning of their careers as artists and start enthusiastically adding them to their work, as if doing so had been the habit of a lifetime. Except that she only wrote a title and the date on hers. She didn't sign it. Nor did she leave at the end of the class.

As she made her way hesitantly towards where I was putting the class register into a locker, I feared I may have been premature in asking to see her work. I worried again that she would say she wouldn't be coming back, but she just stood quietly in front of me and held out her note book. She briefly looked behind her, checking that the others had all left, and then asked if she could leave the book in my locker…because her husband held that drawing is for stupid people, and she didn't want him to know she was taking lessons. She'd told him she was out babysitting so her sister could go to cookery classes.

At the next lesson I gave her a proper sketch pad and both graphite and colour pencils: left-over supplies from the previous season's course. She looked them over carefully, running her hand slowly across the cover of the pad and taking out and inspecting each pencil in turn. Scrunching up her mouth and smiling nervously, she muttered "Thank you. I'll try to use them properly," then turned and made her way to her desk. A little later, I watched as she worked on the lesson, her arms and body still ranged around the pad, protecting her drawing – except now she had to spread her arms a little wider to accommodate the increased size of the sketch pad over that of the notebook.

It was the day after that, in the coffee shop, that I found

myself thinking about her and picked up a pencil. Why I drew the bruise, which I had vaguely noticed on her neck the previous evening, I have not the slightest idea – I had started out intending to draw her face. As I played around with techniques, trying to give the bruise the right prominence on the slope of her neck – strong enough for it to be clear what is was but also faded enough so it didn't dominate – I wondered how she got it in the first place. That's when I became embarrassingly aware that previously I had seen other marks on her as well – but had paid scant attention to them.

It's hard to inspect a younger woman's body without feeling self-conscious, so at the following classes I checked it a bit at a time with just the briefest of glances which, I hoped, wouldn't be noticed. To my dismay, I'd been right. Every lesson she seemed to have some mark or other which had not been there before. I ventured a couple of seemingly casual comments: *quite a shiner you have there*, or more adventurously, *looks like you've taken a bit of tumble*. She would give me one of her painfully awkward smiles and mumble some excuse or other: *I fell off a stool* or *just some rough-play with my son*. Then she would add a little self-deprecating phrase about being *just a clumsy person* or being *all fingers and thumbs*. I had a flicker of understanding for the expression 'my heart bled' each time she brushed off my questions.

At the end of the second to last night of the programme, for which she had turned up with a nasty cut on her lip, I noticed one of the tree-hugger women follow her out of the classroom and put a hand on her arm in the hallway. I couldn't hear what they said to each other but they chatted in what seemed an amicable way for about ten minutes. Eventually, the environmentalist opened her sketch pad, wrote on the corner of a page then tore it off and pushed it into the girl's hand. They hugged clumsily before moving on, one heading for the front door, the other, as usual, heading for the back. I felt a small sense of relief: someone else was taking an interest in her, too.

After the two women disappeared, I looked curiously at her sketch pad which was lying on my desk, waiting to be put in the locker. I had seen much of her work during the lessons – always clearly talented but sometimes naïve, sometimes disturbing. I felt compelled to study it more: study it away from the pressure of her grimaces, her half smiles…and her bruised body. An hour later I pushed back the chair and rubbed my face vigorously. I'd looked again at *Shadows* and then had been amused by another drawing - of the town's errant fountain splashing unsuspecting office workers (subject: landscape of a place away from home, title: *I Ain't Never Been Nowhere But Round Here*).

Three other pieces also drew my attention.

The first was on the subject of 'Space'. She had written the topic and the date, as I had encouraged, but there was no name – indeed I had not seen a name on any of the sketches. Her 'Space' was a police car pulled up at an acute angle to the street with all its doors open. Wisps of smoke from the exhaust pipe showed the motor was still running and lights were showing on the dashboard – everything was working but there was nobody in the car. Effective background lines showed the setting being a housing estate, and a more detailed rendering of the pavement's curb added urgency to the car's position. The whole effect was quite compelling but I was unsure about the implications of the police car - and whether the 'space' was that inside the vehicle or that outside of it.

The second was about 'Perspective' - which she had spelled 'Purspective'. Her composition was a human arm drawn from the point of view of the person whose arm it was. Initially, my attention was pulled to four elongated bruises on the inside of the forearm. Possibly the result of a strong hand having gripped the arm tightly: there would presumably be a fifth bruise – from the thumb - on the other side. My first reaction was a little envy at how well she had portrayed the contusions; she'd done a better job than I had achieved in my first few attempts.

It took me a while to understand that the bruises were not the focus; they were incidental. The real focus was the hand stretching out beyond the arm towards the far distance where a small patch of cross-hatching had been drawn in a pale yellow colour. Her title was *Purspective on…….?????* I could have added quite a few of my own question marks to that. Was the hand trying to get to whatever the cross-hatching represented? Some kind of goal? A saviour? A place of safety? Or was it reaching out to try to prevent the loss of something? Something precious slipping away? Something lost for

34

ever?

The last one was interesting because it was from a lesson at which I felt I'd not done a particularly good job of teaching. I'd tried to set the topic to stimulate divergence away from the tropes of drawing lessons but had succeeded only in reinforcing those tropes with all of the students – all the students except her, that is. The topic was 'Half-full/Half empty'.

Under the title *NOW It's Half Empty*, her picture was a close up of the corner of a room where a tiled floor met two plain walls. A broken cup lay on the floor, fractured ceramics scattered everywhere, but one larger piece, comprising the handle with part of the side and some of the bottom still attached, rested at an angle to the wall. Coffee or tea, I couldn't decide which, was splattered on the floor and up the wall, but some of it also still remained in the handled relic of the ruined cup. It certainly was a trope-evading piece, but I couldn't interpret the sense behind the title. Was it defiant, *There – NOW It's Half Empty* implying the destruction was deliberate, or even violent? Or was it disconsolate, *Oh no! – NOW It's Half Empty?*

Drawings which have the power to captivate are good, and hers definitely captivated. A certain amount of ambiguity is also appealing; creating debate holds the viewer's attention and engages the mind. I vacillated for some time about whether the ambiguity in her work was deliberate or accidental, but settled on deliberate as it was there in so many of her pieces. But I couldn't make up my mind in each of them if the ambivalence was to show an option she wanted, or an option she was desperate to avoid: *freedom/confinement* in 'Space', *something to strive for/something being taken away* in 'Purspective' and *anger/despair* in 'Half Empty'.

Putting her sketch pad into the locker, I snapped the door shut. For once, I felt I could look forward to the final lesson where, instead of starting with a teaching topic, I planned to immediately put the class to work on a single subject – a single subject which would be open to individual interpretation but which would also incorporate multiple topics from the previous lessons. It was only later that I admitted to myself that I was anxious to see what she would produce.

On that last day, there were several groans when I announced

35

the topic as 'Still Life', and even more when I added the other parameters: the subject had to be something organic, and the setting in which it was portrayed was to be somewhere other than where it had originated - *and* their work had to show how the subject had got to the current setting. They had the full two hours of the class to complete it. To avoid debate, as soon as I had given the briefing, I left them to it, walking out of the room and wandering around a small garden beside the building for the first hour.

When I went back in, several faces turned towards me; some appeared pleased, some angry, some hopeful, some were just blank. I tried to avoid them and looked across to her desk, feeling a momentary disappointment as she concentrated totally on her work…was probably not even aware I had not been there for the past hour. Wandering around the room, I was actually quite impressed with much of the work - maybe I was not as weak a teacher as I thought. There was a bit of a theme to several of them – labels on packaged food. Predictable, but even so, some of the settings were very well drawn.

I kept looking over to her desk, and even walked both in front of and then behind it from time to time, but she remained hunched over her pad with the only movement being in her right arm as she sketched away. I announced 'half-an-hour left' and toured the room again, spending time with two students who were putting finishing touches to quite good pieces.

The first was a variation on the labelled food theme but was more imaginative than the others – a wintery railway yard in which pallets of oranges were standing beside a container on which was painted a brightly shining sun over the words *producto de España*. The student, half of the male-male couple, was one of the few who had paid attention to the instruction to show how the subject had travelled from where it had grown. The other interesting drawing was a pumpkin lying on the table of a very modern kitchen. A string vegetable bag lay next to it, once more showing how it got there, and there was a knife on the edge of the table implying that the gourd was about to be carved into a Jack O'Lantern. It told a good story of the pumpkin's journey.

I was about to announce fifteen minutes left when I saw her

36

half sit up and put the pencil she was using back into its box. Walking behind her I tried to look at her work, but she was still blocking it. Talking somehow seemed inappropriate, so I lightly put my hand on her shoulder to move her enough for me to see. A small shock, almost as if it was electric, ran up my arm when she immediately reached up and grasped my hand, holding it tightly as she leaned back to show me the drawing. I felt her body shudder lightly and realised she was holding back tears.

The picture was shocking – there is no other way to describe it. Shocking in the sense of the sheer impact it had, shocking in its brilliance, shocking in its awfulness. And yet it is a scene we all know well, a scene which has been shown time and time again on television, on the web, in newspapers and magazines all over the world – the body of the three year old Syrian refugee child, Alan Kurdi, lying dead, drowned on a beach in western Turkey. The subject for the lesson was 'Still Life'; she'd titled her work *Still Death* and added a subtitle; *Nobody Did Nothing To Help Him.*

"Bloody hell, it's fantastic," I whispered, squeezing her shoulder and leaning forward to see more detail. The viewer's attention was pulled towards the child's closed eye just above the gently lapping tide in which his body lay, peaceful in its lifelessness; the eye never to be opened again. A life wasted before it had properly begun. That little Alan Kurdi had come from somewhere different, that he had come by sea, that the world had let him down - none of it needed explaining: a complete story in one heart-breaking scene.

She moved her other hand onto her shoulder, and then, clutching my hand in both of hers, pulled it down over her heart. Even through the cotton of her shirt, I could feel it beating heavily. Her body tensed momentarily then relaxed a little as silent tears dropped from her face onto our hands. Subconsciously I looked down but then had to suppress a gasp; under her shirt, which had opened slightly from the hands pressed against it, a large, ugly, older looking, discolouration spread across a big part of her chest. In an uncontrolled reflex, I jerked my hand away and crossed my arms behind my back.

She turned her face quickly towards me and mouthed, "Is the picture OK?"

"Very OK," I replied quietly. "It's...very, *very* OK."

Looking again at the picture, she did that small head-nod thing of hers and dropped her hands into her lap. Not certain what emotions were actually running through my mind, I walked quickly back to my own desk.

Closing that final lesson was more drawn out than normal. I couldn't take my mind off her picture while everyone else seemed to want to come up to say goodbye – again and again in the case of a few of them. She and the tree hugger were the last to go, fifteen minutes after we were supposed to have cleared the room. At the door she turned and, for the first time, albeit very briefly, flashed a smile and gave a little wave before leaving. I pushed my things and a few sundry pieces of equipment into the lockers and surveyed the room one final time. It was then I realised that she had left with her sketch pad tucked under her arm and had not, as usual, left it with me - I assumed because the class was over and she wouldn't be coming back again.

I have to admit the days following the last class were somewhat aimless. *Still Death* floated around in the back of my mind and several times I thought I saw her: in the queue at a cash machine, coming out of a fast food restaurant, putting shopping bags in the back of an old, beaten-up car. It never was her, of course – but that didn't do anything to lessen the immediate tension of the next 'is that her?' moment. I googled Alan Kurdi, and reread several of the newspaper reports. She had replicated it exactly but, by subtly changing the perspective, had added even more emotion than the original, dramatic, photograph had captured. I needed to find my own way of drawing it too.

Settling into a corner of the coffee shop, my plan was to recreate her work by doing a charcoal sketch, looking over her shoulder - as I had - at the drawing. What better way to explore the correlation between my fascination with her and my wonderment at her work?

Except it didn't pan out like that. An hour into it, whatever thought came into my head, I still found that I was putting more detail into my hand, which she had pulled over her heart, than I was into anything else. To make it worse, it was not, as had happened, my hand held by both of hers, it was my hand by itself - on the top part of her chest. I felt disquieted, even a little angry, because it hadn't been like that, nor did I really want to think of it that way. It was the same as when I wanted to draw her face and ended up drawing her bruises; it seemed I had no control over my art when she was the subject.

I have always encouraged students to keep all of their drawings, no matter how bad, no matter how many mistakes they contain – they are all lessons which may help later. Now I ignored my own advice, tore the page from my pad and ripped it up into tiny pieces. Several customers looked up curiously from their coffees at this madman who was furiously, and noisily, destroying his work. I frowned back at them, unable to explain that she had pulled my hand over her heart in a gesture of compassion for a dead three year old, and now I had falsely transposed it into a gesture of intimacy between us.

For two weeks, I tried to keep to a regimen of coffee in the mornings, where I drew a series of *how-people-hold-a-coffee-cup* studies and, in the afternoons, walks in one or other of the town's parks where I drew trees, children on swings, and anything else which took place in front of me. In the evenings, for dinner I made a point of trying new but simple recipes, then put on a concert and read or played chess against myself until bed time. It didn't work. I still kept 'seeing' her, still kept running her drawings, and their interpretations, through my mind. I went to the library and got her address and telephone number from the student registration records.

That there was no such address in either our town or any of the surrounding conurbations should not have surprised me, but it did. I tried Google Maps, Map Quest, showmystreet.com, instantstreetview.com and any other site I could find. The road name she had given did not show up anywhere in the area. I tried searching for her name, but, even on Facebook or Twitter, there was no-one by that name who could possibly have been her. And the telephone number she had used was a pizza delivery service. The young man who answered my call was nice enough to even check against their customer list after he had told me there were no employees by that name. I ordered a pizza from him, as if this somehow rewarded him for being so helpful. I don't really like pizza.

And then, the following Wednesday, something drew me to look up at the coffee shop television. I was vaguely wondering why the reporter looked like an ever-so-correct Mormon missionary rather than an ordinary member of the society which he served, when I noticed the housing estate in front of which he stood. It MUST have been the one she had used as the backdrop in her drawing of 'Space'...there was even a police car parked there! While the journalist talked away, a confused looking man in handcuffs was pushed into the back of the police car. The cameraman had to move as the car sped away and hurriedly he changed his angle to the reporter. A shaft of ice ran down my back as *her* picture appeared in the upper right corner of the screen and the commentator pointed to one of the housing units into which investigators, in CSI coveralls, were taking cases of equipment.

Scrambling over the bench, I rushed towards the TV, shouting at a server to *please* turn up the volume. It was her picture on the screen – I was sure of it. The sound increased just in time for me to hear the reporter ask, "Why didn't anyone come forward to help her?"

***

40

Snowball

Phillip Sterling

Phillip Sterling is the author of a book of fiction (In Which Brief Stories Are Told), two collections of poetry (And Then Snow and Mutual Shores), and four chapbook-length series of poems: Significant Others, Quatrains, Abeyance, And for All This: Poems from Isle Royale. He won the 2015 Monstrosities of the Midway contest, and his story 'Registry' was selected for Best Small Fictions 2017. The recipient of a National Endowment for the Arts Fellowship, two Fulbright Awards (Belgium and Poland), and a PEN Syndicated Fiction Award, he has served as Artist-in-Residence for both Isle Royale National Park and Sleeping Bear Dunes National Lakeshore.

In Judge Anisha's words, Snowball is "A tale of kindness told movingly. Well-plotted with plausible characters who effortlessly invoke believable benevolence."

When elephants and roustabouts from the Romanski Family Circus hoisted a gargantuan tent at the county fairgrounds last summer, Don proposed that we take Louie to an afternoon's performance of what was billed as "The Oldest Traveling Big Top in North America." A great idea, I thought at the time. Not only did a genuine outdoor circus sound like fun, given my childhood memories of Dad and me seeing the Shrine Circus in Grand Rapids, but the event was a big deal for North Bank, where family entertainment was typically located somewhere between the Fourth of July Parade and Rent-One-Get-One-Free at Blockbuster Video. I was fairly certain that Louie had never been to a circus before - and even if he had, he'd not likely have remembered it.

We were not disappointed. "Five Generations" of acrobats, animal acts, clowns, and "Aerialists That Defied Belief" had untrailered in the dusty parking area beyond the 4-H building an assortment of sideshows and games of chance, lined them with hotdog and lemonade vans and Elephant Ear wagons, and had assembled in the very midst of our trotter infield a real old-fashioned circus, for "Kids of All Ages," complete with a Big Top half the size of the courthouse.

Louie was the biggest kid there, of course. And not because he is literally three times the weight, a foot-and-a half taller, and more than thirty years older than most of the youngsters that packed the bleachers around the centre ring. Nor because he was able to consume more popcorn and fried dough and cotton candy and sno-cones than a whole den of Cub Scouts. It was more because he laughed the loudest at the clowns. He gasped the most passionately at the high wire acts. And although the barkers could not entice him into some of the sideshows (like the fire-eater), he was the best customer for the elephant ride. A two - dollar ticket bought three circuits of a round pen on an Indian elephant named Mabel - and Louie rode sixteen dollars' worth.

The elephants were his favourites, he said, especially those "Pendulous Pachyderms" that paraded around the ring during the opening act, the ones dyed pink and yellow and blue. Did I remember the pretty elephants? he said, again and again, for days after, and he must have thanked Don and me a hundred times for taking him along. It was the best day of his whole life, he'd said.

A hundred times we assured him he was welcome - that we wouldn't have had it any other way - and he would smile his signature smile, all teeth, like the smile that fills his face in the photo I'd taken of him perched on Mabel.

Don and I are the closest thing to family Louie has. He lives above our garage. Originally a carriage house, my father converted the empty attic space of the building into a studio apartment in 1970, the year Louie's father was diagnosed with cancer. "The Rileys and Lewises go way back," Dad exclaimed at the time, a shot glass of bourbon raised as a toast. "Even before the war. And we'll be like family until the very last battle!" It was the litany of a promise he'd meant to keep.

And he did, for the short time he was able to. Unfortunately, my father's "last battle" came sooner than anyone had expected - within four years of Rick Lewis's - and as I was the only heir, my father's property in North Bank became mine. I inherited Louie Lewis with it.

About a week after the Big Top had been packed into semi-trailers and trucked off to the next county, Louie came around the corner of the garage to where I was working in the flowerbeds and asked if I thought Snowball would look good painted pink.

"Sure, Louie," I said, "wouldn't that be something!" I was so intent on lopping dead heads off marigolds - and so certain that Louie was simply being Louie - that I responded without thinking.

Snowball is a tom cat, a neighbourhood stray. Except for one black ear and two gray paws, he is an off-white colour overall, which accounts for his name. He's widely recognized around the block - praised as a mole deterrent, cursed as a birder - though I've not seen him befriend anyone except Louie. He's never been inside that I know of - Louie understands our no-pet rule - but more than once I've seen the cat gather itself onto Louie's lap as he sat on the wooden swing under our dogwood tree. And when Louie is helping to weed the small vegetable garden by the back fence, Snowball can often be found in the nearest shade.

Silence followed my response, which was unusual. Louie has a reputation for bird-dogging one question with another, and so when another did not immediately follow, I looked up. Louie's face had taken on a kind of squinty confusion - a half-smile - as if he were pleased, but uncertain about the pleasure. As if he'd been commended for doing something he'd not actually done.

"You really think so, Ann?" he said. "You think Snowball would like being pink?"

The impulse of his voice gave me pause. While he was not known to be devious, he could be unpredictable. What came to mind suddenly was Louie chasing Snowball around the yard with an aerosol can of Rustoleum (though at the same time I knew no one at Bart's Hardware would provide Louie with paint without first checking with Don or me). I felt I should sound him out. I was certain I could swing his logic around if I needed to - I had lots of experience at it - but first I had to know what he was thinking.

"Well," I said, tactfully, "I'm not sure that it can be done for one thing, or that Snowball would allow it."

Louie's face scrunched up even more. It looked peculiar, given that it's more likely to present an incongruous, toothy smile, even under the most difficult circumstances. "What about the elephants?" he asked.

Elephants? It was a moment before I realized he was talking about the parade inside the Big Top.

"Those were circus animals," I replied, "performers. They're used to it. Snowball is more . . . independent. [I was thinking *feral*.] Sort of his own cat, you might say. He may not hold still long enough to be painted. Besides, if he was no longer white, then he'd no longer be Snowball, would he?"

"But he'd be pretty - like the elephants - wouldn't he, Ann?"

He was smiling again now, but I could see a kind of discomfort in his eyes, a puzzlement. As if the idea that a cat might not want to beautify itself was inconceivable. Perhaps I needed a different approach.

"I suppose some people might think he would look better with a little colour," I said, "but there may a law against it, or something." Laws, like house rules, were things Louie understood.

"Is there a law?"

"I'm not sure," I repeated. "But I wouldn't be surprised."

"He'd be pretty, though, wouldn't he, Ann?"

"Yes, Louie," I said, finally. "I guess he would be, if you liked pink cats."

Later, Don told me that Louie had asked him the same question, and he'd said he preferred green. It may have been all the encouragement Louie needed.

Louie's level of retardation is "mild," according to the classifications in Nelson's *Textbook of Pediatrics*, a book I'd retained from the Intro to Human Development class I took my first year of college. (The same class, I might add, that introduced me to my husband Don, who "just happened" to sit beside me in the back of the lecture hall one day.) Louie's caseworkers call him "functionally independent," although they've also acknowledged that in a lot of ways he'll never be more than a big kid his whole life - that is, someone who will continue to require a certain amount of guidance and supervision. And although Louie is twelve years older than I am, ten years older than Don, we agree that he's more like a younger sibling than a renter. "Brother Louie!" Don calls him at times, playfully.

Mostly Louie manages on his own. He's employed as a custodian at the courthouse, a job that was initially part of a pilot program sponsored by a grant from the Michigan Mental Health Council. At the time of Louie's hiring, the county chapter of MMHC had been located in an adjacent building, and so the courthouse was a perfect placement for someone like Louie. Not only could his caseworker monitor Louie's progress on a daily basis, but as we live only two blocks away, Louie is able to walk to work. His placement has been so successful that Louie's been able to stay downtown even after social services became the Family Independence Agency and moved to the new government building out by the river.

For the staff at the courthouse, Louie's more than simply a custodian. He's as much a fixture as the portrait of John Foster

46

("the First"), who was North Bank's longest serving mayor. When Louie isn't emptying waste cans or washing windows, he takes it upon himself to be a kind of doorman. In bad weather, he's been known to meet fellow employees in the parking lot with his umbrella. He's done so well, in fact, that he's been recognized more than once as "Employee of the Month." The worst thing I've ever heard anyone around the courthouse say about Louie concerns his unquenchable curiosity and short-term memory, which are manifest in redundant interrogations. Louie communicates largely in questions.

I wasn't terribly surprised, then, when John Foster III called me a day or two after Louie's questioning above the flowerbeds. John spends a lot of time at the courthouse. In addition to his law practice, he serves on the city commission in an advisory capacity - an ill-defined role, to my mind, since he never seems to come up for re-election. I suspect most people in town simply take it for granted that the Foster & Foster Law firm is on some kind of special retainer with the city; John's father - John Foster, "the Second" - had served on the commission for decades, passing on the responsibility only after his retirement and move to Florida. But I'm not so sure.

"So, Ann," John said, "what's this business about a pink cat? What are you telling Louie?" He may have meant for his voice to sound professional, even advisory, but to me the tone was parental, patronizing.

"I didn't *tell* him anything," I said, defensively. "He asked me if I thought the stray cat we call Snowball would look good painted pink. I told Louie I didn't think he could do it."

"He can't." The declaration was followed by a pause, as if John's attention was diverted. I imagined him proofreading a summons as he talked. But as the pause lengthened, I began to wonder if he'd maybe put me on hold by mistake. Then it occurred to me, suddenly - maybe that was all he'd intended to say in the first place, as if saying that much was enough. I could feel my cheeks and forehead fill with blood.

"Then what's the problem?" I asked.

47

"He stopped me in the hall this morning and began asking a million questions about painting a cat pink."

"And?"

"And I told him he just can't. But he doesn't seem to believe me. So I want *you* to tell him. He'll listen to you."

For the record, I should disclose here that John and I have a history, a history of intimacy - something that a good number of North Bank females my age (and younger) could also claim. But past history aside, the tone of John's voice irked me to no end; it was accusatory and presumptuous. Of all people, I thought, John Foster III should be the *last* to be telling me what to do as far as Louie was concerned.

I pulled the phone away from my ear and looked at it, parrying our conversation with my own pause, certain that if I replied too suddenly, it wouldn't go well. My voice was likely to shake as uncontrollably as I now realized my hand was. I didn't want to end up cussing out loud.

Louie's been the brunt of an awful lot of mean teasing over the years, and, sad to say, I count myself a party to it. As an adolescent, whenever I was frustrated with my father - embarrassed by the fact that a preternaturally smiling half-wit lived in our garage - I expended my share of unkind verbal thrusts at Louie. I mean, when he wasn't making my high school friends uncomfortable with his goofy-grinning presence, he was boring them with his interminable questions. Who could blame us if at times we mimicked him, or cut him short, or replied in snide, sarcastic ways? He would just nod and smile anyway, pleased for the attention. We figured he wouldn't understand.

Not until college did I begin to see myself as a spoiled, insensitive, loss-ridden only-child, who had a hard time believing that anyone could possibly be so contented with so little. Not until I met Don, a man with an uncanny depth of poise and good will, did I begin to realize just how irresponsible and mean my treatment of Louie was - behaviours I've come to regret. My decision to return to North Bank and to accept responsibility for the apartment over the garage, in fact, may have had as much to do with Louie as it did with the economics of inheritance or with honouring a father's promise. I may have felt in some way I owed Louie as much, and that by assuming supervision of his welfare, I could in some way make up for the small cruelties I'd foisted upon him during my thoughtless adolescence. Certainly, my going off to study at a large urban university in a distant state educated me in more than just matters of literature and philosophy. I learned that the ways of a small town are not necessarily the ways of the world. But not everyone in North Bank has had the education I have. And the person I was talking to on the phone was a prime example.

Besides, knowing John as I do - intimately - I began to suspect that he had another agenda. Perhaps the phone call was not about Louie at all. Perhaps it had something to do with my husband, who John has begrudged since college, both playfully and publically, blaming Don for our dissolution as a couple. Fearing the worse, I took a deep breath and let it out slowly, through my nose.

"Okay," I said. "So why can't Louie dye Snowball pink?"

"What?" said John, abruptly. I pictured his head jerking up, suddenly attentive to the call, as if his mindless foraging among a stack of file folders on his desk had been interrupted by a casual girlfriend's announcement of an unexpected pregnancy.

"Why can't he dye Snowball?" I repeated. "Just tell me what the law is and I'll explain it to Louie."

"For one thing, it's not his cat," John said.

"It's nobody's cat," I said. "It's Louie's as much as anyone's."

Again there was no immediate response, only what sounded little several quick breaths, like panting. There seemed to be something important that wasn't being said. I could feel my pulse slowing, returning to normal. I decided to play offense: "You didn't answer my question, John. Is there a law against painting cats?"

"Not exactly," John mumbled. "But there *are* ordinances against - "

"Then why should I tell him he can't?"

"Because he *can't!* And don't you go encouraging him." The voice on the other end of the line was beginning to fume. For whatever reason, Louie had stirred up something in John, and, as a result, I suddenly found myself with an opportunity for a little, if not payback exactly, a kind of former-girlfriend goading that would be satisfying and instructive.

"Well," I said, "then Louie can paint Snowball pink if he wants to."

"No, he *can't!*" John roared.

"But you said there's no ordinance against it. Besides, didn't I see you and Geri Tipton at the circus last week, where the elephants were pink. Clearly there's no law against coloured animals."

"Damn it, Ann," said a voice that now seemed in its tenor to be a poor imitation of John's, "don't you start on me with those stupid elephants. I've been over and over that with Louie. Are you two in cahoots or something?"

That thought - that I was in cahoots with a simple-minded and generally agreeable person - struck me as funny.

"It just seems to me," I said, "that if elephants are allowed to be pink, then cats should be allowed as well, as long as it doesn't harm them."

"We'll just see about that," said John, and he hung up.

All through high school - maybe even earlier - John teased Louie relentlessly, called him "Louie Louisiana." During the months that John and I dated - the spring of my senior year of high school, the summer after, up to my first Thanksgiving break from college - whenever we encountered Louie in town, John would ask loudly if anyone "smelled smoke in the bayou," and Louie would take off running for the carriage house - unless I could stop him and convince him it was only a joke. Louie's fear of fire is nearly as legendary as his smile. Even today, if fire engines happen to pass by the courthouse, sirens screaming, Louie will stop whatever he is doing, close his eyes as tightly as he can and press his hands hard against his ears - he will stand stock still - until someone he recognizes comes and reassures him that everything is all right.

"The flames were everywhere - twenty feet high!" my father would say,

recounting the time Rick Lewis - Louie's father - wrapped his best friend in muddy canvas and carried him out of a burning jungle, where what was left of their platoon eventually found them.

"You were unconscious, according to my *recollection," Rick Lewis would* say. *"How can you be sure it was me?"*

"I can't," my father would reply, the banter well-rehearsed. "But they gave you *the medal for it, and that's evidence enough."*

John teased Louie even after I had asked him to stop, after I saw the meanness behind the teasing - after I'd told John the fire story - after we broke up and our friendship dissolved. Maybe, now that I think about it, even to this day.

For the next couple of weeks, Snowball remained white, although I didn't see him around as much as usual. Then Don noticed in the *Banner* that a new ordinance was on the agenda for the next city commission meeting, an ordinance preventing "the colouration, by artificial means, of any living creature, domestic or wild."

We decided that we'd attend our first commission meeting ever, and to take Louie along.

The North Bank City Commission meets in the assembly room at the courthouse, familiar territory for Louie. On the night of the meeting, as we made our way through the maze of vacant folding chairs, Louie couldn't help but stop and straighten any that weren't perfectly in line. I told him that he didn't need to do that, that he wasn't there to work, but he just grinned sheepishly and then sat down between Don and me. The meeting started about five minutes after seven. By seven forty-eight, when the New Business items were introduced, there were still fewer than twenty people in the audience, and only five of the eight commissioners - plus John, and the mayor - following the agenda. "Sports banquet," I heard someone whisper.

Louie fidgeted right up until the new ordinance was introduced. At one point-during the approval of the previous meeting's minutes - he interrupted the proceedings by exiting through the door behind the commissioners and returning with a pitcher of water and seven glasses, which he placed directly in front of Joyce Stelling's microphone. Joyce is the current mayor.

"Thank you, Louie," she said, and they continued.

John had barely introduced the proposed ordinance when Louie raised his hand. At that point in the proceedings, Mayor Stelling reminded us - the public - that there would be ample opportunity to voice opinions "at the appropriate time." Don whispered something to Louie, and he lowered his arm. I scooted his way and took his hand in mine. If Louie was listening as intently as his tense arm suggested, he was unquestionably the most alert person in the room.

After a short, uncomfortable silence, Milt Aston asked John why such an ordinance was necessary. "Don't we already have an animal cruelty law?" he said. "Shouldn't this be covered under that?"

"The animal cruelty law doesn't technically address painting or dying animals different colours."

"But who in their right mind would want to do that?" one of the other commissioners asked. I looked at Louie; he hadn't flinched. He was staring at the pitcher of water in front of Mayor Stelling.

"Let's just say that I've been approached with such an idea," John said. He looked my way. I had to give him credit for not mentioning Louie's name.

"Does colouring animals hurt them?" Joyce asked.

"Sometimes," John said.

"Then it seems that we should amend our animal cruelty ordinance instead of creating a new one."

"But it goes beyond physical injury," said Dr. Johnson, our dentist, another long-established commissioner. I suddenly recalled that among the plaques and diplomas on the walls of his waiting room, there was some recognition for his work as an animal rights advocate. By my quick estimation, at least three of the five commissioners in attendance were on John's side.

Louie began to look at Donald and then at me and then back

at the ice water on the table. Dr. Johnson continued: "What about the emotional trauma or embarrassment that a purple poodle goes through. I think a separate ordinance is a good idea, and I move we accept it."

"Second," someone said.

After a few rephrasings of the same opinion were bantered about by other commissioners, public comments were solicited. That's when Louie stood up.

"The Mayor recognizes Mr. Lewis," Joyce said.

I was concerned at first about how well Louie would do in front of a group. But he held himself in control. He said, "The elephants were pretty. Wouldn't Snowball be pretty, too?" He turned to face me. "Wouldn't he, Ann?"

I began formulating what I knew would have to be a convincing argument, figuring that I'd need to help make a case for Louie, when Becky Reynolds spoke up. Becky had been a year behind me at school; she was now working for Legal Aid in Grand Rapids, commuting there every day, as many people from North Bank do.

"It seems to me," Becky said, pacing her words carefully, "such an ordinance is unnecessary. If colouring a dog purple —"

"Pink," said Louie suddenly. He was still standing.

"- or *pink* would harm that animal, then the animal cruelty ordinance could be applied. On the other hand, if there was no injury to the animal, then what harm is there in rendering it any colour we wish? Remember the purple ducks that were part of the window display at Bart's Hardware last Easter? And how many of you bought those green and blue chicks that the Athletic Boosters sold to support Special Olympics?"

"Water colour," John said. "It came out in the first rain."

"A blue chick is not the same thing as a purple dog," someone said aloud.

"*Pink*," Louie said again.

Suddenly, everyone began talking at once, and it became very difficult to hear what was being said. Strong polarization about the issue apparently existed among the members of the public in attendance; the commissioners became restless; along the length of the table was a marked increase in attention to water refills. John was either taking copious notes on the legal pad in front of him or was intent on doodling a masterpiece.

Finally, Joyce Stelling, enforcing her prerogative as mayor, acknowledged that it was obviously an issue that needed to be addressed more completely before a vote could be taken at the next meeting. She asked that a public hearing on the proposed ordinance be scheduled in the meantime, for two Mondays hence.

On the way home, Louie wanted to know why so many people were concerned about Snowball. "Nobody cared about him before," he said. I noted that it wasn't in the form of a question.

"It's not about Snowball," Don said, in a tone of voice that fell somewhere between reassurance and condemnation. "It's about politics."

And character, I was thinking. But I didn't say it.

Don and I had expected a certain amount of controversy, especially after the *Banner's* somewhat biased coverage of the commission meeting, yet we never imagined that so many people would raise issue with "Pink Cat" ordinance - as it came to be called - that the hearing had to be moved from the assembly room in the courthouse to the auditorium in the middle school. By the time we got there, fifteen minutes before seven, the only three vacant seats together were in front, the middle of the second row, and so Louie, Don, and I had to apologize our way to them.

Louie remained quiet throughout, less riled than Don even, who, for once, was huffing and snorting audibly at some of the speakers' thoughtless remarks. I'm not sure that Louie completely understood what was going on, for, quite frankly, I was having trouble following it all myself. The logic of public opinion, it seems, is written on scrap paper with unsharpened pencils.

Mayor Stelling began the hearing with a summary of the ordinance and the issues that had been raised at the prior commission meeting. She reminded everyone that this was to be an open forum and that as a community we could benefit from it only if we treated opposing views thoughtfully and with respect. But even as she talked, hands were waving all around the auditorium.

"I think it's *disgusting*," one woman said. "Why would anyone want a blue or green dog anyway? Anyone who done that should be put in jail."

"But it's a question of personal freedom," said a long-haired man in a voice that seemed to mimic Clarence Darrow. "Why can't I paint my cat purple if I want to? Isn't it a question of art? Next you'll be telling me that I can't paint my garage any colour I want."

"You *can't*, if I can help it!" someone shouted.

"That's a good point," Becky Reynolds said, when she was finally able to be heard. She'd been recognized by Mayor Stelling some time before but had to wait for a lull in the cacophony before she could speak. "If I want to express my individuality by painting my cat pink, I should be allowed to, if it's not hurting the animal. My neighbours shouldn't be able to prevent me from doing so just because they don't like it. Should we pass an ordinance against crabgrass if we don't like the looks of someone's lawn? I think such an ordinance may well be unconstitutional - it infringes on personal expression."

"A pink cat is *obscene*," John said, without looking up from the yellow notepad he'd been studying. "And obscenity is outside of the First Amendment. You should know that, Counselor - *Roth vs. the United States*, 1957."

"But, *Counselor*," Becky retorted, "the community needs to decide by its own standards what's obscene and what isn't - *Miller vs. California*. That's the case here. I'm not sure the rest of us are willing to go that far in sanctioning expression. We'd be opening ourselves up to Federal recriminations, which could get expensive."

A man dressed in a flannel shirt and a brown insulated coat shouted: "I don't know of nobody that would want to paint their cows, but I'd sure as hell like to know I could if I wanted to."

"Didn't Jerry Kraals paint *COW* on the sides of his Holsteins a couple hunting seasons ago?" someone asked. "Would that still be legal under this ordinance?"

"What we're talking about here is censorship," said Carl Fowler, the editor of the *Banner*. "Let it go on record that the *Banner* supports Freedom of Expression."

"What we're talking about is protecting a helpless animal," John said. "A cat that can't protect himself. Wouldn't you want to be protected if you were as helpless?"

"If you've ever seen Snowball go through my garbage," someone joked, "you'd know he ain't helpless." Laughter moved through the sweaty audience like a breeze from an open door. Even Louie laughed.

"What we're talking about," said someone in the back of the room, "is a stupid cat. How do you know he wouldn't *like* to be pink?"

What could only be called pandemonium followed. Angers flared and tempers were stretched taut. A straw vote seemed to indicate that the people in favour of the ordinance outnumbered those who opposed it, though no one actually counted the number of hands, and it looked pretty equal to me. Finally, after nearly two hours of bickering, Mrs. Rupert, whose hair was the colour of tarnished aluminium, raised her hand to speak.

"Does this mean," she said from her seat, "that I can no longer have Joanne do my hair? After all, doesn't the ordinance say 'living creature'?"

Once the laughter stopped, Becky, in response to the commissioner's silence, said, "Under the ordinance as it's proposed, I'd say that most of the beauticians in town would be considered liable. Unless we are not defining people as living creatures."

"Is Mrs. Rupert proposing an amendment to the ordinance?" asked Joyce.

"We could reword it," said John abruptly, and he began to scribble on his yellow pad. From my perspective, he looked a little sheepish.

"What I'm suggesting," said Mrs. Rupert, as she rose from her seat, "is that the elected officials of this fair city should have more important matters to spend their valuable time on than such silliness."

The auditorium broke into applause. Almost immediately people began excusing themselves and manoeuvring to the aisles. With the commotion, we could barely hear Mayor Stelling acknowledge the lateness of the hour, thank everyone for coming, and proclaim that the commission would take all the helpful comments into consideration before they voted at the next regularly scheduled meeting.

Back home, Louie thanked us several times for taking him along, then said good-night and went up to his apartment. Don fixed vodka tonics, and for a long time we sat on the wooden swing in the yard, listening to the neighbourhood settle as the light faded. There was no sign of Snowball.

"It's funny," Don said, suddenly, "how some people have such a need to foist their pettiness on others. Funny, in a sad way, I mean."

"I know what you mean," I said.

"- and how so many of us get caught up in the *pet*tiness." He gave a slight laugh. "Excuse the pun."

I laughed as well, a different kind of laugh. Not so much for the play on the word *pet*, as for the recognition that I could be one of those people.

In the morning, the *Banner*, as expected, gave a slightly biased description of the evening's event. The "freedom" fighters came out ahead. Fortunately, neither John nor Louie were mentioned. During the rest of the week, the editorial section of the *Banner* offered a score of disputatious letters from both sides - much of which simply repeated the basic contentions.

By the day of the next commission meeting, however, the discussion had long been stalled.

Nevertheless, we had to stand in the back of the assembly room at the courthouse because every folding chair was taken. The commissioners - all eight of them - were playing to a crowd that spilled into the hallway. At two minutes after seven, Mayor Stelling began the meeting by announcing that, in the best interests of those involved, the commission had decided to remove the proposed animal colouration ordinance from consideration - that the motion and second had been withdrawn. There would be no more discussion of it.

At that announcement, the crowd, clapping and yelling, began to disperse. Very few individuals would stay for the rest of the agenda.

Several people congratulated Louie as we were leaving, which sort of struck me as odd, since his association with the ordinance had never been made public. But a small town being what it is, he was treated like a celebrity - if only briefly. Even John made a special effort to say something to us as we were leaving. "See you tomorrow, Louie," he said, and he shook Louie's hand.

Don suggested we celebrate at the Dippy Quick.

"Well, Louie," I said, watching him suck strawberry ripple through a hole in the bottom of his sugar cone, "now you can paint Snowball pink - or whatever colour you want."

"Green," said Don. "I vote for green, Brother Louie."

"Oh, no," said Louie. "Don't you like Snowball the way he is?"

He was smiling. Like the biggest kid at the circus.

***

How It's Always Been

Jake Teeny

Jake Teeny is currently pursuing his PhD at The Ohio State University, where he researches the psychology of persuasion. In addition to his scientific work, Jake rites all kinds of fiction, appearing in literary magazines like the Saturday Evening Post as well as placing in nationally renowned short screenplay competitions. For a list of all his publication credits, along with his weekly blog (discussing useful and fascinating findings in social psychology), check out his website www.everydaypsych.com, where you can find more short stories and free psychology eBooks.

"The language is rich in romantic imagery" says Judge Brett about *How It's Always Been.*

"**H**ere's something unusual about me," says the woman I'd spend all three of a genie's wishes on just to meet. "Every night before bed—and this is true—I have to...check the freezer to make sure my cat's not locked inside."

I laugh like it is natural to walk outside naked. Like if I jumped, my ankles would fan wings and gust me skyward. "That is pretty unusual," I say. By accident (subconsciously on purpose?) our swinging hands graze.

Sunlight. I have been reborn as sunlight.

"All right, your turn," she says. "Tell me something really unusual about you."

"*Really* unusual?" I peek at her as we stroll through the humming courtyard of our *alma mater*, beneath the first cornflower sky in weeks. Frisbees floating. Baseballs buzzing. People sprawled on towels like cats draped across windowsills. "Are unusual things even possible on a day as perfect as this?" Away from her, my words and thoughts are like my handwriting, full of cockeyed "r's" and jerky "e's." But beside her, I know only sweeping calligraphy.

"Having to check the freezer for my cat was kind of weird."

"Yea, it was."

She laughs, her face half concealed behind her hair. Which is necessary. For should I witness her full smile, my bones would turn to parchment and my blood to lighter fluid and there are no lakes near enough with water deep enough to prevent my prodigious combustion. "Then it's your turn," she says. "Tell me something about you that makes me wince."

I'm smiling so hard I'm dizzy. Or maybe it's the heat. Or most likely it's her. "You want to wince, huh?" I muse over every eccentricity I comprise, but only one fact keeps battering at the bridge of my nose: *The four women I have ever loved, I loved at the wrong time.* My heart a series of Venn diagrams, where it's always the rejected third. "My ring fingers are different lengths."

"*Bor*-ing," she chimes.

We are both in our mid-twenties, the most fertile time for love: the gardens of romance trimmed by the reason of experience. "Let me think…" I skim thoughts for something clever but can only meditate on metaphors about her. Those images between my ribs, Easter marshmallows inside a microwave set to max. "You know," I say, "you knit galaxies together when you smile."

In an instant, her radiance flattens. Is culled and crinkled and clutched inward.

In an instant, my radiance is bled. Sucked through the arteries in my wrist until I cough dust and blink ash.

The first girl I ever fell in love with was Tessa Danners. She had strawberry blond hair and one dimple and fingernails that were always painted in shades of blue. We were six and in the first grade and when she spoke to me, she turned my heart to dandelion seeds and blew on them with her giggles. Halfway into the school year, though, my family moved to another county, and one day my mother received a phone call that I should stop sending her letters.

"You want to sit?" she asks, and I nod, ready to nod at anything she requested—to sprint away from her, to solve a dozen Rubik's cubes, to buy her a mountain and then fill it with dynamite.

We head toward a bench with a concealed view of the main path. I sit first, and when she follows, our arms press against one another.

"What's the last movie you cried at?" she asks. "I think you'd be a funny crier."

I laugh. I can't help it. She makes every one of my organs feel like they're aligned for the first time. "The Little Mermaid," I say. "Two years ago."

"You're lying."

"But I'm not a funny crier. I'm a manly crier."

"What does that even mean?"

"Just one tear," I say. "And it's flexing the whole time it rolls down."

She half-conceals her grin behind her hair again, and my fingers crave to stroke her cheek.

The second girl I fell in love with was Katya Bader from my high school English class. She had hazel eyes and symmetrical freckles and she started on the school volleyball team. We dated for a few months, her whispers capable of painting murals—of convincing those walls that the paint was already tucked inside their cracks. But I was too cowardly to do more than kiss her. Too fearful. Too craven. Too gutless. Too yellow. I looked at her Facebook the other day and saw she was getting married to one of my best friends from middle school.

"How long does it take you to get ready in the morning?" I ask, when really I mean: *How long does it take to comb sunlight into your hair? To brush moonlight around your eyes?*

She puzzles her face. "An hour maybe. You?"

"Similar."

"Why do you ask?"

"It was...the first question I had to prevent awkward silence."

She smiles the solution to infinity.

"You know what I like to do sometimes?" she says. "You know how you hear all this ambient noise. The cars on Pike Street.

The leaves on the cement. Your own breath."

With our arms still touching, my breath must sound like waves cresting a cliff.

"If you close your eyes, though, and just focus on one sound. Just the cars. Or just the leaves. Or just your breath…"

And there, in that moment, it feels like the world has misplaced our names, like we exist in one of God's few sighs.

"It's nice," she says. "It's really nice."

The quiet between us is now different than before. The right kind of quiet. Like the creases of a map refolded perfectly. So we sit like that. The trees, the sun, the bench, the people, our socks, our shoes, our day still golden.

"Do you think…" She pauses.

The wind, the grass, the birds, the laughter, our shirts, our hair, our world still waiting.

"Do you think we tell each other too much?"

The dirt, the concrete, the shrubs, our hopes, our lips, our arms still touching.

"By asking," I say, hesitating, "you must think we do."

I had been raised to believe that good things happen to good people. That you should try to fill the world with love—to make people smile, to plant happiness—that the goodness seeded today will be the harvest of tomorrow. In college, I fell in love with Erin Lassiter. But I don't think about her anymore. The loneliness she caused me…a hundred sculptures I could chisel from it and still have enough stone to build the vault that kept them.

"It's just…" She twists the blue diamond of her wedding ring to face her palm. "It's just...you know."

From the prism of heaven's star bursts, down and deeper down to the splintered shells and sand of the ocean's floor. "I know," I say—and I do. I have known. Since the moment I first fell in love with her. But hearing her say it, her need to acknowledge it—I feel like...I feel...

Silent.

"It's not fair," she says. "You... Never before you was there... But now..." She looks away. She says nothing. No, she says the anti-matter of words.

In fairy tales, conversations like this never happened. So many stutters and pauses, so much melancholy and emptiness. In front of us, college students begin filling their backpacks, stretching, wandering from the courtyard, taking with them the slap of baseballs and the sinking glide of Frisbees. Afternoons always finish like this, though; never a bang, just a burning wick you some point realize is no longer burning.

"This... It doesn't... We don't have to stop talking," I say. But why I do I keep talking now? "We're good people," I assert. "Good people can still talk." For my execution, instead of the electric chair I choose to be hanged by a thousand, neon balloons. *And for your final meal, sir?* A jug of helium to stretch the ascent before I strangle.

"You're... you're a good person," she says without looking at me. "I like talking to you. I like... It helps."

Every night, she goes back to him, back to that image in my head of her flush and naked body pressed against a stranger. "I like talking to you, too," I say. And there it was, all the love I could have added to the world, and instead, I produce a heart full of milk

65

I can only drink from when curdled. "Maybe we should head back, though?" The truth behind my words turn her eyes doleful, and for a breath, I relish that hurt I cause her. For a breath, I don't feel so alone.

"Yes. All right," she says.

The hollow wind blows at my shoulders as we stand.

Love…

I used to think that love and fate were the same thing, that you could find the right person at the wrong time and still make it work. Really, though, love may start that way but it never ended so. If one person doesn't leave the other first, then one person always dies second. "I thought of something unusual about me," I say, the courtyard around us accepting a paler hue, a light coat of beige leaked over the entire world. "I've never once cried in a movie."

"What? What about The Little Mermaid?" She smiles so broadly it makes my teeth hurt.

"No, not even The Little Mermaid," I say.

She snorts. "I don't believe it. Who hasn't cried in at least one movie?"

I shrug. "Maybe something's wrong with me."

***

Have a Nice Day...

Diana Powell

Diana Powell was born and brought up in Llanelli, South Wales, and studied English at Aberystwyth University. Her stories have won, or been placed, in a number of competitions, including the 2014 PENfro prize (winner). Last year, she was short-listed for the Over the Edge New Writer award, long-listed for the Sean O'Faolain prize, a runner-up in the Cinnamon Press competition. Her work has also appeared in a number of magazines, including 'The Lonely Crowd', 'Crannog', and 'Brittle Star'.

She now lives with her husband in west Wales, and is currently working on a novella and a collection of stories.

Of her entry to Nivalis 2017 Judge Sandra says "very topical and well-written, Have a Nice Day was an intriguing read about a conflicted character, which was handled skilfully and, most importantly, convincingly."

The characters in "Have a Nice Day..." are real, the incidents and thoughts are not – they solely represent what could have been.

Martyl. She paints pictures. Abstract landscapes. Of waterfalls, rocks, the sky. The kind that makes you feel warm inside.

Martyl Langsdorf. She made a Doomsday Machine, ready to blow the Earth into a million, trillion particles of star dust.

'We had a class about it in school,' the girl who brings her morning coffee tells her. 'Our topic of the week. Scared the crap out of me, 'scuse the language. I had nightmares for months after. I thought the countdown to zero had already begun. Guess that can happen to a twelve year old.'

Doomsday. She gets it all the time. Fearful children, ignorant journalists, misguided adults. In California, a man jumped off the Golden Gate, because he heard the Clock was only three minutes from disaster. And who made the Clock? She did.

'I'm sorry,' she tells Tannie, the coffee girl. 'But, really, it's not my fault. All I did was sketch two lines and four dots on a piece of paper. For my husband.'

They were sitting at a concert at the time, she thinks... she seems to remember, though, suddenly, she is not sure if Alexander was there. He was always so very busy. The drawing was on the back of the program. Or the musical score, maybe.

'It's easy to get confused,' she tells Tannie.

People have always been confused about it. They can't even decide if there is a real clock, for a start. Someone from the Board will explain patiently that it's a metaphor, a symbol, and, would you believe, the very next day, there will be an article stating that it's really there, in a room in the University of Chicago, big, round and plain for all to see. And how many times has she seen an interview with some so-called expert saying the hands were closest to midnight during the Cuban Missile Crisis? 'Hogwash,' she'll yell at the screen. But it never made any difference.

'I get confused myself sometimes.'

'Well, you're old,' Tannie tells her back. Meaning, your mind's gone. Meaning, you'll soon be dead anyway, so it makes no difference to you.

When she'll die is something that bothers her – not the hour the doctor will scribble on a piece of paper; she doesn't care about *that*, you don't when you're ninety-five. But Clock time, that's what matters. It's five minutes to midnight, right now, according to the latest Bulletin (she checks online regularly, she likes to keep up to date, the same as she's always done) but, with the conflict in the Middle East, nuclear modernization, etc, she's sure Time is going tick on down any day soon.

And that's what the obituaries will headline with. 'Martyl Langsdorf, creator of the Doomsday Clock, dies at four minutes to!' Or three minutes to! Two minutes to! No surely, not that. It hasn't been that close since 1953, when they tested the H-bomb – the worst it's ever been (N.B. NOT the Cuban Missile Crisis). | And only six years after she set it on the seven.

'They blew a Pacific island to bits. Well, not really to bits. There was none left.'

She sees Tannie's face. She remembers the nightmares.

'Oh, sorry... I was just thinking about my obituary. How it will begin with wherever those minute hands are at.'

And then they'll go on and on about it, saying how it was one of the most significant graphic representations of the twentieth century; quote Michael Bierut again, no doubt, who created a new version in 2007. All those things he said, praising her... 'Cry at midnight/traditional imagery/using an everyday object/something so complex reduced to something so simple. A magical achievement!'

'As if I'd waved a magic wand, and there it was! Well, there was something spontaneous about it that night at the concert, I'll allow. After all, two lines and four dots don't take too much contrivance. It's not rocket science. No, I left *that* to my husband and his pals. But, of course, they say it's the concept that matters. And *that* was brilliant. Apparently.'

Of course, she was already ninety in '07, so most people probably thought she was dead already. But with all the fuss about the 're-imagining', the media were reminded of her existence, and tracked her down, and wanted to interview her all over again, or put her on a stage, or in some television studio. So she got herself into 'Clock Lady' mode, because if she's honest, she's always been able to do that – adopt that particular persona when necessary, where she would tell them what they wanted to hear, answer as she was supposed to. Resurrecting the sound-bites she had perfected down the years.

'They couldn't pay me much.' She liked to slip that one in. The audience always liked it! They laughed, she laughed. And 'a clock is an instrument for measuring, and that's what scientists do!' And there was her line about the importance of art, how this design was a clear example of how much it could achieve. 'Artists have the power to change the world!' On and on and on.

So, yes, there were these moments when she enjoyed the attention of it all, as the Bulletin has always been ready to point out in its publicity. And will no doubt point out again, when she dies, glad to get another slice of air-time, eager to hang on the coat tails of her recognition, one last time.

'But that's not what I want to be remembered for! I don't want *that* as my legacy. It's not what I want my obituary to say. Then again, maybe if I'm lucky, they'll add a paragraph about my paintings as an afterthought!'

It is different on her own website, because she's got one – that keeping up to date thing, again. On there, it is the Clock that gets relegated to a line towards the end. There, it's all about her life as an artist for over eighty years. And her travels. And her wonderful home and how she saved it for the nation.

So why does the press, and most of America, including Tannie, insist on calling her the Clock lady?

'It was just a magazine cover,' she says. 'And that tight budget meant there were only two colours! Still, the design was purely aesthetic. (Does Tannie know what that means, she wonders?) That's why I picked seven minutes to. It looked good to my eye. Of course, some argued it looked more like an eight, had the nerve

71

to point it out to me, but whose clock was it? Wasn't even a whole clock, in fact. Just the top left quarter. So… no Clock. No machine, Doomsday or otherwise. Our aim was to prevent nuclear catastrophe, not start it.'

'That's what my teacher said the next week, when my mom phoned to complain about the nightmares. And the hysterics. And the not eating. But it was too late. I'd got the notion fixed in my head that there was this clock attached to some device that was connected to a nuclear bomb, that it would blow up the world when it struck midnight. Like what happened in Japan, like they showed us in that film. 'Cept it was going to be far worse than that, on account of the new weapons being a hundred times more powerful. ARMAGEDDON. The coming of the APOCALYPSE. The END of the WORLD is NOW!

That's how these things look when you're twelve.'

When she was twelve, she was going to make music. When she was twelve, there weren't any A-bombs, any H-bombs. There wasn't even any uranium back then. Well, there was, of course. It has always existed. Just such a shame that Klaproth found it. Just a pity that Becquerel discovered its radioactive properties, and that Fermi, Oppenheimer and the others, including Alexander… Well…

Uranium. Atomic symbol U. In the beginning, she was going to go with a U, because that's where she thought it all started. 'Uranium, with its naturally occurring fissile isotope.' No uranium, no nuclear bomb. No Hiroshima, no Nagasaki, no arms race, no Cold War, no sixteen thousand three hundred nuclear warheads in the world.

A bold **U**, perhaps, that she could draw following the edge of the cover round, with the contents of the issue inside it, nicely contained. The title above, perhaps, or stretching from side to side. A plain U, no fancy font, so that it was clear, the meaning was clear.

How boring, she thinks now; how uninspiring, how pathetic. How she so wishes she'd gone with that U. No Clock, no Clock Lady, no nightmares, no suicides, no obituaries that don't mention her hundred solo exhibitions, her displays in galleries stretching from New York to L.A. Her work on archaeological sites. Her social conscience murals on public buildings. Her skies... How she loves her skies! Once upon a time, all she wanted to do was capture air and light, then set them free on a canvas. But did anyone else love them as much as she did? Did anyone pay them any attention at all?

Perhaps she should have stuck with music.

'Truth is, I wasn't good enough. But my paintings... did you know that I was regarded as a child prodigy? And of course, my mother was an artist. And my father took photographs. And we had these artists' communities and summer schools, where we... Oh, did you know that Gershwin...'

'Yeh, you told me.'

Had she? She doesn't remember. But she remembers Gershwin, coming through town, buying one of her early pieces. The thrill it gave her, making her think 'This is what I want to do.'

'Because I so admired Gershwin. Do you like Gershwin, Tannie?'

'Not really my scene, Mrs L.'

'Oh. What kind of music *do* you like?'

'Rock. Heavy metal. That kind of thing. Alt rock, too. Wouldja believe that some of those guys have written songs about your clock? Imagine, these wild long-haired rockers draped in metal and leather, bawling out about your creation? Iron Maiden. The Smashing Pumpkins – have you heard of them? One of their songs about it got used in a movie. All these robot machines fighting to your tune. And wrestlers, and monster-trucks – they do it, too!'

'Well, it wasn't really my tune, Tannie, just like it isn't really my clock.'

'No, but you inspired it. You're really quite famous. When I told my mother you were in here, she didn't know whether to come in and ask for your autograph, or punch you in the face, on account of those nightmares.'

'Perhaps you could explain to her that really, it was nothing. A sketch for the cover of a magazine that nobody read. It wasn't even all my idea. Egbert made some suggestions, said about keeping it going. But if you look up Egbert Jacobson on the Internet, not a word about the Clock, not a word! And – think about it – it's only when they decided to move the hands, that the image got changed into an icon. And I had nothing to do with that! That was in '49, two years later – the Board deciding they'd have these get-togethers to discuss the fate of the planet, and change the minute-hand up or down, according how close we were to nuclear disaster. Moved it to three minutes to then, things having already got a lot worse. Same as it is now, things don't look good at all, climate change unchecked, huge nuclear arsenals… Oh, sorry.'

Tannie picks up her empty cup and heads out the door. 'See ya tomorrow, Mrs. L. Have a nice day.'

'Have a nice day,' it's what people say these days, even if they don't mean it. Even if it makes no sense, saying it to an old woman lying in bed in a nursing home. As if … what's she going to do that's 'nice'? She hasn't got the energy to lift her paint-brush any more. 'Still painting at ninety-five,' she liked to say, until the last attack put paid to that.

'Have a Nice Day!' It's something else, too. Her work based on her painting of Tent Rocks, New Mexico. 2002.

'Have you ever been there?' she asks Tannie, who is no longer in the room. It doesn't matter, she can still talk to her, just as she can still talk to Alexander, even though he's been dead for such a long time. Or anyone she likes, really.

'You really should go. There are these amazing rock formations, pointed at the top, like tipis, hence the name.'

She remembers her amazement when she first saw them. She clambered through them, in and out of their caves, knelt to feel their texture, worshipped them you could say, as she did with all her landscapes.

The colours at sunrise and sunset, the way they played on the folds in the rock. How she loved that place… But then, she loved most of the places she had visited. Greece, Egypt, Iraq, Turkey. Such wonder in all. So much time spent looking and absorbing them and then, they gave her her art, like a gift. That waterfall…

'Have you seen my waterfall, Tannie? I remember that day so clearly. I sat there, watching the water, hour after hour. Alexander got quite fed up waiting for me. *How can you stare for so long? At nothing but water going over some rocks.* But of course, there was so much else – the movement, the energy, change, slow to fast, still to rushing. Mind, he wasn't in the best of moods in Japan. Perhaps it was a mistake to go there. The train had stopped at Nagasaki. We were supposed to get out, to meet the people, to see… But he couldn't. He just stayed in his seat, staring straight ahead. He said he felt ashamed. And it was so awful… the way those people had died… Oh…'

Better not to mention that, perhaps, better to get back to New Mexico. Not that there was anything to be proud of there, with Los Alamos, and the first bomb test. But, hopefully, Tannie doesn't know about any of that, and won't make the connection.

'Of course, Georgia O'Keefe rather steals my thunder when it comes to the New Mexican landscape, but still, I'm happy enough with my efforts. I didn't use the pointed summits in the 2002 work. I wanted the larger, chunkier faces of the rocks. It was that texture that was important. And their power. And then I placed all these representations of the Clock over and around it. Through it, even…'

She shouldn't have. A mistake. She should have left well alone. It was another of those instances that reminded people of her link to the Clock, dragging it all into the limelight again. And, as usual, she had enjoyed playing to it, going on about Art and Science, Science and Art ('the cover of our '59 Bulletin!').

'The fusion of two distinct disciplines!'

Just like her marriage.

'Is that where it all went wrong?' But there's no-one there to hear her, because Tannie's gone, hasn't she?

And really, she's glad. She shouldn't have said it. She shouldn't have thought it. Though Alexander has been dead these …however

75

many years, it still seems like a betrayal. And she loved him, didn't she? And they were a great couple, weren't they? Except... And yet... What if...? What if she hadn't met him, fallen in love, married him? What if there'd been someone else? A farmer. A carpenter. Another artist best of all, perhaps, so that they could have stayed in her mother's communes, spent their lives just painting, with music playing in the background. All these quotes of hers about her interest in the interplay between the forms. But is it true? Was it true before she met Alexander? She cannot remember – it is too long ago.

Happenstance, that's what it all comes down to. Happenstance that she'd got talking to him that day. Or happenstance that she'd gone to *that* university, where he also happened to be studying– a scientist who went on to work on the creation of the atom bomb. Who helped make 'Little Boy', that got dropped on Hiroshima, killing sixty-six thousand people outright. And they were the lucky ones. Following it with 'Fat Man' on Nagasaki (oh, the silliness of those names!) Okay, so he and some of the others soon realised the error of their invention. 'We made something that can kill us all. Imagine that. That's how clever we are.' So they got together – the Board of Atomic Scientists – and decided to form a protest group to campaign against nuclear proliferation, sent a petition to Truman, which he may or may not have received (another of those confusions). And in 1947, they started a magazine, the Bulletin. And whom did they ask to design the cover?

'Me! I was the only artist they knew! Who else could they ask? Hyman – Hyman, it was, who said 'Just have a think, Martyl. See what you can come up with'. So I thought of the U, and dismissed that as hopeless. And then I just sat around listening to them, and picked up on their urgency, how anxious they were that something needed to be done NOW. Before it was too late. Time was of the essence. TIME. And what tells the time? A clock...

So I drew a clock. Not even a whole clock. Just the top left quarter on a piece of orange paper...'

Or a giant, lead-weighted monster that hangs around her neck, keeping her chained to it forever, pulling her down towards the Earth, an Earth she is going to blow apart when midnight strikes.

76

'Who am I, Tannie?'

Tannie's here again. Tomorrow must have come, though she can't say she noticed it. After all, it's been turning up every day for the past ninety-five years, by some miracle, both for her and for the planet.

'Who am I? Am I the Clock Lady, famous for two lines and four dots? An abstract landscape painter, or the Scientist's wife? A social commentator; an archaeologist; an architectural conservator? The saviour of our planet, or a threat to our democracy – have I told you about that, Tannie? How I once got followed by the F.B.I, or C.I.A, or both of them? These silly little men, who were always so obvious? Sometimes, I would wave at them, offer them a cup of coffee. They couldn't even decide why they were after me – because I was a liberal artist, or because I wanted the government to change its nuclear policy. Idiots!

All these Martyls... Plain Martyl, Martyl Langsdorf, Martyl Suzanne Schweig, Mrs Alexander Langsdorf, your Mrs L.

Which is it, Tannie?'

But Tannie's gone again, until tomorrow, anyway. Providing tomorrow decides to dawn one last time.

**

The Mimsy Borogove

Megan Waters

Megan Waters currently lives in Bayport, New York. She graduated from Binghamton University with a Bachelor of Science in Biology where, ironically, she never took one writing course. Her flash fiction piece "Lies of a Certain Nature" was a runner-up in Wow-Women on Writing's Winter 2017 Flash Fiction Contest.

An avid reader, Megan enjoys all styles and genres, but loves writing flash fiction and short stories. This is Megan's first short story to be published in print.

An impressed Judge Anisha says of her story "Told from a child's perspective, this is a tale of preferred inevitability made utterly believable."

The boy walked along the dirt road, chugging his water and tossing the plastic bottle into the tall grass. He took care to avoid the potholes and puddles, keeping his one good pair of school shoes clean and dry. The white bedsheets hung on the clothesline behind the small shack of his house. He noticed they didn't flap much in the strong spring breeze; Mama must've just washed them.

He approached the rickety fence and stopped. Sticking out just beyond the house was the back end of a beat-up red pick-up truck.

The Jabberwock was back.

He took a deep breath before turning left onto the worn footpath leading up to the front porch. The boy paused when he reached the door, listening through the screen for voices, movements, anything that would suggest he do an about-face. The only sound he heard coming from inside was that of running water. Mama must be doing the dishes.

He opened the screen door and gently closed it behind him. There was a good chance Lily was taking a nap. Mama always said you had to be extra quiet when Lily was sleeping, because ruining her nap was like waking a sleeping monster.

The boy started down the hall, past the washroom, and he could see Mama standing over the kitchen sink when a strong hand grabbed his overalls and yanked him backward into the washroom. The door shut, and he was swallowed by complete darkness. Stale smoke and an acidic tang polluted the cramped space.

"Now you listen here, boy," the Jabberwock said, spitting the words into his ear. "I thought I told you to get that patcha dirt ready by week's end. Ain't no way nothin's gonna grow up next to them weeds." His voice was a low growl, a controlled sort of fury that could explode at any moment.

"And what about that water hose I left in the barn for ya? Did ya patch that up like I said?"

The boy didn't say a word.

81

The Jabberwock leaned in even closer.

"Seems to me like you gotta bit of a listenin' problem... like your Ma." The words singed the hairs on the back of the boy's neck.

"You best get busy outside and have that yard ready by tomorrow or you ain't gonna sit for a week. You understand me, boy?"

The Jabberwock didn't bother waiting for a response and shoved the boy out into the hallway, sliding past him and out the front door.

The boy looked at his Mama. She hadn't moved an inch, still bent over the sink. He stared at her back with anxious eyes, silently pleading with her, willing her to turn around. Realizing his mental powers of persuasion were perfunctory, the boy looked back at the screen door once more, ensuring that the Jabberwock was gone before he dared to move a muscle.

He found the power to move his feet, and walked down the short hall which opened up onto the tiny kitchen, cramped and relatively dark; the only bit of natural light coming in through the one window which sat over the sink and looked out onto the backyard and the decrepit old barn. The boy walked up from behind his Mama and stood next to her at the sink, looking out the window, watching thick, grey clouds roll in from the west.

"Is Lily still taking a nap?" he asked her.

"Yes." She didn't take her eyes off the soapy water, vigorously scrubbing a frying pan.

"I got an A minus on my Greek mythology report, and Tommy only got a B, and he worked twice as long on his," he said.

"Uh-huh," she replied.

Her disinterest made him feel like a pesky gnat being swatted away with dismissive responses.

"Mama, why do you…"

She slammed the pan into the water and snapped her head in his direction.

"Not...now!" she said in a very loud whisper.

He stared at her face: her eyes were glassy and tired; strands of hair were coming loose from her bun, sticking out the sides of her head like wispy, brown tentacles; and the right side of her bottom lip was purple and swollen.

She dropped her gaze back to the sink.

The boy stood there in silence, lowering his head, staring down at the dirty linoleum floor. He felt sad, like he wanted to cry, but then his insides bubbled up with anger, because his Mama's face shouldn't look like that, all fat and coloured. Who on earth would do such a thing? And how? And why? His brain was scrambled with so many questions, all of which he knew the answers to. He couldn't stand there any longer, so he turned away and left the kitchen.

He stormed down the hall to his room and flopped backward onto his bed, completely forgetting about his outdoor chores. On a normal day, the boy would keep busy out of fear, doing something, *anything*, which tended to keep the fury of the Jabberwock at bay. But today was not a normal day. He stared at the ceiling for a moment, then shut his eyes real tight, trying to make the image of his Mama's fat lip go away.

He remembered when his Mama used to smile a lot, and laugh, and act like a kid. His happiest memories were of her reading books to him and Lily after dinner. Mama's favourite book was *Through the Looking Glass, and What Alice Found There*, and his favourite part was the Jabberwocky poem. He knew the whole thing by heart. She would read it aloud with an exaggerated silliness, which distracted the boy from the fact that the Jabberwock was a monster.

But then *he* started coming round.

Mama met *him* at a church event, and they immediately took a liking to each other. Occasional visits became regular occurrences. She would tell the boy it was nice to have a man around the house again. At least that's what she used to say. Then *he* started acting like Mama's stuff was *his* stuff, and saying things had to be done *his* way. That's when Mama got all quiet, and not fun. Mama wouldn't read books after dinner anymore.

The last time Mama read the Jabberwocky poem was months ago. Her voice was dull, and her eyes that once were bright blue and dancy now seemed grey. The made-up words were different, too; they were a bunch of strange sounds all jumbled up in his head. And for the first time, the boy understood that the poem wasn't a funny tale about a brave young boy, but one about a monster with jaws and claws. The memory made his stomach flip-flop, and a tingling sensation rippled down his spine.

Lily's cry aroused the boy from his sickened melancholy. He walked to her room, going to comfort her, to reassure her that everything was going to be okay.

*

The boy was startled from his sleep. Soaked bed sheets and the severe darkness of his room were tempered by the rhythmic sound of the rain beating down on the roof.

He gathered his wits and slithered out of his bed. He shuffled quietly down the hall to his Mama's room and leaned against the door frame, slowly peering inside. He could make out the silhouette of a female body asleep in the bed, alone. The sight brought him temporary relief, but not complete comfort.

The boy continued down the hall and into the kitchen. Without turning the light on, he grabbed a glass from the cupboard and walked over to the sink. He filled the glass with cold water and looked out the window as he drank. An orange glow emanated from the barn. He knew the Jabberwock was holed up in his lair.

A fire, like the glowing light in the barn, grew in the boy's belly. He remembered standing in this very spot, this very afternoon, looking up into his Mama's eyes thinking she looked like a delicate bird with a broken beak.

The glass slipped from the boy's hand and shattered in the sink. Shards of glass and droplets of water sprayed everywhere. Completely unphased, he broke his gaze from the barn and headed for the back door, grabbing the butcher's knife from the block on his way out.

The rain was coming down hard, soaking the boy's pajamas, making the ground soft and squishy between his toes. The light from within the barn acted as a beacon, shining through the wooden slats of the wall, comfortably allowing the boy to traverse the yard in the middle of the night.

He slid the barn door open a few inches and peered inside. He spied a gas lantern burning on the workbench alongside numerous tools and contraptions. The water hose he was supposed to have patched up sat coiled on the dirt floor next to a solitary metal chair, upon which sat the Jabberwock, his back to the boy.

The boy opened the door and let himself inside, slowly crossing the short distance from the door to the workbench, avoiding substantial puddles which formed over the past few hours due to the heavy rain and leaky roof. The Jabberwock was slumped over sideways in the chair resembling a lifelike statue that had fallen asleep. A strong odor hung in the air, and an empty container of ethyl alcohol was lying on the workbench on its side. The boy maintained a distance of an arm's length, and gently poked the Jabberwock's shoulder with two of his fingers.

Nothing.

He did it again, but harder this time.

Still nothing.

The boy leaned in closer. The Jabberwock's breath was hot like fire on his face. The boy reached in and brazenly lifted one of the Jabberwock's eyelids, revealing a red eyeball, unfocused and seemingly misplaced in his head. But the boy knew it wouldn't stay that way forever. It was only a matter of time before *he* would be awake. And like Mama would say, you don't want to wake a sleeping monster.

The boy felt the knife in his hand. He knew if he waited too long, he would run out of time, or worse yet, lose his nerve.

Pressure was building in the boy's head. His heart was racing. His knees felt weak. He took a step back and tripped over the coiled water hose. He fell into a large puddle, his bottom completely immersed, his pajamas thoroughly soaked and muddied. He sat there and started to panic, looking up at the Jabberwock, waiting for *him* to wake up, waiting for the moment when *he* would come along and scoop the boy up with his jaws and his claws, like a helpless fish flapping about in a shallow pond, struggling to live...

In that instant, it all became clear. He knew what to do.

The boy stood up quickly and placed the butcher knife down on the bench next to the empty bottle of ethyl alcohol. He worked swiftly and diligently as if possessed by the spirit of a warrior, armed with nothing but his mind and his mettle. The simplicity of the battle and the defeat of his adversary justified his actions, and left him with a strange sense of peace.

The boy retrieved the knife from the workbench before exiting the barn. He closed the door and walked back toward the house in the dark and the rain. Once inside, the boy wiped the blade dry and placed it back into the block. He went directly into the washroom and removed all his clothes, placed them in the small wash basin and ran warm water over them. He grabbed a towel from the shelf, dried himself off, and wrapped it around his waist. He walked quietly down the hall and paused outside his Mama's room. She was still asleep, her silhouette rising and falling in even meter. He watched her like this for a minute, and smiled.

"'And hast thou slain the Jabberwock?

Come to my arms, my beamish boy!

O frabjous day! Callooh! Callay!'

He chortled in his joy. "

***

Bullets

Colum Sanson-Regan

Colum Sanson-Regan is an Irish author and musician whose debut novel, a psychological thriller, 'The Fly Guy' was released by WordFire Press in March 2015. He has had several short stories published. As a musician he has released several albums and toured extensively over Europe and the US. He now performs mostly in Wales, UK where lives with his wife and two children and develops creative teaching programmes for international projects, and delivers creative writing courses.

Judge Brett says, "the beautiful ending to this coming-of-age tale of friendship, amidst the distorting shadows of the Irish troubles, is cathartic in the most wondrous of ways: a perfectly paced tension and foreboding that bursts forth into an unexpected peace. A triumph of hope for these seemingly worst of times."

Long before Alan moved away, me and Ronan and him collected bullets. There was a loose flagstone with a hollow underneath it, and we put the bullets in there. Our secret stash of gold. The artillery range was more than a mile from our little street. At the back of the terrace the hill was covered with old woods. So many of the trees were twisted, the ground was dense and pitted and we made thin paths around mud holes and over rotten trunks. Up at the top there were the broken walls of an old castle. From there, where it levelled off at the top was a flat field where the fences started. You could hear the snap of the guns there, especially early in the morning. From the hedges at the edge of the field we'd hide and watch the men aim and crack and reload and aim and crack and reload and aim and crack and reload. When they finished and the vans drove away we'd climb the fences and go to where they'd been shooting and scour the ground for shells. Not the empty cylinders, there were hundreds and hundreds of those, but the ones with the points still on. There were a lot fewer of these, but they were there, dropped carelessly in the rush to reload. With so many soldiers training, there were a lot of bullets to collect. When we got them, we brought them to the back alley behind our houses and put them under the flagstone. I think maybe Alan started it. He was the oldest. I never remember the hole being empty, and over the years the little collection grew and grew. It was our secret. That little pit of gold.

The first time I met Connie was during the summer. I was seven. She was sitting on the footpath across the road, outside Dempsey's house, playing with marbles. I wanted something to swap with her. I'd never seen marbles before. I ran out to the alleyway. I got my fingertips under the edge and bit by bit I lifted and dragged the heavy flat stone. I'd never done it alone before, usually there was at least me and Ronan doing this and it slipped and scraped the concrete. As soon as the gap was big enough I squeezed my hand into the blackness. The bullets were cool in there and rattled like boiled sweets in a bowl as I grabbed a handful. I knew that they were rare. She probably wouldn't have seen them before. I ran back through the house. My dad stopped me.

"What's in your hand?"

"Only something. I want to swap it for some marbles. I have a new friend. She's visiting the Dempseys."

"Oh, the English girl. Show me."

I hesitated.

"Connor, show me."

I opened my hand.

"Jesus," he said, "give me those."

Before lunch there were army vans and Garda cars blocking the street. There were men with guns guarding the end of the road, stopping the cars, leaning in at the windows. In the alley the flagstone was up. The hole underneath was bigger than I thought. We'd never taken it all the way off before. It broke up the little alley and now men with helmets and big gloves crouched at the pit looking in. They looked like they were friends, like the way that Ronan and Alan and me did when we were putting the bullets in. If we were grown up we'd be working together dressed like that. They were taking the treasure. Our treasure. I wanted to cry but I held it back. When they asked me, I said the same as I had said to Connie and my dad. I didn't know how they got there, I just knew they were there. I said that Ronan and Alan had shown me, that we were the only ones who knew about it and no, we didn't know how the bullets had got there. They said they'd ask me more questions later. They never did. Some more people had come around now, curious about the army vans in the village. Me and Connie sat on the footpath and watched. I'd never heard an accent like hers before, not even on TV. I remember she said, "It's only my first day here."

The news said that a store of bullets for an IRA cell had been found in a rural village. Earlier in the year a stash of guns and rifles had been stolen from a barracks across the border. They never found the guns, but now they had found the ammunition. Everyone said what a great job the Gardaí had done.

We kept that secret. Me Alan and Ronan. We never told

anyone.

Connie came back every summer. Her dad was a cousin of the Dempseys and was in charge of the factory that was going to be built near the village. She had her hair in a high ponytail and she wore t-shirts with logos, tucked into her shorts. She chewed gum and knocked on my door. We'd trek into the woods climb on trees and swing from branches. We'd go up to the old castle. They didn't have old ruins like that where she was from, she said, but they must be all over Ireland. Little castles? I didn't really know. I'd never thought about it. I just liked hearing her talk. We'd try and copy each other's accents. She told me about the Irish people in Nottingham. They were dangerous, she said. They collected scrap iron and raced dogs. Her mum told her to watch out for them. The Irish people in England were not to be trusted. I didn't know any English people. Ronan's dad sang rebel songs. We could hear him from next door sometimes and I knew that the IRA fought the British Army, but that was it.

She started playing football with us on the road, but she kept her hands in her pockets. When we went to the village green and played there she'd sit on the wall and watch. Sometimes Mike, Ronan's older brother would wheel Brian to the green and leave him sitting there. Brian was the youngest and had always been in a wheelchair. We didn't know if he was watching the game or not, it was hard to tell. Ronan said he was born that way. That was why his dad was always singing. There was no point talking to Brain, he couldn't talk back, but he liked the songs, Ronan said. The songs were old rebel songs and he'd sing them over and over but I could never make out the words. His voice was deep like an old farm engine and I grew used to hearing the run of a melody coming from next door. I'd forget about Mr Brady. The song was coming from the thick stone. The walls were singing.

One of those summers I had my first seizure. One evening on the village green. I just remember being pulled away, a sudden distance opening between me and everything around me, and then waking up on the ground. The light had changed. It was darker than usual. From the look on Alan's face I knew something was wrong. He'd never looked at me like that before. He was kneeling next to me and behind him Connie was standing with her hand to her mouth, looking pale. Ronan and Mick were crouched over me too. Brian was still in his chair near the wall, but no-one was with him now. When I got to my feet I was aching and my tongue was swollen. I wanted to know what time it was. Connie was gone, she had run back to get my parents. While I waited I sat on the wall. The village green was different, like it wasn't the real one. I felt like I was visiting. I waited for that feeling to go away but it didn't. That distance that had opened up, that change of light, remained. It never went back to normal after that. Summer was nearly over.

The village was growing. Fields were cleared and flattened. The little road had been widened, a new one was put down, two new estates were being built. Fine white cement dust covered everything like a baker's board. The windows of the houses, the bushes, the broad leaves on the old trees all the way up into the woods, had all been sprinkled in a dirty white. Everyone on the street took to washing their cars but as soon as they did the cars were covered again. They couldn't do anything about it, it was just there in the air. When Connie came back we climbed up to the old castle again. The shell of the factory lay across the back of the village like a huge abandoned ship, and at the edges of the new estates were houses waiting to be finished, with empty windows and doorways like missing teeth. The children from new families that were moving in were all playing in these half-built houses, the boys running around with sticks from the old wood playing war and the girls on the driveways planning dance routines or making houses into girls only zones. By the time the younger ones were rounded up by their parents and the others were at the village green, we'd hang around there until the sun went down. I was on medication now and the days were longer but still never as bright as before. I felt sleepy all the time. On one of those long summer evenings, we kissed, Connie and I, in a cold concrete corner of what would, in a few weeks, become someone's living room.

Almost as soon as she left the factory opened. The school was suddenly full that year. Next door Ronan's parents started fighting. His dad's voice changed. Whereas before I could hear him singing his rebel songs through the walls, now there were voices that were hot and sharp and stripped the air. Mike and Ronan's voices joined

92

in too, shouting their dad down. Mike was big now, he was out of school. He was working at the factory and drinking at the pub. During the cold winter and spring months me Alan and Ronan stayed out later and later. We'd steal cigarettes from our parents and smoke them on the corner of the new estate. If we were short Ronan always had a stash, or we'd ask Mike for a few when he was on his way to the pub. Alan was the first one in the village to get a leather jacket. His dad had bought an old motorbike and was showing him how to fix it. We'd spend time in Alan's garage, while he'd take apart the metal jigsaw again and again before reassembling it and revving it, bringing it to life. Ronan never spoke about what was going on at home. I used to see his mum getting Brian in and out of the car. The only times I'd see his dad was when I called in. He'd be in the back room. There never seemed to be any light in that room, just the glow of the TV. From the hallway I couldn't see the screen, just Mr Brady on the sofa, illuminated in a shaky light. He never spoke to me. He'd only give a grunt of acknowledgment. Upstairs, Ronan had a Walkman with big headphones. Mike's old comics were piled on the dresser and we'd read the comics and go through his tapes, taking turns with the headphones. Sometimes Ronan would be called to help and we'd hear the wheelchair being moved around downstairs. I'd try to sound out the action noises in the comics – Whap! Booom! Ssshriing!

One night on the way out, his dad shouted at me and Alan, calling us into the front room. He was sitting on the sofa. There was a confusion of voices coming from the TV and the colours on his skin moved. Brian was sitting in his chair, motionless.

"You're hanging around with the English family, aren't ya?"

"Well, the Armstrongs. They're the Dempseys' cousins."

"That English girl."

"Yes."

"Careful what you bring into your family boy, into this community."

He was leaning forward and pointing at me now. The light from the TV changed and it shimmered on his face. The lines at the edge of his mouth and eyes were deep and sharp.

"Mr Brady..." but he cut me off with a grunt. He squinted. The lines moved in splinters, cut deeper. Brian moaned. Mr Brady didn't move, he was still pointing at me. Alan tugged at my sleeve. I didn't want to leave. I wanted to see it, I wanted to see his ugly disapproval shatter his face. Alan tugged at my sleeve again and we left.

Outside, just before Alan turned to go his way home he said, "When Connie comes over again I'm going to ask her out. She likes me. She's nice isn't she?"

"I kissed her." I said

"How many times?"

"Once."

Then the summer came around and when I saw the car with the roof rack parked across the road it felt like I had jumped and stayed in the air. All I wanted was to hear her talk again and my impatience of mind was unbearable until she knocked. She had a new football and stood at my door with it under her foot with a big smile. Soon Alan was playing with us on the village green. I went in goal and he and Connie tackled and took shots. He had gotten better, he was faster. He was taller this year too. So was she. Her hair was longer and her tucked in white t-shirt was showing the shape of her chest now. I could see the straps of her bra underneath as she tackled the ball away from Alan and he chased her.

Later on I heard Connie promising she'd go and look at his new bike with him. He said he'd take her for a ride. Alan started hanging around with us all the time then. He asked Connie all about Nottingham, about the differences between there and here. I heard her tell him about the castle in Nottingham right in the middle of the town. It wasn't a little ruin like ours. They walked together while me and Ronan kicked the ball around the road after them. I was sure there was an excitement in her voice. Alan was making her laugh more than I did. Because he was taller the way she turned and looked when he spoke was different, and there was a way she held herself when she walked next to him. When I saw it I felt a sickness, like the moment you hear the branch snap. One day she told us about some bombs that were found near her street. If they had gone off, her street, her house would have been blown up.

"What's it got to do with me?" she asked. "I can understand if it was an army base, but what's it got to do with me and my neighbours?"

Some evenings she wouldn't call. When I went and knocked across the road and she wasn't there I'd end up just sitting by my window so that I'd see her when she came back. My embarrassment when it was dark and she still hadn't walked through the door stuck in the air around me, I felt it push against me every time I turned around. It made my day an empty cartridge, hollow and useless. The thoughts of her with Alan kept me awake even after my medication. It felt like I would never sleep again until I talked to her. On the day before she left, she called for me and we walked up through the woods beyond the old castle and sat on a fallen tree looking onto the flat field where they used to shoot.

"What was it like on the motorbike?"

"Oh, yeah. A bit too fast. He asked me to be his girlfriend."

"Are you?"

She shook her head.

She leaned in to me. We kissed. She tasted like gum.

"When you go back to Nottingham, do you have a boyfriend?"

"You're my boyfriend now aren't you?"

Alan stopped going to school then. He worked in the local garage. On our way to school the shutters were open and we'd see his shadow and clouds of breath. On the way back we'd call in, and he'd lean up from under a bonnet or roll out from under a car and wipe his hands. Sometimes he'd take a break and share his cigarettes and we'd smoke. One day he was sitting sideways on his bike, his overalls covered in grease and he told us that his dad was going to pay for him to go to England to get work there. We smoked in silence for a while.

"Are you going to stay here, work in the factory?"

"Maybe. I don't really want to."

"Everyone else around here is going to."

"Exactly."

"We should have held onto it."

"What's that?"

"The pit of gold."

We laughed.

"Did you ever tell anyone?"

"Sure that's a good secret. Don't want to spoil that one."

"That's long gone."

Ronan said, "I've still got a little stash."

We all laughed some more and threw the cigarette ends on the floor of the garage. Alan left soon after that. He was gone by the summer.

The next time she came over Connie got a job, packing in the factory. On the village green a football league with teams from each estate started up. Soon teams from other villages were coming to play during the holidays. We'd sit and watch them play and the other people on the green would shout and cheer and joke and the more noise they made the less it seemed we needed to. The players' boots dug into the grass. The kicked up soil and the scent of the earth textured the evening summer air as the light thinned. We held hands when we walked. I kissed her every night before we said goodbye. Ronan's mother left that summer too. He said that she had just been waiting until he and Mike could look after each other. She took Brian with her. Ronan got a little van and took every opportunity to get away from home. He took Connie and me to the coast a few times. We'd sit for a while on the beach, never stay long. Ronan didn't seem to have much to say anyway. The closer me and Connie got the further away Ronan seemed. Then we wouldn't see him for a while. He'd be gone for days, sometimes weeks at a time. His father stopped shouting and went back to singing rebel songs. Some nights after I'd said goodnight to Connie and counted my medications, I would start thinking about how it would feel to be together, and there would be the voice, some muffled stories about some kind of glory, coming from the walls.

Before she left that year, Connie said she was going to move to Dublin to study. Ronan didn't go back to school. It was just me now, and I wanted to get it over with as soon as I could. I knew I could just keep my head down and work hard. School was nearly over. Summer was waiting for me, and like every summer since I was a boy, so was Connie. I was eighteen. I got a job in the offices of a newspaper in Dublin. She had started in Trinity, studying International Law. We got a place together. She made a chart to put on the wall. I had to tick it when I had taken my medication.

"Just so I'm sure" she said, "I need to know you're not going to have one when you're on the bus or in the street."

The next time I saw Ronan was six years later. I was back in the village and I saw his van outside. The local football team had made it to the county finals. The game was being played on the new pitch up on the hill. Everyone from the village and the new estates was out, walking to the game, already jubilant. The fact that the game was happening at all was a cause for excitement. There were banners proclaiming good luck hanging from windows and cars honked their horns. I called in. His dad was still there, in front of the TV in the dark back room. He grunted at me. I said, "I'm going to marry Connie Armstrong, Mr Brady, I'm going to marry her you know." Ronan grabbed a pack of beers from the fridge and threw his coat on and pushed me back out the door.

We joined the throng.

"I didn't know there were this many people in the village," Ronan said. "Are you really going to marry her?"

"I think so. I haven't asked her yet. But I think we'll do it."

"I bet she's even more gorgeous now. You hung on to her alright."

"It's not even this busy in Dublin."

"It's not even such a big game."

"Well, come on, county league final."

"Yeah but it's not much of a county." He opened a can as we walked. Around us, groups of men with team shirts and scarves joined colours and followed the road out of the village until the crowd was thick. Someone had made a flag and when it was hoisted and waved a cheer resounded. The road wound up to the new pitch, onto the flat of land at the top where the supporters for the other team were gathering on the other side. By the time the teams came out of their dressing rooms, the sidelines were packed, and as soon as the ball was in play the noise back and forth was as much of a competition as what was on the field. I wasn't going to drink, but the atmosphere was fuelled so we finished Ronan's six pack before the second half started. When the teams came back on there was still only a goal in it. Ronan produced a naggin from his inside pocket. He had stopped cheering long ago. Another goal halfway through and our crowd jumped and hugged and cheered like we'd made it to salvation day. One more goal and we'd all be there. Ronan supped from his naggin and leaned into me and talked right into my ear.

"Mike and Dad didn't know it, but I was seeing someone last year. From over the 'Cross. We've broken up now. It's such a fucker."

The fans were really shouting from the sides now, throwing their arms about and the captain, a skinny player with a scraggly beard, kicked the ball right to the feet of a winger who rushed past two men and put it to the other wing. There was a scuffle and two men went down. The ball went out. Everyone was shouting at the linesman now as the players got up and pushed each other. The ref blew and it was our free. The captain roared and the team surged to the box.

"I couldn't tell her what I did."

"What do you mean? What you did?"

"What I do."

The free kick was cleared but we were on the attack again, but every time we tried to get through the ball was cleared, but we kept the possession and kept setting up another attack. All the supporters on our side of the pitch were on the balls of their feet, dancing around the edge of a celebration. Voices clamoured – C'mon lads! – Go on! – Ref! – Go on boys!

"What I do."

"Ronan -" I wanted to tell him to shut up for a minute, Jesus, this was important, it looked like we were going to score. Of all the games played, this one could be the one that makes the village proud. Players collided, the ball skimmed across the grass, was controlled, – Your ball! –Watch the wing! Then a tackle brought it back – C'mon boys! – Mark him! – Get it in! It went to the wing, – This is it! – Keep them out! – C'mon boys! – Guns Conor! –

"Wait, what?"

There was a pass to the centre, another player ran in from the edge of the box, shouting for the ball.

"I've been working in a southern cell. Small one. Mostly dumping guns brought over the border."

"Ah Jesus," and there was the shot. I jumped, tight with everyone else but the keeper put it out to the side and we all exhaled. I looked at Ronan. He was looking at the pitch now and sipped from his naggin as the players rushed forward again, jostled for position, back in the box. They looked fevered now, and elbowed and pushed each other as the captain stepped back to take corner. – Yes boys! – This is it! – Get it in! – C'mon! – This is it! Ronan was still looking ahead. The captain kicked it into the box.

"Mike and Dad don't know that either."

We scored. There was a noise like a spike going through their crowd, and we exploded long wordless sounds, sheer joy, faces reddened with triumph, fists beat the air and strangers exchanged fevered embraces. Within a minute the whistle was blown and we'd won, our little village had got to the top of the county. A torrent of triumph roared down the hill and celebration resounded around the streets of the village. Everybody gathered in the green, and was drinking and cheering and laughing and chanting and toasting the provincial victory. We sat on the wall.

"I didn't think you'd do that. Guns, Ronan."

"Well," he said, "and coke. They don't need so many guns now. And there's more money."

"So the girl from the 'Cross, did she find out?"

"No. I just couldn't tell her. You're lucky. You got lucky."

We kept going back to the pub and bringing out pints and sitting on the village green wall, watching the celebration around us.

"So do you have some in the house now?"

"Guns?"

"Coke. Come on now. What would I want with guns?"

"Ah yeah. There's always a bit yeah."

By the time we got back to Ronan's I realised how drunk we were. I'd forgotten to take my key out, so Ronan said I could crash at his. The TV was on and his dad was asleep, sitting upright on the sofa. Ronan took me up to his room and opened the bottom drawer of the cupboard. He took out a hand gun.

"This is mine."

He handed it to me and I held it for a while as he cut up a few lines on the dresser. It wasn't as heavy as I thought it would be. It could have been fake for all I knew. He inhaled.

"I've never used it."

"Put it away." I stood up and gave it back. I rolled up a note.

"Connie takes care of you right?"

"Well, I mean, we take care of each other I think." I covered one nostril and inhaled. "It's like the dust from the old factory." I dabbed a finger on the leftover grains.

"You're on the sofa. Let's move the old man."

We couldn't wake his dad. He was cold and his breath was

shallow and weak like the sound of a pencil scraping a desk. We tried to lift him, but he was too heavy. His breathing stuttered. There was a gap, then a sound like twisting a bottle cap, then he stopped. We froze, holding him like that and waited for it to come back. In that silence Ronan and me just looked at each other. Fear was filling the space where his father's breath should have been.

"Ah shit," he said. "Now look what's happened."

"Call an ambulance Ronan," I said and we put him down on the sofa again. The breath returned. I could hear the thin stream of air, but it didn't seem like it was going in or out. Ronan was giving his address and rubbing his hand up and down over his face, tilting his head and checking his nostrils in the mirror and slapping himself on the back of the neck.

"Yes I'll stay on the line".

It took two weeks for Mr Brady to die.

The church wasn't full for the funeral. The village had grown but Mr Brady's friends were part of the old village, before the factory. I couldn't remember a time when he wasn't old. Me and Connie were just two seats behind Ronan and Mike. His mum was there, with her partner, a lean straight looking man in a well-fitted suit. Brian wasn't there. He was in a home, being cared for. As the casket was carried out I saw Alan at the door. He had his suit jacket over his shoulder, his tie was slightly askew, his chest defined beneath his shirt. His hair was shaven and he had stubble that was thick and crept up to his cheekbones. He looked like it wasn't his suit, or he had been wearing it for days, but there was a solidity to him, a sense of consequence. We hugged. He hugged Connie too.

"You guys, still together!"

"You look good Alan," Connie said.

There were tears in everyone's eyes when Ronan came out, he looked skinny and grey and streaked with grief, as if this wasn't the real Ronan, he was already gone. His mum and Mike walked behind him and held each other up. We walked with the procession to the graveyard behind the church. As they lowered him in the priest intoned a prayer. There was freedom to be found in the grave, rest which comes in the arms of the earth, an end to the struggle, peace at last.

"You still in England?" I said to Alan.

"On and off, I've been in the Middle East for a bit."

"What have you been doing there? Still working on engines?"

"Not really, well sort of. How's your health? Still on the meds?"

"Always."

"But you're okay?"

"Oh yeah, fine. We're living in Dublin."

"Good, good."

He and Connie walked together to the pub. She was telling him all about her studies and her job, all about Dublin. I stayed close to Ronan. Ronan's mother reminisced about the old village, the small school, the little shop, and about that time when they found the bullets under the flagstone. We didn't say anything about it. There was no point now, it felt so long ago. Later Ronan said, "Wasn't that Connie's first day?"

After the pub emptied out we went back to Ronan and Mike's. Though we clowned and threw laughs and teased the air had a heaviness of inevitable defeat. At the door, Mrs Brady didn't want to come in. Her partner said again how sorry he was, and then there was just us. We ended up in the back room, Connie and Ronan on the sofa Mike on a chair and me and Alan sitting on the ground. A bottle was being passed around.

The talk turned and Mike asked Alan again what he was doing in the Middle East.

"I'm in the army," he said. "I've been sitting on top of a roof under a plastic sheet in the baking fucking sun and dust with my rifle waiting for someone to walk out of a door. Twenty days."

Connie sat forward. "What? You've been what?"

"What army, the British Army?" Mike said, "The British Army?"

"In the Lebanon."

"A sniper?"

"Sometimes. That's what I've just been doing"

"Jesus."

"I know."

Ronan didn't sit up. He had his hand to his forehead holding his eyes closed.

"Did you get him?"

"What?"

"The target. Did you get him?"

"Turns out he wasn't there."

"Or he got away without you knowing."

"Yes."

Ronan stood and crossed the room and looked down at Alan.

"British Army. Alan."

Alan half-laughed and put his hands up in surrender. "I know. It's a strange world Ronan, it's a strange world."

Ronan went upstairs.

Alan started to talk about how he got into the army, all of the training, how tough it was. Connie asked what other things he did. Protect people, rescue fellow soldiers, combat, kidnap hostiles, wait a lot. Ronan had been gone a while. I stood up, patting Alan on the shoulder as I made my way upstairs. He was in his room, leaning over the dresser. He had a rolled up note and was just about to sniff a line.

"Do you want some?"

"Sure, a little bit"

He inhaled, and straightaway set up another one. The top of the dresser was dark wood, the streak of powder glowed white. There was a little ornamental bowl and a glint of gold caught my eye as I took the line. I took a bullet from the bowl and looked at it. When I turned he was sitting on the bed looking tired, resting the gun on his lap. I sat next to him. Alan was talking downstairs. We listened to the mumble.

"Would you have guessed?"

"Jesus no. I thought he'd be working in a garage, playing in a local football team, hitting on the English girls. I honestly thought that that was why he left. To get an English girl like Connie. Is that loaded?" I turned the old bullet in my fingers.

"No. Well, a bit. Those are old rifle cartridges. Those old bits of gold. They're not for this."

"All the things he's done, none of them have been over here. It's all the Middle East."

"Fighting in a country that isn't even his."

"Well, leave him. It's not really fighting for anything is it? It's just fighting Ronan, really. It's just an excuse to shoot a gun."

"Conor, he's sitting in the room where my dad was. Dad's not even cold and there's a British Army Officer in our front room."

"It's Alan. And Connie."

"And Connie."

"Ronan, you were mad at your old man, all the time, for the way he was. Weren't you? C'mon, we'll go downstairs."

"I'm just going to line another one up."

"I'll wait then."

"And I bet he still hasn't got a girl like Connie."

"You're going to put the gun away?"

"Do you think he's killed anyone?"

"Yeah. Probably. Just, well, when I saw him at the church and now he's said it, it makes sense, the way he looked. He looked…"

"That's what I'm supposed to be doing isn't it? A rebel? Fighting the Brits? Isn't that what I'm supposed to be doing?"

"I don't know, Jesus, don't ask me. I just have word counts and medications, and I can barely get those right without Connie looking out for me. But I know that that gun, it's just for show. Ronan. Come on. It's Alan. Alan."

Ronan lined up another two thin rows of coke on the dresser and sniffed one. He put the gun into the belt of his trousers and covered it over with his shirt.

"Let's go," and he went out the door and down the stairs.

Back in the room, Connie and Alan were talking about England. Connie was listing what her friends over there were doing. She missed it sometimes. Ronan stood there, took the bottle and started singing a rebel song. Mike joined in. Connie and Alan fell silent. I went and sat next to Connie, and said to her quietly, "It'd be a good time for us to go."

She shook her head and edged away from me. The brothers' voices were strong together, the song increasing in volume as they continued through the verses. Ronan's eyes were filling with tears. Mike had his closed.

O come, come from o'er the river, and raise thy hands chained,

Dark Rosaleen, though gentle are thy graces, now your freedom unrestrained

Shall flow from e're our fathers fought and e're our brothers died

And Ireland born anew united in blood will in glory rise.

When they finished, Alan and Connie clapped. I raised my glass. Mike stood and put his hand on Ronan's shoulder. Alan said, "Your dad was a proud patriot, and was always good to everyone here in the village. Long may his memory last." He picked up the bottle and went around the room filling a glass for each of us. We all stood. "To Tom Brady!" We drank.

Connie sat down again and said, "Sing another, another one

105

of your dad's songs."

I sat, close to her. "Connie, we should go soon."

She ignored me. "Have you got anymore Ronan? Anymore of your dad's songs?"

Mike sat down. "He used to sing to Brian all the time."

"Were they all like that? Irish Army songs?"

"No, Jesus, no. That was the only rebel song he sang. And not that often."

"Hang on, Mike," I sat forward. "I remember hearing him singing all the time, there were more songs than that. Sure half the time it was when I was trying to go to sleep. And when your mum left, he didn't stop. I mean, he didn't just sing to Brian did he? He'd sing half the night in an empty house."

"But not rebel songs Conor."

"What? Well what the hell was he singing then?"

Alan leaned forward and topped up my glass again. Connie held out hers and he filled it too. He passed the bottle over to Ronan and Mike, before he sat cross-legged on the floor.

"Go on lads," he said. "Sing us another."

Ronan started to sing. He had a voice like his dad's, a kind of a plodding, workman's tone, but a sure handle on the tune. He knew what he was doing with it. I knew this tune, it was a part of my growing up, the song through the walls in the evenings. The melody quickly came round to the start again, it was hypnotic, but for the first time I could hear the words. It wasn't a song that yearned for liberty or revenge or freedom. It was a love song. A song of a brief passionate love which had to be abandoned, a love unfulfilled but that lives on in the song, and the song will be sung and the love will live on. A song of the heart. By the end Connie and Alan were crying. And Ronan didn't stop. He sang another, and with each song he revealed another story which I'd thought I'd heard, songs I thought I knew, but I never knew really. And they were all about love. About tenderness. About innocence. Love. That's what he'd been singing about.

Ronan sang Raglan Road. He sang about Nancy Spain, the Parting Glass, the Galway Shawl, he sang The Star of the County Down. We stayed there till dawn.

***

Scarecrows
Eileen O'Donoghue

Eileen O'Donoghue lives in Killarney in the South West of Ireland with her husband and three kids. She is a lawyer by profession. She is currently completing her thesis for an MA in creative writing at University College Cork and this story, Scarecrows grew out of a writing prompt at a fiction workshop on the MA programme. It is her second story to be published, the first one was included in The Quarryman, the literary journal of University College Cork earlier this year.

On Eileen's entry to Nivalis 2017, Judge Sandra says "Scarecrows is certainly an ambitious short story. I liked how it experimented with the linearity and perspective."

Today.

Carrie is washing up at the sink, all the while watching Shay through the kitchen window. Shay is watching something too but he cannot tell her what it is. The summer was easier, when he was happy in the garden in the afterglow of the day. As autumn settles, she has noticed his increasing agitation when he goes outside in the evening. She turns back to the sink, staring down at the white foaming water and making a mental list of the jobs for tomorrow. That is when she hears the commotion outside.

"What the hell...." Carrie drops the bowl into the water and runs out through the open sliding door that leads onto the back porch.

He is chasing the crows with a stick.

"Jesus Christ!" she swears and suddenly she knows what he is doing and she is bent double with the force of it. It's the apple trees. He's minding the apple trees. He remembers. Straightening up, she moves forward to join the fight.

Last night.

Red digital numbers say it's 2.15. Where is he? Panic rises. Is he there? She reaches in the dark. It's okay. He is here. He is asleep. She checks again that her boots and down jacket are within reach. The nights are sharper and she can't afford to get sick if she has to go looking for him in the cold dark. She lies back against her pillows, exhaling. Her thudding heart is slowing but she knows she will not be able to sleep anytime soon. Awake at night, she is falling more and more into the rabbit-hole of their memories. Shay is losing his and it feels like they are pulling her underwater, trying to make space in her head as if they are looking for a new place to live. She is defenceless against their surge and pace, these flickering refugees that were once moments of their lives, fleeing for survival. They come at night, while she cries for the loss of the man lying next to her in the bed.

D-Day.

After the scan, the consultant bluntly says its dementia, a rare and progressive form, a degeneration of the frontal lobe of the brain. His office is in a prefabricated building. It's shabby and bare, making all speech sound hollow and distant. The rain falling on the roof sounds like ping-pong in a bucket. They had to climb two uneven steps to get into the building and it felt like stepping into the dimness of a circus tent. Pulling his sleeve over his wrist-watch, having checked it twice, the doctor explains that Shay's dementia is further complicated by a form of motor neuron disease. It has a rapid progression but that could be a blessing of sorts. He will grow more childlike and hyperactive and possibly more affectionate at first. Later he will become withdrawn and disinterested in life. At that stage he might react to things that had been very important to him, strong feelings or memories but perhaps not, this varies between patients.

"He's only forty-seven. Are you sure this is right?" she asks, pleading silently with all the gods that there is something wrong here, a simple mistake, anything else, please! No, there's no mistake. He is very sorry. He says she will need a lot of help. Shay stands up, walks around the desk and hugs the doctor. It's comical and she thinks of Groucho Marx because Shay is so tall bending over the doctor seated in his swivel chair. Afterwards, she wonders why she thanked the doctor.

Little things.

It's their wedding anniversary. Shay is already up and gone when she wakes. They have never accounted to each other, never needed to, but lately he comes and goes without a word. It has been niggling at her but does not seem worth going on about. She lies in bed a while. She's not bothered about the anniversary. It has never been their thing to celebrate something on the prescribed day - they might do something at the weekend, if they can be bothered. Deciding that she might as well get up, she stands and moves to the window. Moving the curtain, she checks out the weather. There's a light drizzle with a brightening sky behind it and everything is a polished dark green, washed in the morning mist.

Stepping into the bathroom, she curses Shay for leaving the sink in a mess after shaving. That's another thing. What's with all this shaving? Why is he shaving in the morning before going out on the farm and then again in the evening? And, was she imagining it, or did he shave before he going to bed last night, as well? Brooding about this, she cleans up and follows her body's coffee alarm to the kitchen. Shay is at the sink, washing what looks like dozens of empty plastic milk cartons.

"Shay!" she says to his back, "What's going on?"

He turns his head around to smile at her and goes back to his work at the sink, whistling "Raindrops keep falling on my head". The whistling is new.

"Shay, please, what's going on! Are you taking the mick or something?" she asks.

He wipes his hands on the tea-towel and comes over to where she is standing by the table. He hugs her and lifts her off the ground.

"Happy anniversary, love." He kisses her on both cheeks and the on tip of her nose. Then putting her down, he says "Look what I've been collecting for us!"

Before.

The apple trees survive her gardening efforts because Shay knows what to do and quietly tends to them, when she is busy with something else. She knows he wants her to believe she has made a success of it by herself, that something blossomed at her hands. They are happy and proud when the first crop of apples come. It seems like first steps.

Early harvesters, the apples appear in the last shortening days of August. The crows are a pest though, vandals intent on damage for the sake of it. Their black beaks savage the fruit leaving deep brown holes, mortally wounding but never taking a whole apple. Carrie asks around about learning to shoot. She would get such satisfaction in shooting the bastards. She has never hated anything as much in her life as these crows. Someone said you wouldn't get close enough to actually hit them, the murdering bastards.

The day the trees were bought.

She is going to walk to town to vote in the divorce referendum. It's as good a day as any to meet people. Everyone will be out to vote and she hasn't been in town for ages. She tells Shay she needs to do something physical. He says voting isn't that strenuous. She smiles and walks out into the day. It is cold and crisp, the countryside covered in a clear blue light, like a village Christmas card scene. The sparse clouds are long sheets of white and the birds fly high above the skeleton trees. She feels him watching her go. It has been three weeks since their last loss and the doctors have advised them to stop trying. Four is enough, four small souls that had almost been people.

Later, she comes home in John Tarrant's garden centre van. Shay is outside, sitting on the windowsill and smoking when they pull up at the back door. She calls him to help John, who is taking out plants from the back of the garden centre van. They place the four of them side by side against the wall of the house.

"You need a hand with the planting, Shay?" calls John, the keys of the van in his hand. Looking at Carrie, he answers, "No thanks, John. We'll be ok."

"Good luck so. Better get them in soon. We'll hardly escape the frost much longer." He raises his arm pointing, and adds "the corner of the south wall and the hedge there is a good spot. Good shelter with the hedge. It'll break the wind and there's plenty of sun."

That's what I was thinking" she says. Turning to Shay she adds, "They're Irish Peach and Kerry Pippins, something to do with boys and girls." He smiles and the fragile winter sun appears behind him. Moving away, he says,

"Sounds good. I'll get the shovel so."

"Is it getting a bit dark?" she asks.

"Ah no, not too bad. No time like the present. You have a look there and see where exactly you want to put them, and we'll belt into it together when I'm back with the tools."

She hears the small catch in her own voice saying: "Ok."

When all the trees are in the ground, they stand back to admire their work. Suddenly the sound of crying takes her by surprise. For a second her brain searches for who is crying. Then the low keening sound he is making frightens her.

"Don't, don't," she pleads. He throws the shovel against the wall and sinks to his knees. She hasn't touched him for so long, has never allowed that he feels the same way, owning all the sadness herself. She puts her arms around him and when he turns to her she sways and they tumble into the grass together. Crying and then laughing a little, they lie together in the grass until they have to go in out of the cold.

"Look on the bright side" she says, going in the back door, "It looks like divorce is in. He kisses the top of her head and says "Yeah, at least there's that."

Home from London.

Because Shay's father is sick, his parents are too busy dealing with medication and schedules and doctor's appointments to say too much about Shay bringing a pregnant girl home with him from England. His mother gives the customary "We are very disappointed..." speech but soon the idea of the baby takes hold and she warms to Carrie and is good to her. His father says: "At least she's Irish."

Shay carries her over the threshold of a house in the village. He says they can't start their life together in the farmhouse, the way things are with his father. She grows more rounded and is happy and lazy. He is up at the farmhouse when the baby starts to slip away. At first, there is no pain, just blood. Later it is like some cold claw tearing the baby out of her. She lies curled up on the kitchen tiles, tracing the pattern of the grout with her finger, listening to Axl Rose singing "sweet child of mine" on the radio. The phone on the wall is not connected, another job she's been meaning to do.

London.

He says he has some news when she runs into him in the hotel. He grabs a quick kiss before his supervisor, Tony, roars at him to "Keep up, Paddy!" He turns to follow and mouths "See you later", his eyes lingering on hers a moment longer. She has booked their favourite Italian restaurant for later to celebrate Shay's twenty-fifth birthday.

She has her own news and she practises the telling of it while she is getting ready to go out. Dancing around her room to "I've got to let you know", she laughs and puts on her most girly dress. The room is light and summery with the sound of INXS and the smell of apple blossom shampoo.

"Mam has asked me to come home." He says when the waiter comes with the coffee. "Dad's sick. It's nothing bad or anything, but she says he can't manage the farm on his own anymore."

"Oh? Like, in a few months or so?" she asks, her hands now starting to shake a little. She places them in her lap under the table.

"No, sooner than that." He is looking at the table cloth, slowly turning the teaspoon over and over, not looking up.

"You'll have to be a farmer so," she says quietly.

"Maybe," he says, raising his hand to call for the bill.

"I'm getting this!" she protests, "It's your birthday!"

"With what?" he laughs; "Tony told me you got fired, when we were clocking out. So, what you do this time?"

She smiles up at him under her eyelashes, containing her laughter.

"I just gave chef a helpful tip. It could be life changing for him. Anyway he was picking on the new waitress, the Spanish girl, Marisa and I couldn't take the way he was treating her!"

"What tip?" he asks, on cue.

"Oh, just to go fuck himself 'cause it's probably the only way he can get it up." She smiles innocently, totally enjoying herself now.

"Jesus!" he laughs. "Wasn't it enough to tell the poor man, last week, that he could have an operation to have his finger removed from his nose!"

116

"C'mon! It's a kitchen. He's got to have some standards."

"So what's next then?" He's not asking about her job. She understands that.

"Well, I'll have to marry you anyway," she says.

"Don't do me any favours!" he counters beaming from ear to ear.

"You see, you're pregnant," she explains, "and I wouldn't like to leave you up the pole."

He reaches for her hands. "So, you think you can handle a farmer?"

"I already have," she teases, "but you can forget about me working outside in the muck! I couldn't grow mould in a damp corner. I will take up a bit of knitting, join the ICA and bake pies for our apple-cheeked offspring."

"I could always make a scarecrow out of you. You can be scary some times. The poor old chef knows that!"

"A pair then, hanging out in the fields together!"

"We'll make some pair, alright." He strokes the back of her hand with his thumb.

They sit, holding hands across the table, like the happy couple in a wedding snow globe.

Hello.

It is the first time he sees her. She is shouting at one of the hotel porters. The man is livid red in the face and inhaling through his teeth. It's Bobby, the one the lads called Brando because of his swagger. She is rubbing the old dog Belle, who is always hanging around the basement door near the clock in machine, begging for scraps. Shay sees the porter, a fat lock of his combed back raven hair hangs loose, over his forehead like a sharpened beak. He feels the hair rising on the back of his neck. His fists are clinched, ready. Her Irish accent is enough.

He sees her stand up to her full height and look the guy

straight in the eye, her index finger wagging at him like an Irish mammy. "If you ever, and I mean ever, kick this dog again, I will break your greasy balls with the nearest blunt instrument I can find. What did the poor fecker ever do to you, you bloody coward!" Brando leers and she counters, "Oh go on! Hit a girl next, why don't you. Come on dickhead. Make my fucking day!" Maybe because he sees Shay in the shadows, Brando backs off muttering "Crazy Irish bitch!" She shouts "Fucking sissy!" at his dark retreating back.

He sees her rubbing the cowering dog's neck, talking to it in a crooning voice, "Don't worry about him, darling. I'll mind you. I'll look after you. He'll be missing some important equipment if he goes near you again, won't he? Yes he will, poor baby."

Watching her with the dog, he sees a beautiful girl in a faded hotel uniform. He sees kindness and courage. He sees a loving hand on a creature who only wishes to survive a while longer. He sees a girl who is brave, a girl that will stand up for something. In her Irish skin, he sees the clean air and mist of home. Looking up, she sees him watching her. Still cross, she warns him, "And what are you looking at!"

"You." he smiles, walking towards her and the dog and something that could be theirs.

***

There are two of me. Not twins. Me. I am in two places at once, always. If there was a map of my world I could place my finger on one part of it and say 'I am here'. But it would be equally true for me to place my finger on a different part of the map and say 'I am here'. It's true. There are no two ways about it: there are two of me, and I live in two different places.

I live in a world of grass. Grass that spreads out as far as the eye can see. The stalks are long, elegant; they are the colour of spun gold and they shimmer in the light of the day. They undulate in the wind like a sea and when the wind is rough I can hear the sound of waves breaking on a shore. It is just the grass, rustling, but when you look at it through squinted eyes it can look like golden water. There is just the grass and the blue sky and the sun in my world. Sometimes I sit and strain my eyes, gazing in every direction by turns, thinking that perhaps I will see something that wasn't there before—something that is not grass and sky and sun. But there is nothing. This doesn't make me sad.

This empty place revolves around one solid thing: my house. It is plain, made of bare, dark wood that was almost black when the house was built, but has since been bleached a paler colour by the sun. It is strange, you must think, that there can be a house of wood in a place where there are no trees. I built this house. But I built this house in another place and somehow it appeared here. To explain it better, perhaps I should tell you about that other place where I am.

I live in a world of snow. I live high in a mountain. I believe the whole world is covered in snow. The snow never melts. It is white and powdery in some places. In others it is darker, wetter. Sometimes it is icy or crystalline. It has a variety of forms and I know every one of them. The air is cold and usually quite dry. Dark coniferous trees rise up out of the snow and surround the house that I built with my father. I built the house with wood from some of these trees. The cedars are my favourites.

Sometimes, when it is quiet and sunny outside and the snow is shining, I go up to my favourite cedar that stands at the top of a slope, right behind my house. I wrap my arms around it and press my face to its rough bark and I breathe in deeply and smell its beautiful perfume. When I leave the tree, a perfect imprint of its patterned trunk comes away with me, pressed into the skin of my cheek.

I live by myself in my wooden house, but the town is not so far away and I am not really alone. I have the dogs and a few goats for company. Not many things can grow up here, so I go to the town for my vegetables. I usually make the trip once a month. I have many friends there from when I lived in the town with my father, before he died. They sometimes make the trip up the mountain to visit me. Sometimes I spend a night down there with them.

I spend my days quietly, carving little figurines of animals out of wood and looking after the house. I have no job. The town is like a family. We share. I like this but I also like being away from everyone. I am a child apart. I was not born in the town, but brought there as a baby. And I feel different from the others. My father often told me stories of his snowy homeland and of my mother and I always had a feeling that one day, perhaps, I would journey beyond my borders to another white place with different trees and different people and different ways. But I would feel at home because no matter where I went the snow would be just as beautiful as it is here.

When I built the house with my father, it assembled itself around me here. I sat, staring into the golden, blue horizon, and the foundations of the house were laid down beneath me. Sometimes I would move to get out of the way of the build, but mostly I was still. The house was built from the bottom upwards. Of course. I watched as the sky was covered up with roof. And when the house was finished, I stepped outside onto the wooden porch and sat on the steps that led into my sea of grass. Soon the house began to fill with furnishings. A bed appeared and I slept in it during my star-filled nights. The shelves slowly accumulated wooden figurines of dogs and wolves, of lynxes and snow foxes, and even the occasional squirrel. These were creatures I was unfamiliar with and yet so very familiar with. I saw the dogs every day. I stroked their grey and white fur and felt their wet muzzles, which they pressed into the palms of my hands. I knew their long tongues. I knew the steady whack of a wagging tail against my leg as a content dog stood by me and allowed me to scratch its back. These dogs were here with me but they were not here. Not here in the grassland.

Just as there are two of me, there are two houses and two of every figurine I have ever carved. There are two beds, two stoves, two of every pot and pan and there are two kettles. There are two bathrooms, both crude. There are two fireplaces and every log I chop has its duplicate, safely stacked, here. There are two rocking chairs, two sofas, two of every stool and table. But there is only one of each dog and one of each goat. Sometimes I see the goats when they are dead and the meat is in the freezer.

One day I met a man. In town for my monthly visit, I went to the public house. The pub is run by Eyulf, an old friend of my father's. He brews all of his drinks himself and they are very good. I often sit with him and we reminisce about my father.

The pub is always quite full and I know everyone there. The atmosphere is usually relaxed and restful. But this time the place felt different. There was a tension in the air that would have been unnoticeable to an outsider. It was not as full as usual either. There was a man that I did not recognise, sitting at the bar. I sat down a little distance from him and greeted Eyulf, who hugged me then poured me a drink. I gestured to the stranger with a twitch of my head.

"Wanderer," Eyulf said. "Arrived this morning. Been in here all day."

The townspeople are unused to visitors, other than nearby traders; and most of those traders are as familiar as a neighbour in the next house. They are afraid of real wanderers. The last strangers they had let into the fold were my father and me, a good many years ago. It has been long enough for everyone to have forgotten that we really were outsiders.

The townspeople gave the wanderer a wide berth, afraid of being too curious. Afraid of what kind of a man he might be. Afraid, not of the difference that there might be between him and us, but rather of the possibility of them being unable to bridge any divide. They are good people. I stood up and took a place beside the man. He looked at me. I studied him. It was easy to see why one might be nervous of such a man. He was weather worn and wary; he looked wild and tough and hardy, like an animal. He sat still under my scrutiny and studied me in return.

"Where did you come from?" I asked.

"I left Finnur country some weeks ago."

His voice was rough, almost hoarse. I nodded and sipped my brandy. We sat in silence for some time.

"Are you from Finnur?" I asked eventually.

"No. Can't say I remember exactly where I'm from," he said with the hint of a smile that made me wonder if he was telling the truth or not.

"Where were you before Finnur?"

"Herleif, Asgeir, Babak, Ymir, Lodur, Masashi... I forget..."

"Ymir?"

"Yes."

"Do you remember Ymir? What was it like when you were there?"

The man gave me a long look.

"Why?" he asked me.

"It is where I was born. My father was Ymirian."

The man and I talked for some time. He told me about his travels, he told me about the world. He was a wanderer. He had no place to stay that night. There was room on my sled. He had few belongings, all of which fit into a rucksack. He came with me. That night we made love. It was not my first time, but it felt as though it was. The next day I knew that there was life within me.

I woke up and knew that there was life within me. Another living creature just like me, with another creature that was itself somewhere else. I rose from my bed and went outside. I looked over the grasslands into the distance. This empty space would soon have two souls within it. I lay down, nestled in the gold grass, and looked up at the clear blue sky above. I felt the sun inside my skin. I felt the life in my belly and stroked it with my hands.

I lay, nestled in my furs in the snow and looked up through the branches of the trees at the clear blue sky above. I felt the cold creeping through me. I felt the life in my belly and stroked it with my hands. I heard the man come out onto the porch. Time passed. I grew colder. He came and sat with me. He took me in his arms and I curled up against his chest. I could hear his heartbeat through his thin clothes for he had not bothered to put on a coat.

124

"What are you thinking about?" he asked me.

"Our child," I said.

I felt his surprise. He rubbed my arms to warm me up.

"How do you know?" He asked.

"I feel it. I'm certain."

I felt him nod. He felt my conviction. He was not afraid. A man like this could not be afraid.

"Will you move on?" I asked.

"Perhaps," was his answer. "We'll see." He bent down and kissed me softly. I felt he would not leave.

The months have been passing. I am living with a man in the snow. I am living by myself in the grasslands. I know the man well. Every inch of him. Every wrinkle and scar. The exact shade of his eyes (a mixture of grey and blue). His hair is dark with the occasional streak of grey. I know him bearded and bare faced. I have never touched him and yet I have and know the feel of him. I know his love for me. I know love. I have felt it before for the people I have known and yet not known. My belly grows and swells. The baby moves a lot. I feel it kicking, and as I feel it kicking here so too do I feel it kicking in the other here. I wake alone every morning – just me and my belly – and I wake up with the man. I eat the same meals as myself, alone and in company.

Eight months. I wake up. The man is lying beside me. I watch him sleep. Some minutes later he wakes up also. He stretches, opens his eyes and searches for me with them. He finds my face and smiles. He reaches up and kisses me. Suddenly he pulls away. He jumps out of the bed, never once taking his eyes off me.

"Who are you?" he asks backing away across the room.

"I'm me," I say.

"No," he shakes his head. He runs outside. He runs around the house. He runs into the grass. He runs but there is nowhere to run to. I follow him. I can't walk fast on my swollen feet. Eventually, I find him, sat on the ground amidst the grass. He is shaking.

"This is a dream," he says when I get there.

I crouch down beside him.

"No," I say.

"It has to be," he says.

I smile at him. He sees I am the same as me. The same open smile, the same wrinkles at my eyes. He reaches out and puts his hand to my cheek. He strokes it with his fingertips as if searching for the imprint of cedar wood in my skin.

"How can this be?" he asks and his voice trembles.

I shake my head and stand up slowly. I offer him my hand. He takes it and rises up. As we walk back to my house I tell him:

"There are two of me. Not twins. Me. I am in two places at once, always. If there was a map of my world I could place my finger on one part of it and say "I am here". But it would be equally true for me to place my finger on a different part of the map and say "I am here". It's true. There are no two ways about it. There are two of me. You," I tell him, "have known one of me. But now you know two."

"That's impossible," he tells me.

"Perhaps," I say, "but the impossible has occurred. Surely that means it is possible." I take his hand and place it on my belly. "This is our child," I say.

He tears his hand away and looks at me with fear and something else – an expression I have never seen before.

"No," he says, shaking his head. "I don't know you. I am having a child with a woman that looks just like you, but you are not her. That is not my baby," he says pointing at my stomach.

"It is," I say. "I met you eight months ago at Eyulf's pub. You were sitting by the bar alone. The place was not as full as usual. I sat beside you and asked where you were from. I asked you about Ymir. We talked for some time and—"

"Stop!" the man begs me and I see that there are tears in his eyes.

I take a step towards him. I want to comfort him but he pulls away. "Who are you?" he asks. 'What do you want?"

I continue walking. He follows me at a distance.

"I am aware of the me that lives in the snow. I experience that life if I close my eyes and think of it. But the other me, knows nothing of me here. I – the me in the snow – woke up this morning. You were not in the bed. I got up and pulled on my boots and coat over my woollen nightdress. I pulled the hood up over my loose hair, still messy from sleeping. I went outside into the snow and called for you. There was no answer but I was not worried. I thought perhaps you had gone for a walk. I made breakfast. You did not return so I ate my share before it got too cold. I did not bother to dress as few of my clothes fit me now and my nightdress is comfortable and warm. I sat in the rocking chair my father made for me and decided to finish knitting the little cardigan I have been making for our child. The wool is burnt orange, bright. I'm sitting there now, knitting and waiting for you. I'm not worried yet." I stop and turn to look at the man. Tears are still running down his face. "I never thought I would see you cry."

A flicker of anger crosses his face like the shadow of a fast-moving cloud.

"You don't know me," he says. His tears have stopped.

"But I think it is clear that really I do. I know you as well as I know you. That is—"

"Stop," he says. "It... confuses me. How can you know about another you and yet the other you not know about you?" he asks.

"This is the way it has always been, ever since I was a little girl. I lived alone in this grassland all my life and, at the same time, I have had a father and a town and a life full of company. Sometimes I forget that I am me here and believe that I am me in the snow. I can't call it there because, strictly speaking, it is not there if I am in it. One could say it is neither here nor there."

He smiles at this.

"That is a joke she would have made," he says quietly.

"There is no she," I say. "It's just me. I am me whether I am here or here."

We begin to walk again and after some time we get to the house.

"Are you hungry?" I ask him.

He shakes his head, sits down on the porch steps and gazes out.

"Can I go back?" he asks.

I sit down beside him and take in a deep breath. I smell the grass and the wood of the house.

"I don't know. In truth, I don't know how you got here. No living thing has ever done it... I am still sitting on the rocking chair and knitting, but since some time has passed I am beginning to grow worried. I wonder where you are. Did you go to the town? Why didn't you take the sled?"

"Please... don't," he says. I nod.

127

"I have always thought that this grass world was only full of doubles. I wonder now if another you will appear in the snow. Then maybe you won't leave. But perhaps when you fall asleep you will wake up in the snowy world again." He looks at me hopefully.

"Do you think I will?"

I shrug.

"I couldn't say. Stay for the day. Talk to me. Although I have spoken with you I haven't spoken with you. This is a first as well as a thousandth for me. We'll only be able to say what might happen when you wake up. If you wake up in the snow then maybe you'll never return to here. Or maybe you will. If you wake up in the grass then it is less likely you will return to the snow, I think. But who can say for sure? As you said before, this is an impossible thing. So now we can believe all manner of impossibilities."

"So now we can believe all manner of impossibilities."

He seems to like that phrase. He turns it over on his tongue several times. I get up and make us some food. The day passes. He talks to me, but not as he usually does. Wariness, revulsion and fascination temper his tone. He moves between creating a distance between us and closing the gap, repulsed and drawn in by the fact that I am me. The talk between us and the way it is conducted makes me feel strange. It is an emotion that neither myself nor I have ever felt before. And both myself and I are worried.

Although I am in no condition to drive the sled, I harness the dogs to it and get on. We travel faster than we should. I am no longer worried, but afraid. When we get to the town I rush to Eyulf.

"What the... What's the matter? Have you gone out of your mind?" Eyulf asks as he sits me down.

"He's gone, Eyulf! I don't know where he's gone!" I say, and I finally burst into tears.

I feel a surge of emotion and have to hold back the tears.

"Are you alright?" the man asks me. I nod. Yes. Keep talking. He goes on.

I am crying in Eyulf's arms. He tries to console me. Darkness falls. Eyulf calls one of my old friends, Inge. She takes me to her house and puts me to bed. The stress is not good for the baby. I

128

can't stop crying. I did not think that he would leave.

I feel desolate, abandoned, and yet I am with him now, he is talking to me and it is different from all the other times we have spoken. Although I know him and can experience him whether he is here or not, I find myself wishing that when he wakes up tomorrow morning he will still be here, with me.

I finally fall asleep, exhausted by the tears.

We go to sleep. He refuses to get into the bed with me but chooses instead to sleep on the old sofa. I am disappointed.

I wake up. My head hurts. I am dehydrated. I feel uncomfortable and anxious but it takes me some minutes to remember why. Then it comes back in a flood. He's gone. But maybe he's back. I leave Inge's and hurry to find my dogs. Eyulf has taken care of them. I thank him silently and harness them. We drive back home, faster than we should and when I get there I rush into the house full of hope.

I wake up. Immediately I sit up and look at the sofa. I breathe a sigh of relief. He is still here. He is awake. He is watching me, an unreadable expression on his face.

I feel a weight crushing me. I sink to the floor. Where is he? I know he has not left me. I know him too well. He would not do that. Not without some warning. Not without leaving a note. Besides, all his things are still here. His rucksack is still in our wardrobe. I sit on the floor for hours and think of him, wondering where he is and why he is not here.

I am thinking of him, all of the time we have spent together, and wondering why he is gone. I can't tell him this, as it will only upset him. I am thinking of eight months together and I am also thinking of one day together. Yesterday is all the time we have had.

Eyulf finds me. He has brought the doctor with him. Doctor Lyal helps me to my feet and tells me I can't stay up on the mountain in this state, especially now. I might go into an early

129

labour. I must come down. I nod. I haven't the energy to argue.

"I've organised a search party. We're heading out in about an hour," Eyulf tells me. I nod again. I have a feeling that they won't find him. I have a feeling that something impossible has happened to him. All I can do is wish for him back. They take me away. I find myself in Inge's house again and realise that this may become my home for a time.

He doesn't want to talk to me. He doesn't want to have anything to do with me. All he wants is to return to... her. Yes. For the first time I am thinking of the other me as 'her'. And yet she can't be simply she when she is me. I'm confused. Unable to think clearly, I pour the water I have boiled not into the teapot but onto my hand. I cry out and part of me expects him to act, to move, to do something to help. He doesn't. I go to the sink and run my hand under a steady stream of cold water, watching the angry skin cool and pale. When I look up I see him studying me.

"Yes. It's true that you are you. But yesterday you were more definitely you. Today it is perhaps less definite."

And he is right. I am less sure of myself now. I wonder if I am becoming someone else. He sits on the porch outside and wills himself away. It does not work, much to my relief. I rub my stomach.

"Baby," I whisper, "maybe you'll have a father,"

The days pass. A week passes. Another passes. Time flows. Every day he sits out on the porch and wills himself away. I bring him food and he eats because he needs to. I sit with him sometimes. Sometimes I work around the house. Today I caught him watching me as I cleaned the windows. I'm sure he was seeing me as the woman he knew. He seemed embarrassed when he realised I was looking back at him. I wonder when he first began to watch me. Thinking of it makes me oddly pleased.

I sit inside on the floor and I rub my belly. The baby is kicking. I begin to sing to it.

"What's that song," he asks, startling me.

"I don't know the name. My father used to sing it to me. I never grew out of it. He sang it to me even when I was fully grown."

"Yes," he agrees quietly and he comes to sit down next

to me. "Tell me more about yourself," he says.

And so I do. I tell him everything, and he has heard it all before from the other me. But as I tell him everything, I wonder again if I am talking about me or about someone else. He seems soothed by the stories. He takes my hand and presses it gently.

"I like that story. About your cedar tree." I nod. I smile, but the smile is strained. "You look worried," he says and he brushes the wrinkles out of my forehead with his hand.

He smiles at me. I lean into his hand and close my eyes, memorising this moment, this touch. Tentatively, he kisses me as though testing waters. The kiss does not last long but he does not look dissatisfied as he pulls away.

"Why?" he asks me, "are you so sure that you and you are the same?"

I can't answer him. I am not sure. I stand up. I hug my belly and walk out of the house, into the grasslands, far into them. I know he is following me. I stop, far from the house and close my eyes. The wind is blowing and the grass sounds just like the sea. I saw the sea once as a child. My father took me to it and we walked along the beach. It was freezing.

I spread my arms out and feel the wind rush around me. It whips my dark dress around my legs, and it whips my dark hair around my face. I stand straight, my stomach protruding before me, and savour the air. He is right behind me, watching me. The wind here is my favourite cedar tree there. I turn around.

"I was alone. There was nothing. Just golden grass and blue sky and sun. I did not know that there was anything else just yet. I crawled through the grass. I was looking for something, but I did not know what it was. I stopped when I realised I could not find it. I wanted to cry but I did not know what crying was or how to do it just yet. And then the wind blew around me. It wrapped around my naked body and rushed through the grass, sending it rustling into a noise I could not describe at that time. It ruffled my hair like a mother or a father, though I did not know what mothers or fathers were, and I felt at ease. It blew all the feelings away. I stayed in that wind for days and nights. I stayed there until I experienced being the other me. And then I began to learn about the world and people. That is where it all began. The first time I was me, the me in the snow, I was standing in this spot in the wind. And I was standing by a cedar tree on a slope. There was no house yet. I was on a hiking trip with my father. I was here in the wind."

He walks towards me and takes me into his arms. My belly gets in the way of any proper embrace but I feel his sentiments all the same. I am not the me he knows. I am someone else. It has taken another living being in this world to show me this.

"Stay with me," I say.

"Come back to me," I say – she says.

My heart feels as though it is being squeezed. I must give him back. I can't.

"I can't," he says.

"Are you sure?" I ask.

"No."

"Are you alright where you are?" I ask and Inge asks me whom it is that I am talking to.

"I'm fine," he says.

"Do you want to stay there?" I ask and Inge gives me a strange look.

He looks at me.

"Yes," he says.

I begin to cry.

"No," he says.

He hugs me and disappears. I sink to the grassy floor and cry. I know now what solitude is. I rub my stomach and feel a surge of fear. My baby will come into this world without any help from anyone. I will be on my own. And then this baby will inherit my life. Only it will be harder for my child. The child will grow up with a companion. But one day I will die.

I sit up in my chair. I feel a change. He's back. I know it. I rise to my feet and brush away Inge who is worrying at me to sit back down. They have hidden my dogs from me so I cannot use the sled. I begin to walk. Inge runs after me and tries to stop me but I will not be stopped. Inge fetches Doctor Lyal. He cannot stop me either so he fetches a sled and takes me home.

He is standing some distance from the house, amidst the trees. I heave myself out of the sled and call out to him, but he does not turn. I struggle through the snow and Doctor Lyal is yelling after me to stop. I don't. I reach him. He is standing quite still as though petrified. I take his face in my hands. I am crying.

"Where have you been?" I ask.

132

He finally stirs.

"With you."

He is serious. It makes me angry. I hit him. Not hard, not properly, but I hit him. He takes a step away from me. He turns around and runs to the house. I cannot follow him. I'm tired and weak and the snow is too hard to walk through. I struggle forwards. The doctor is watching from the sled track.

When I finally get to the house I find him walking around and around its confines, opening doors and cupboards and then closing them, only to open them again some minutes later.

"What are you looking for?" I ask. He does not answer. "What are you looking for? What are you looking for?" He never answers. Eventually he sinks to the floor. It is getting dark.

"I don't know," he says and he looks unbearably sad.

I go to the window and look out. The doctor is gone. The baby kicks inside me.

"The baby is kicking," I say.

He looks through me.

"I wonder if the baby is kicking?" he says.

"I just said the baby is kicking."

"Yes. The baby is kicking here. But is the baby kicking there?"

"What do you mean?" I ask and again I feel angry.

He smiles.

"It's neither here nor there."

I crouch beside him and put a hand to his forehead. He is not running a fever. I wish the doctor had not left. He would not have left if he were a good doctor. He would have stayed to see what had happened to my man, to check if he was well.

He looks up at me and finally he sees me.

"I love you," he says.

I smile and wrap my arms around his neck.

"I love you too."

He kisses me on the neck. Not a real kiss. Just a brush from his lips and then he pulls away from me. He pushes a lock of my hair behind my ear and regards my face admiringly.

"Yes. You're strong. You'll do well."

"What?" A sudden fear twists my stomach. "What are you saying?" and again I can feel anger and tears tying knots in my throat. I feel sick with myself. This is not the reunion I was expecting, if I was expecting one at all. I should be happy, relieved.

We should be sitting by the fire, eating a good meal, while he tells me everything that has happened to him, where he has been and why he disappeared so suddenly. He interrupts my thoughts with another kiss, this time a proper one. I lean into him, but as I do he pulls away again and rises to his feet. Offering me his hand, he pulls me up.

"You should not be all the way up here. You're about to give birth. It's dangerous. Come. I'll take you to the town." He takes my hand and leads me to the door.

"No," I say pulling back. I am afraid. I know what will happen. He smiles at me sadly.

"I'll take you tomorrow," he says. "Let's have an early night. I'm tired."

With that, he climbs into bed. Reluctantly, I follow suit, but I feel better as he wraps his arms around me and nuzzles his face into my neck. I have missed him so much.

I wake up. The man is lying beside me. I do not believe he is really here. This is just a dream and in this dream I watch him sleep. Then he wakes up. He stretches, opens his eyes and searches for me. He finds my face and smiles. He reaches up and kisses me. Suddenly I know. He is here. He is with the me in the grass.

He was a wanderer.

I am alone in the snow. But not so alone. It is a boy.

***

Zag
Steven Fromm

Steven Fromm is a writer and journalist currently living in Robbinsville, N.J. His work has appeared in several publications, including Inkwell and Salamander. He recently completed his first novel.

Judge Sandra was delighted by this story. In her own words "I must admit Zag has been my favourite short story of the bunch. It was stylish and didn't pull any punches. It's a real skill to tell such a intricate story in such a small word count. I was really impressed."

Our wives' funerals were at the same time, about 40 yards apart, two separate constellations in the middle of that vast stretch of cemetery in the middle of an inappropriately beautiful fall day.

The only thing to connect us, at least physically, were the sprinkling of TV news cameras hovering like satellites at a respectful distance to take the requisite shots of the husbands delicately placing flowers on the caskets. Ishaan Deshpande sprinkled a handful of rose petals. I had six sunflowers, which were Emma's favourite.

The services ended at about the same time. We each stood where we were as the mourners formed a line for hugs and breathless encouragements, a blurred amalgam of tears and mumbles that seemed necessary to bring the ceremony to a close before they started drifting toward their cars. I watched them threading their way slowly through the grave stones. It seemed to take forever.

"Excuse me."

I turned to find Deshpande standing about five feet off to my right. I looked over his shoulder. There was a small cluster of relatives still standing around his wife's casket.

"Excuse me," he said again. "Mr. Moore? May we speak?"

He was waiting for some kind of assent to approach, like someone asking permission to come aboard a ship. I took a step toward him, my right hand out.

"Mister?" I couldn't remember his name from the police briefings.

"Deshpande," he said, stepping toward me. "Ishaan Deshpande."

He was wearing a navy suit, white shirt and black tie, his receding black hair and moustache cut short with an almost military precision. Nothing was out of place.

"I was wondering if I could speak to you," he said.

"Sure," I said. "What is it?"

He gave me a tolerant little smile, as if I wasn't following.

"I do not mean here," he said, glancing past me to my wife's casket. "Not now."

"I see," I said. "But what about?"

"I wish to discuss matters associated with our—" he stopped and looked into my eyes, "with our mutual experience."

I felt my face tighten. I didn't want to talk about our mutual experience. It wasn't mutual.

"I know this is not the proper time to ask," Deshpande said, reaching into his jacket pocket and withdrawing a small black wallet, "but I did not know when I would see you next. The court dates, the media requests. They are so—what's the word—random. The phone rings and we must be at these places. It is a blur. Some of the families show. Some do not. You never do. At least not at the public events."

He stopped, shot me another embarrassed smile, shrugged his shoulders then turned back toward his wife's grave. All of his relatives stood there, looking our way. He raised his hand, then turned back toward me, opening his wallet and taking out his business card. He held it out to me. I hesitated for a few moments, then took it.

"This is my cell. I always have it with me. Please call."

"I will," I said. "And you have my condolences, Mr. Deshpande."

"You have mine," he said. "And please call me Ishaan."

Then he turned and began walking back through the gravestones.

"Ah. You are here."

I looked up from the menu to find Deshpande standing over me, looking pleasantly surprised that I hadn't stood him up. I made a show of rising partially out of my seat to shake his hand, then

138

motioned for him to sit down. When he had settled in he asked me how long I'd been waiting. I said six minutes. He seemed like the type who appreciated precise answers.

The waitress appeared. Deshpande ordered an egg white omelette and iced tea. I ordered a tuna sandwich and water. The waitress went away, leaving us without the shelter of our menus. The place was beginning to fill with the lunchtime crowd, the buzz of conversation growing around us. There was a time when I would have launched into some small talk to avoid the silent stretches, but those days were over. I could have sat there for an hour without talking. Deshpande sat straight in his chair, his hands on the table before him, his fingers intertwined. He was neatly dressed in a white, button-down oxford cloth shirt and a narrow maroon tie. A gold Parker pen was clipped into his shirt pocket.

"You have a very interesting occupation, Mr. Moore," he said.

"Call me Eli, please," I said, even though I knew he wouldn't call me Eli anymore than I'd call him Ishaan.

"I have a subscription to your paper, and have read many of your articles," he said.

"I'm glad someone's still reading them," I said.

"What?" he asked.

"It was just a remark," I said. He kept looking at me. "A remark about the fact that people don't read as much as they used to." He still didn't say anything. "You know. Newspapers in general."

The waitress came and set down our drinks. I made a mental note to cease all self-deprecating and ironic remarks around Deshpande. It was a waste of energy. I didn't bother to ask him about his profession. I read it on his card. He was some kind of software engineer. Deshpande took a sip of his iced tea and cleared his throat, as if preparing to give some kind of presentation.

"As you know, the district attorney's office very quickly made their decision not to seek the death penalty against Alfred Romero," he said.

"Yes," I said. "I was at the meeting."

About a month after the shootings, the DA's office herded us into a conference room, offered us cheap coffee and bottled water and for the next 90 minutes explained their decision to seek life imprisonment. They said his age, the complications of a capital trial and possible mental health issues influenced their decision.

"Did you agree?" Deshpande asked.

"With their decision?"

"Yes," he said. "And their reasoning behind the decision."

They asked us the same question at the meeting, but it was clear they really didn't care. The decision had been made.

"Well, the whole issue of mental competence—"

"—there is no issue," Deshpande said. It came out hard and quick. He paused a moment to take another sip of iced tea. "He was examined by two state psychiatrists who found him mildly sociopathic, but quite competent."

"I know, the DAs told us that. But they also told us that defense counsel would just come up with a few shrinks who would find him just this side of Josef Mengele. A battle of the experts. It's a wash."

"Maybe there should be."

"What?"

"A battle of the experts."

"Toward what end?"

"An exchange."

"What exchange?"

"Of opinion. Of fact. A jury should be given the opportunity to view the full panoply of evidence."

"It still wouldn't work."

"Why not?"

"A guy goes into a donut shop and shoots up the place for no reason? Of course the jury's going to think he's bughouse."

"Bughouse?"

"Nuts. And worse, he's a *young* nut."

"So he commits mass murder. And because he commits mass murder, he must be insane, therefore we cannot hold him to any standard?" Deshpande's voice got louder with each word. He was leaning slightly forward, the tips of his fingers on the edge of the table. "It makes no sense. Perhaps if he'd worn a suit and tie and killed only one person rather precisely and politely, *then* he could be tried for a capital crime."

Deshpande stopped and leaned back in his chair. Perhaps he felt his anger was rude. We stayed silent for a few moments, staring at our empty place mats.

"That's why I possess an abiding love of mathematics," he finally said.

"What?"

"Mathematics," he said. "There is always a solution, and it is linear and completely logical. It is the most beautiful language. It is God talking, and without passion. Or at least without a destructive passion."

I started smiling.

"Do you think that is amusing?" he asked.

"No. It's just that you hear the language of God in mathematics, and I nearly flunked high school geometry."

Deshpande regarded my statement for a moment, trying to decide if it was funny, but only a wistful expression came to the surface.

"I suppose we all find divinity in different things," he said.

"And some of us don't," I said.

The waitress brought our food. We made a show of eating for a few minutes. I was able to steal a look at my watch when I wiped my mouth with my napkin. He didn't eat much of his omelette, but busied himself by moving half of it one from one spot on the plate to another.

"May I ask you something of a personal nature?" he asked. Given the situation, it struck me as an odd question.

"Fire away," I said.

"Are you a religious man?"

"Is that a delicate way of asking what my religion is?"

"Yes."

"I'm Jewish. Technically."

"Technically?"

"My mother was Jewish, my father Presbyterian. I wasn't raised religiously."

"Your name. Eli. It is an abbreviation for Elijah, yes?"

"That doesn't mean anything."

"How so?"

"My mother was fond of the name Eli. And he's mentioned in the New Testament and the Qur'an as well as the Old Testament."

"And the Mishna as well, yes, I know," Deshpande said. He was cutting a tomato slice in precise quarters, but still not eating anything. "I was perhaps hoping that you may identify with certain aspects of the Old Testament."

"Like an eye for an eye?"

"Precisely."

"Exodus 21:23."

"Yes, but you will also find that sentiment in Leviticus, Numbers and Deuteronomy."

"And you'll find the opposite in the New Testament. Jesus was no fan. Take a look at Matthew, Luke, John and I think Romans."

Deshpande stopped slicing his tomato. "You have read the Bible quite carefully," he said. "So did my wife. She was from a Catholic family." He remained silent for a moment, then shrugged. "The problem with building an argument on the Bible is that you

142

really cannot build an argument on the Bible," he finally said.

"A user's guide with too many users and not enough guidance," I said.

The waitress came up and asked if we wanted anything else. Deshpande shook his head. She looked at our plates and walked away without leaving our check.

"Are you a religious man?" I asked.

"Religious is probably not the right word."

"What is?"

"Spiritual," Deshpande said. "I am a spiritual man."

"Hindu?"

"Yes. I am Hindu."

"So, what does Hinduism say about the death penalty?"

"Unfortunately, this is a case where Hinduism's flexibility is a liability," he said. "The Dharmasastras name many offenses that may invoke death. The Mahabharata also supports it. Later scriptures indicate the opposite."

"You get to choose," I said.

"Yes. I get to choose."

"And you have." It wasn't a question.

He gave a little smile, but it wasn't the same as the others.

"Yes," he said. "I have chosen."

The waitress appeared and asked again if we wanted anything else. I looked at Deshpande. He shook his head. She pulled a pad out of her apron, tore off a piece of paper and put it between us. I was about to grab it when Deshpande reached out and put his hand on it. I looked up at him.

"I want you to go see him," he said.

"Why?"

"Someone, one of us, needs to go and ask him."

"Ask him what?"

"The question."

"What question?"

"Please do not play stupid games."

"Ok. Fine. You want someone, one of us, to go and ask him why."

"Yes."

"And what do you expect?"

"An answer."

"Right. He is asked this question, and he just sits back, twiddles his thumbs and gives us a complete, articulate answer. And it's not an answer, it's *the* answer."

"That is not what I mean."

"What *do* you mean?"

"Whatever answer he gives will be better than what we have now, which is nothing but what he took from us."

"You want an answer? *You* go ask him."

"I have tried already."

I blinked at him. "You tried?"

"Yes. I had my attorney contact his counsel. My request was rebuffed."

"Why?"

"He did not say. He is not very proficient when it comes to providing explanations."

"What about the others?"

"Others?"

"The other spouses."

"I've asked them. They do not wish to even attempt a meeting."

"You've asked everyone."

He gave me a nod.

"He said no to you. What makes you think he'll say yes to me?"

"You can try."

"Why give him the satisfaction?"

"Satisfaction of what?"

"Of saying no."

"You can try," he said again.

We looked at each other for a few moments. I could have said something else, but he'd just keep repeating the same thing. I reached for my wallet, took out a few bills and put them on the table.

"There is no chance," I said, standing up.

"I beg your pardon?"

"There is no chance," I repeated. "That's the problem with all of you. You want to control what happened even though it's happened. It was a point in time. One small speck in time, and something imploded in all of our lives and it's over. It's gone. You want a say in something that's history."

"In this case perhaps the past begins where we choose," Deshpande said.

"The only one with a choice was Alfie Romero, and he made it," I said. "There are no choices left. That's what it means to be a casualty."

I started walking away from the table. Deshpande said something, but I didn't hear him. The place was filled with people chattering over their Caesar salads and hamburgers about work and children and mortgages and little league. People from a different planet.

When I reached the door I turned back, half expecting to see Deshpande following me, but he still sat at the table, facing my empty chair. And it was at that moment, standing there looking at poor little Deshpande sitting at that table, ram-rod straight but still broken, completely broken, that I made up mind.

Brookens stood stiff and nervous just inside the prison's General Intake Security Section. He was wearing a short-sleeve, white shirt with faint sweat marks in the armpits, a maroon tie and slightly-too-large glasses that were at least five years behind the fashion curve.

"Right on time," he said as I cleared the metal detector.

Brookens handed me a little visitor's decal. I unpeeled it and slapped it on the right side of my chest.

"If you'll step into my office, I need you to sign a G-9 before we proceed."

"A G-9?"

"It's a waiver of liability in case of injury or damage."

We went into a small side office with no windows that held a desk with a computer, a filing cabinet and a few chairs. He handed me the G-9, which was two pages with print that belonged on the back of a pill bottle. I pretended to read it, waiting a semi-plausible 30 seconds or so, then signed it and handed it back. Brookens scanned the document, slid it into manila folder and then put it into the top drawer of his desk.

"I need to explain a few procedures to you before we proceed."

"He's in D Block, right?" I asked.

Brookens looked at me for a moment, then nodded. "That's right," he said, "you've covered corrections."

D-Block was where they kept PC inmates. PC stood for protective custody. In a state prison, you want as much PC as you can get.

"That's where we're headed," Brooken said. "Both the DA and defense counsel have agreed to a one-hour meeting. Wait. Sorry. The DA and the defendant have agreed to a one-hour meeting. Defense counsel, at least technically, object to the meeting."

"Maybe they'll come around," I said.

"Excuse?"

"Sorry. A joke."

"Yes. Right," he said, trying a quick smile that looked more like fleeting spasm. "The meeting will take place in a MPCR," he said.

"That's one acronym I've never heard," I said.

"A modified protective conference room," Brookens said. "It's a separate room divided by two-inch Plexiglass. You are on one side, Mr. Romero will be on the other. You will be able to hear each other through a self-activated, two-way voice-amplification system, which is implanted in the glass at about chest level. Any questions?"

"Will we be alone?"

"Yes, but both defense counsel and the DA's office want the conversation taped. Also, corrections officers will be monitoring the meeting offsite via a TV monitor."

"Offsite?"

"In the next room. Anything else?"

"No."

"Mr. Romero will be wearing ankle chains, but we will remove his waist chain upon his delivery to the MPCR. Also, you will both be permitted to smoke."

"I don't smoke."

"Mr. Romero does," Brookens said.

We were silent for a few moments.

"Anything else?" Brookens asked.

"No."

"Let me call down to D-Block."

He picked up his phone, dialled an extension, exchanged a

few clipped sentences to whomever was on the line and then hung up.

"They're ready," he said, rising from his chair.

I followed him out of his office, turned right and proceeded down a long, concrete corridor lit by fluorescent tubes overhead. We went through one more metal detector before coming up to a steel gate. Brookens looked up to a surveillance camera and gave a slight nod. The gate slid open, then slammed after we passed with a doomsday clang, the echoes pulsing down the corridor and fading like rumbles of thunder on the horizon.

We made another right, then started walking down another long corridor, passing two housing modules, which were now in prison vogue. They were circular units, two stories high and lined with cells, anchored by a ground floor with eight round steel tables and stools, all bolted to the floor. The inmates were monitored from guard units on the second floor, where we were. As we walked past and behind them, I looked at the guards, hunkered down behind a console of television screens that covered the module from all angles. They looked more like pilots in a cockpit.

We arrived at a second steel gate. Brookens did his thing with the camera, and someone from within the catacombs remotely opened and shut the gate once again.

"Just one more section," he said.

We turned left once again down a short hall with several steel doors. A guard stood outside the third one on our left. Brookens nodded and gave him a yellow piece of paper. The guard gave me a quick look. Our eyes didn't meet. He turned and punched a code into a little key pad just above the door knob. There was a whirring noise, then a loud click, and the door popped open by about an inch. The guard stepped back. Brookens opened the door wide.

"The hour begins as soon as Mr. Romero sits down."

"You're timing it?"

"We time everything," Brookens said. He gestured toward the room. "Have a seat."

The room was pretty much as he had described. It was halved

by a wall of thick Plexiglass with a speaker a little lower than chest high, a yellowy florescent cast from the light above gave it a darker, more subdued atmosphere than I'd expected. The other side of the room was identical to mine, a little counter empty with the exception of a tin ashtray screwed into it, a metal folding chair and a door on the back wall. It smelled of sweat, industrial cleaner and cigarette smoke.

I sat down on a folding metal chair and waited. I thought about taking off my jacket, but the thick concrete seemed to hold the air conditioning in place, saturating the air with a chilly stillness. I kept myself distracted by looking for the cameras. There were two, one on each side, bolted to the side walls, about six inches down from the ceiling.

Another minute passed, maybe ninety seconds before I heard a faint clicking, a slight whooshing sound, and then the door on the other side of the glass popped open. It stayed that way, about six inches ajar, for half a minute or so, then swung wide. Alfie Romero came in, looking directly at me with a vague smirk on his lips, as if he was on the verge of saying something slightly amusing or borderline insulting.

A guard came in behind him, produced a key and unlocked his hands from his waist chain. The cuffs hung down almost to his knees. He was wearing a red jump suit with a long sleeve white t-shirt underneath. He stood there compliantly, rubbing his wrists as the guard told him to sit down and not rise for any reason until the meeting was over. During the little speech, Romero didn't stop staring at me. I sat still, arms folded over chest, staring back.

He sat down with a grunt. I heard it through the speaker. He reached up under the right sleeve of his jump suit and pulled out a pack of Camels and put them on the counter. The guard dug into his pocket, produced a pack of matches, and placed them by the smokes.

"You know the drill," he said. "Leave all the used matches on the counter."

Romero didn't answer. We were still locked in our stare.

The guard walked out the door, shutting it with a decisive clang. It's like they weren't capable of shutting a door quietly.

Romero waited a few moments, then reached for the pack and tapped out a cigarette. As he fiddled with the matches, I took him in. His hair was shorter than when I saw him during sentencing and combed straight back, which made him look slightly older. He had about two days of stubble on his face.

He lit up and shook the match while blowing out a thin, tight stream of smoke. He placed the spent match on the counter.

"They count the matches," he said.

"What?"

"They give you a full pack, with, what? Twenty matches in it. When you're done you have to give back all the used matches."

He waited for a reaction. I didn't have one, so he went on.

"Of course, that's only in PC. In general stir, it's gotta be one of the COs. They've gotta light them for you." He paused for a moment, maybe for dramatic effect. "That's how they watch you in here."

"Am I supposed to be impressed or something?"

Romero ignored me. He shifted in his seat, took another hit from the cigarette and put it in the ashtray.

"My biggest fear is kind of weird. I mean, it sounds weird if you just say it, but if you *think* about it, it's not so weird. If I get placed in gen-pop, I'm gonna have to take a crap in front of all those people. Or at least a cell mate or two at the least. The idea freaks me out."

"I think that's going to be the least of your worries," I said.

It felt good when I said it. He picked up his cigarette, which had burned down to its last few inches, and let it hang from his lips. It bounced up and down when he talked.

"It's funny you should say that," he said. "But the truth is I don't worry about much of anything. I did something, you know, that took 20 minutes. Just 20 minutes. And it changed everything about everything. It kind of *removed* everything."

Maybe he wanted me to take the bait on his mentioning the 20 minutes. Maybe I should have. "Remove all what?"

"Decisions. My ability to make them." He took a final drag from the cigarette and snubbed it out in the ashtray. "Ability is probably the wrong word. You're a journalist, right? You care about the right word."

I didn't know if I was supposed to be surprised that he'd taken the time to find out what I did. I didn't answer.

"Peace," he said. "That's the right word. I can't make any real decisions. When I eat, when I shower, who I talk to. I don't have a say. Maybe forever. I know it, so do you. Everything's pretty much going a certain way, and that's it, and it's ok. It's peaceful."

I couldn't decide if he was taunting me, or just running out the hour. I looked at my watch. Fifty minutes left. "*We time everything*," Brookens had warned.

"They time everything," Romero said, as if reading my mind. "Think about that. We're all locked up, going nowhere, doing nothing, but they have these schedules that need to be followed to the minute. To the *minute*."

It was the closest I'd seen him to being exasperated.

"I thought you said you were at peace," I said.

He smiled, picked another cigarette from the pack, struck a match and lit up. He shook out the match and placed it next to the first on the counter.

"Ok," he said. "*Mostly* at peace. That's better than most. It's better than you, right, Eli?"

It was my turn to smile at him. There we sat, lost in the bowels of some mouldy, sweat-stinking tomb scoring little points off one another, points so paltry they couldn't carry the weight of their own echoes.

"This isn't the reason I'm here," I finally said.

"I know."

"You know?"

"You have questions, right? Everyone has questions," he said, taking the cigarette out of his mouth and jabbing at the air with it. "They really don't want the answers, because they probably won't

151

like them, or they're not what they want to hear, or they don't seem to be the right ones or they don't *feel* right. So you people ask and I answer and then you just go away with your own answers anyway."

"You people?"

"You know. Like that one guy who's been sending me those weird letters. The Indian."

"Deshpande?"

"Yeah. You talk with him?"

"Yes."

"He wants more than answers. He wants to be *satisfied.*" Romero took a long drag from his cigarette, then let out a long thin stream of smoke. "How about you, Eli? Do you want to be satisfied?"

"I'm not sure what I want."

"Sure you do. You want something else," he said, ignoring me. "Something *deeper.* I wrote Deshpande once. Even got it through my attorneys. I told him there was nothing to tell. I did what I did and there is no reason. Did he tell you that?"

"No," I said. "Not about any letter."

"Right. Of course. He didn't say anything because I didn't give him *the* answer."

"Sounds like you didn't give him *any* answer."

"Ok. Right. I didn't."

"Why not?"

"What difference would it make?"

"Sounds familiar," I said.

"What does?"

"That's what I told him. About meeting with you."

"But you're still here anyway. Why?"

We looked at each other in silence, through the glass. I held out my hands, palms up.

"Ok," I said. "Ok. I want some answers."

Romero smiled, shook his head. "Was that so hard?"

"Was it that important? That I say it?"

"Yes," he said, taking a final drag from his cigarette, its little red point flaring, then fading. He snubbed it out, sat back in his chair and expelled the smoke as if releasing the debris of some kind of inner tension.

"How much do you know?" he asked.

"What?"

"How much do you know? From the paper? The cops?"

"Not much. You were on spring break, at your mother's house. You took her gun, the one she told the cops she bought for protection, then went to the donut shop."

"Nothing else?

"No."

"The DA didn't give you any other details?"

"Not really. None that stand out, anyway."

"Ok. I see." He leaned forward. "The truth is they didn't hold much of anything back. That's what there is."

I didn't say anything, waiting for him to continue.

"In fact, what they say is almost too much, like I had some kind of *plan*. I didn't have a plan. I just woke up that day, took a shower, ate some toast and sat there in the kitchen listening to the house creak."

"Where was your mother?"

He looked annoyed at the interruption.

"She was at work," he said. He went silent for a few moments. "That's not it, you know."

"What's not it?"

"She has nothing to do with it. I'd tell you if she did."

He said it so calmly that I believed him.

"So you were sitting there listening to the house creak," I said.

"Right," he said. "I just sat there perfectly still and I don't know why, but I just thought about my plans for that day, which were none. Absolute zero. Then I thought about the next day, and the next after that and there were none. Nothing all the way to the morning I was due back at Rutgers. Ok. Fine. And then I go back to school. And then what?"

He looked up at me like I was supposed to understand something. I shrugged my shoulders.

"A spring break with no plans," I said.

"You're missing it," he said, shaking his head. "Back at school. And *then* what? It's not the no plans, it's the nothing."

"The nothing," I said.

"Yes, the nothing."

"You had nothing to do. Is that what you're telling me?"

"No, Eli, you're not seeing. It's not the nothing to do. It's the *nothing.* You've probably felt something like it."

"Have I ever felt nothing?" I asked. "Is this some pimply college bullshit screed about nihilism? Is that what we're talking about?"

"No, no," he said, this time reaching for the cigarettes and tapping one out. "It's not feeling nothing. It's there and you're aware of it, and then all of a sudden it's *in* you. It's in your blood and bones or something and that's the end of it. It's in you and it *is* you. It's not feeling nothing, it's feeling *the* nothing. See?"

"It's in you," I echoed, trying to play it dumb.

"You know, Eli, right? You can fuck around all you want, but you know."

"Right," I said. "I do." I leaned forward and tried not to say it, but I did anyway. "We both know who to thank for that."

Our eyes locked for a moment, and then we both looked away. He took out a match, lit up and placed the match by the others. He was smiling now.

"Good," he said. "Ok. Now I can tell you the rest. We've got 37 minutes. That's plenty of time, don't you think?"

"It depends on what you're going to say."

"It's about perfection."

"Perfection."

"Right. Perfection. A *moment* of perfection, and it happened right there, right in the middle of that greasy little donut shop. I left the house that morning, with the gun in my back pocket. You know what kind of gun, right?"

"A 9mm," I said.

"Right. I had it in my back pocket and I left with absolutely no fucking idea where I was going. I just started walking, you know, wandering. I came across that little strip mall and thought I'd mess around, maybe go into that comic book store at the end. I used to hang out there in high school sometimes. So I'm walking through the parking lot and all of sudden the donut shop is there, and that was it. I knew I was going in there. I don't remember feeling anything, not even a higher pulse or sweat or anything like that. It was where I was going to go, and that was that."

He stopped and took a drag from his cigarette.

"That was your moment of perfection?"

"No. I'm getting to that. I was in the store. I don't remember going in. But there I was. I remember the donut and coffee smells and the warmth and I knew that was where I was supposed to be. Right there."

"Right there," I said, "for no reason."

"That's right, Eli, no reason at all. I guess that's the worst of it for you, right? I mean, think of the mathematical odds. Of all the places I could have chosen, of all the things I could have done. How often do you think about that, Eli?"

"I don't."

"Why not?"

"Because it changes nothing."

He gave me a long look, the smoke from the cigarette lazily threading its way to the ceiling.

"I can't tell if you're practical, burned out or just plain fuckin' dumb."

It was my turn to smile. "Which do you think?"

"The first two, for sure. Haven't decided on the third. Maybe it's not, you know, dumbness. Maybe it's because you're just in the dark."

"Enlighten me."

"What?"

"Enlighten me. With perfection."

For a couple of seconds it was like he didn't know what I was talking about. His eyes were almost glassy.

"You know," I said, "with your moment of perfection."

"Right," he said, giving his head a little shake and glancing at his cigarette. It still had a few pulls left, but he snuffed it out in the ashtray. The smell of smoke was heavy in the room. He stayed silent for a few more moments.

"It was your wife," he finally said.

"What about her?"

"When I was getting them into the back room, she stopped for a moment and looked at me and our eyes met up," he said. "I don't know. It was like I *liked* her, you know?" He was looking down, as if the right words were scattered on the floor. "She seemed so, what's the right way to say it? So uncomplicated. So simple. Not simple dumb. Simple clean. That's it. *Clean.*" He looked up at me. "You get it?"

"Yeah," I said. "She was my wife."

He laughed as he picked up the cigarette pack and tapped another one out. He put it in the corner of his mouth, lit up and took another long pull.

"How old was she?" he asked.

"Thirty one," I said.

"How does a person, a 31-year-old person, get to be like that at that age?"

"Like what?"

"Like I said. Clean."

I knew what he meant, but I didn't have an answer.

"And you take some of us, some others," he said, "we can be eight years old, and just be, you know, unclean. Right? Just *filthed* up."

He took the cigarette out of his mouth and tried picking a speck of tobacco from the tip of his tongue. He couldn't get it out, so he turned his head and spat.

"How much time we got?" he asked.

"Enough," I said.

"Ok then. This is the thing," he said. "There was that one point, right after we looked at each other, when she started getting all pale and dizzy."

"Her blood sugar."

"Right. The whole pregnancy thing. How far along was she?"

I looked from his eyes to his burning cigarette. It made it easier to answer.

"Six months," I whispered.

"Six months," he said, almost absently. Then he refocused. "I asked if I could do anything."

"I know. The police told me. You came out and got her something."

"Yeah. A corn muffin. I have no idea why I chose the corn muffins. There must've been, like, 80 varieties in there, but they looked the freshest."

I didn't answer.

"Ok, right," he said. "So I got her the corn muffin and went back to the storage and she was sitting there with that Indian woman—"

"—Deshpande's wife."

"—Right, yes, Deshpande's wife was holding her hand, and I stood there and handed her the muffin and she took it and even without waiting took a bite. And this is where it gets tough to explain. The expression on her face. It showed I guess something like—" he shifted in his seat, flicked out some ash, "—something like relief. Perfect relief. It was a complete moment, you see? Ok. Relief is a lousy word. It doesn't do the job. What's the word I'm looking for. What?"

I didn't answer. He took a deep drag from his cigarette, leaned back and exhaled. We both watched the smoke churn and curl and disappear against the dirty yellow fluorescent lights.

"*Fulfilment*," he said suddenly, snapping his fingers. It sounded sharp and dry through the little speaker. "That's the word. It was one tiny moment of beautiful perfect fulfilment in this filthed up, piece-of-shit world. I saw it in her face the very moment she bit into that muffin. It may seem like nothing to you or anyone else, just a speck, this tiny thing, but it meant *everything* to me. It was perfect. Absolutely perfect, and it was mine. Or ours. I made that happen. I changed one moment that changed a string of moments that led up to *that* moment and it happened and its mine. It's permanent."

He leaned forward, stubbed out his cigarette and looked at me.

"You can look all confused if you want," he said. "But you know. You knew her and you know this. And it happened. And here's the last. The other part. I can come up with all the right answers, but it doesn't matter. You can sit there and wait, or bounce off the walls trying to come up with them, but the world has to give it. Has to give the right answers. If you're very lucky, it does, but for most of us it doesn't. You have to make some kind of guess. So I came up with my own. My own answer. The world maybe wanted me to zig, so I *zagged*. Does that make any sense? I zagged in world of zigs. I did what I did. I sealed up that one

158

moment and I sealed up the rest."

He leaned back in his chair, his hands limp in his lap, and let out a long, low exhalation. It was like he was deflating. I don't know how long I sat there. I had nothing left to ask. The hour hadn't run out, but the meeting was over. There were two sharp taps at the door on his side, and it swung open. A CO, different than the one who'd led him in, stepped inside. Alfie Romero stood up. As the guard cuffed Romero's wrists to his waist chain, there was a tap at my door. I could feel the air stir as it opened. They led Romero out. He didn't even turn to look at me. He walked through the door and it slammed shut.

I got up from my chair and turned. Brookens was waiting. He didn't say anything. He turned left and started walking. I followed. We went down a series of corridors, turning left, then right, then left again, passing through two security gates before coming into the lobby where we'd started earlier that morning.

"Anything for me to sign?" I asked.

"No."

"I can leave? Just like that?"

"Just like that," he said.

I was waiting for him to say something else. He didn't.

"Ok," I said.

I walked through the two sets of heavy glass doors into the visitor's parking lot. As I walked to my car, I felt slightly displaced, the sights and sounds of the physical world held off at a slight distance, numbed and softened. I sensed somebody coming up from behind me and turned. It was Deshpande. He saw my face and stopped.

"Are you all right?" he asked.

"Yes," I said. I stood there by the side of my car with my keys in my hand.

"I am very sorry to not wait for a phone call, but I felt I should be here," Deshpande said.

"That's ok," I said.

We looked at each other for a moment. I didn't know what I was supposed to do. His eyes went down to my chest. "You don't need that any longer."

I looked down. It was the decal with my name on it. I peeled it off, crumpled it up and put it in my pocket. "Well," I said. "That's that." I turned to my car.

"Is that all?" Deshpande asked.

I turned back to him. "All?"

"What did he *tell* you?"

I thought about it for a moment, my mind running over bits and fragments of Romero's words. One splinter made it to my tongue.

"He zagged," I said.

Deshpande kept staring at me. I don't think he was even blinking.

"Excuse me?" he said.

"He zagged," I said, turning to my car and inserting the key. "And now everything is different."

I unlocked the door, opened it and got into the car. There was just enough room for me to shut it without hitting Deshpande. I started the ignition and put on my seatbelt. Deshpande started tapping on the glass. I didn't look at him, and slipped the car into drive.

"But what does that mean?" he called through the glass, still tapping away.

The car started moving. Deshpande walked along side, his palm pressed against the glass. He asked something else, but I didn't hear it. I looked at his palm, still pressed against the glass, and knew it would be gone as soon as I could move fast enough. It would disappear.

***

The Post-Mortem Composer
Laurence MacDonald

Laurence MacDonald is a musician and tutor. A fresh fabulist, Laurence began writing in the summer of 2016 and has embarked on writing a series of short supernatural tales. So far, all of his work is set in the 19th Century and either in the U.S.A. or Scotland but he is contemplating starting a bigger writing project in a different period setting. His first published work in print appeared in July 2017 in the anthology "Evesham Festival of Words – 2017", and another of his stories has been featured and read in a podcast from a river history website in the U.S.A. (http://riverhistory.com).

Judge Sandra says, 'I liked the voice in *The Post-Mortem Composer*. It instantly pulled me in. The plot was well-constructed and original, too."

Have you heard of the violinist Jacques Moreau? Perhaps not, for though he is highly regarded by his peers and is gaining some renown as a talented composer, his name is not yet widely familiar. I though, have known him as a friend for a number of years and regularly attend his concerts in the south-eastern states. I admire Jacques greatly as a musician but when I think of him now the first recollection is of the peculiar events that he and I witnessed in a house in New Orleans in the month of August in 1856.

I had attended a concert given by Jacques with his quartet in Natchez and as is our custom when circumstances allow, the following day he and I took luncheon together. He seemed somewhat fatigued on this occasion, and when pressed, admitted that he had been wrestling with a difficulty encountered in the *Allegro* section of a *Sonata* he was then in the process of composing. Despite this, he was cheerful and spoke expansively and our discussion touched upon a great many topics. Of particular interest though, he made mention of a relative of his - 'some species of cousin' were his words - who sought an explanation and end to what she described in a letter to him as *'perplexing and troubling occurrences'* at her home. She had written that a recently deceased member of the family had not quite relinquished all earthly attachments and the hours of darkness in the house were now beleaguered by a persisting manifestation of his ghostly presence. Knowing that I held a keen, if perhaps slightly sceptical, interest in all things *'other-worldly'*, he invited me to accompany him to New Orleans to assist in the matter. With no engagements in my diary I had the prospect of a few days of leisure ahead and so, being sufficiently curious about the affair, I readily agreed to go with him.

Thus, two days later we met upon the arrival of my boat at a levee wharf in that city, and from there proceeded by carriage directly to the house. He told me *en route* that we would soon meet the widow Madame Claire Montgomery and her daughter Emily; the two women having moved into the old place three years previously to look after Madame Claire's father. The old fellow had begun to decline in health after the death of his wife and they had attended him until his own demise three weeks prior to our visit.

Presently, we arrived at the large and imposing residence situated on the splendid *Rue Royale* and in good time for dinner. Over a most excellent repast I was able to make proper acquaintance with the two ladies. They were charming and attentive hostesses but, although vigorous, both did appear troubled if not overwrought. Before long, the elder gave forth on the unusual circumstances that prevailed in the house and her account ran as follows:

Her father, Nathaniel Norton, had been a banker who had grown wealthy by his trade, but, after his wife's passing, music had become the principal passion and interest in his life. He had been a fine pianist and violinist and on becoming a widower soon after his retirement from banking he had, from that time forth, dedicated himself chiefly to composing works of serious music. Madame Claire had laughed a little and said that he had turned his energies from creating paper notes to musical ones.

However, during this time, the old man complained of worsening lung and digestive ailments, but refused to be seen by any physician. In the weeks before his passing, he had eschewed the society of others almost entirely to closet himself in his chamber for most of each day, only to emerge around midnight to take up work on his piano - sometimes until daybreak - in the study adjacent to his bed chamber. Of course, these nocturnal habits greatly inconvenienced Madame Claire and her daughter and, the house being rambling and spacious, they vacated their bed chambers near his rooms to take up sleeping quarters in the west wing to be free from the nightly disruption. On the day of Nathaniel's burial, they had returned to their former rooms, but that very night, both were awoken and again tormented with the sounds of the piano clanging and echoing through the dark hallway! Indeed, doubly tormented because now there could be no sensible explanation for it. They quit the rooms and fled back to the west wing in perfect terror. Madame Claire had, once or twice since, ventured into the passageway after midnight and listened keenly for any disturbance of the nocturnal quietude. Finding that the unwholesome music continued as before and utterly despairing of a remedy, she had at last written her entreaty to Jacques for assistance.

As I listened to this account any scepticism that I may have harboured dissipated. The two women were perfectly sound of mind and neither of the type given to fancy: there could be no doubt that the freakish travails as described were genuine. Jacques too had listened without giving interruption and, on completion of the account, had asked that certain items be brought so that we might later make a watch outside the haunted study. His demands were readily acceded to and after dinner a maidservant conducted us to the old man's hallway. She took with her a basket containing the smaller items that Jacques had ordered, namely: an oil lamp, a bottle of wine, glasses and, oddly, a quantity of flour. Jacques and I each carried a table chair and as we made our way upstairs the girl spoke freely. From what she had to say, it was well that the orders had been given at dinner as nothing would succeed in persuading her, the cook, or the kitchen girl to visit that part of the house after darkness fell.

Having situated our little camp in the vicinity of the door to the study, Jacques suggested that we retire to our chambers and rest so that, later, we might remain alert to better meet whatever events occurred. I was wearied after the journey and readily agreed; he however, said that he would make an examination of the music room before taking his repose and would set his travelling timepiece (a necessary possession for any touring musician) to sound one half hour before midnight.

He roused me at the appointed hour and we took up our station; both of us very anxious to see what the wee small hours might bring. All other occupants of the house having long since retired, the place was perfectly quiet save for the occasional scrambling of mice behind the wainscoting and an owl's infrequent hooting from a tree outside the hall window. I poured wine while Jacques lit the lamp and we settled in wordless silence and waited. Our patience was not to be tested though, for it wasn't long after the clock in the great hall below had struck the hour of midnight that something began to occur in what had been Nathaniel Norton's bed chamber.

At first it sounded like a hollow cough, then there followed a faint and rasping wheeze, as if someone - a person of infirmity - was arising from bed and struggling to stand up. This sound quieted, but we were then startled to hear the chamber door creak open. Yet, in the dim yellow light of the lamp, we could plainly see that the door from whence the sound came remained firmly shut. We exchanged glances but remained seated and still; both of us eager for whatever would come next. Shuffling footsteps in the hallway drew closer to us, then halted, and again we heard rather than saw a door open and close - this time that of the study - a mere six or seven feet distant from where we sat in rapt attention. Nothing that I could see struck me as out of the ordinary, but Jacques, situated farther from the light of our lamp, later vouchsafed that the sounds had been accompanied by a faint passing luminescence of a deep violet hue. Surprisingly perhaps, the effect of all this was not so much a cause of fear or alarm but rather to induce a feeling of solemnity. I will, though, freely own that a prickling sensation ran over my arms and neck upon hearing those first stirrings.

After a few moments of renewed quiet our expectancy was rewarded and the piano within began to give forth loud and sonorous music. Jacques started and he took on an expression of deep contemplation as one ominous chord followed another while a lilting and melancholic melody line floated above. After a few moments the sad and tuneful air gave way, leaving only a run of declamatory chords - the last of which was sustained and left to fully decay into the tranquillity of night. In all, the music lasted but a few seconds; certainly no more than a quarter of one minute. I asked Jacques what the piece might but, he too, found it unfamiliar. There could be no possibility of any mundane explanation for the thing; no cat nor mouse running atop keys or strings could have produced what we had heard. This was music, fashioned and played by *someone* not *something*, and the disturbing truth of the matter was, of course, that our someone was dead.

I took up the lamp and, steeling myself for whatever discovery I would make inside, I made for the study door. I thought that Jacques would follow me but he stayed put and stopped me abruptly:

"No, we must not interrupt! There may be more to come."

He was right, for thereupon the music started again, the piece repeated, chord for chord, note for note to the end and, when it resumed for a third time, Jacques said:

"There is nothing to be gained by lingering longer. We may take our rest now but we shall return at the same hour tomorrow, and do so better prepared."

Though burning with curiosity and impatient desire to intrude and determine by what mischief the confounded piano played I acquiesced and we made for our rooms. And all the while, the portentous music resonated in the study and dark hallway behind us.

At breakfast, we recounted our experience to the two ladies and they evinced little surprise to our summary of events; though they did exclaim when Jacques announced that he might put the matter to rest that very night. Later, he beckoned me to accompany him to the old man's study and upon entering I discerned the faint aroma of aniseed in the air - evidently the fellow had used it liberally in life. Once inside, I surmised that the furnishings and possessions had been left undisturbed since his death as it gave every appearance of a room still in use. Jacques drew me to the piano - a very fine square Pleyel of handsome rosewood - and I observed, spread out upon its rack, a large manuscript written in a spidery hand and marked with many scoring-outs and substitutions. On a small table next to the piano there rested a pen, an unstopped bottle of ink, and an untidy collection of papers and books of notation. Jacques then brought my attention to the piano's keyboard and said.

"*Regarde!* The flour I spread on these keys last evening is perfectly undisturbed," he smiled. 'As we both know, it was not some prankster that played this piano last night. By what means our phantom coaxes these strings to give voice I know not, but be sure those keys didn't tickle them at all!'"

We left the room in a condition similar to that in which we found it and I divided my time that day by reading in the library, joining the ladies for luncheon, and later, taking a stroll to the riverside. In the intervening period Jacques had gone into the city to purchase 'a few necessary things' and returned later with a violin case in one hand and sheaves of blank music manuscript in the other. At dinner, by some unspoken mutual understanding between us all, the conversation scrupulously avoided any reference to the doings of the ghost but, as the ladies took their leave and made for the drawing room, Jacques said to me:

"For now we rest. Later, we take our place in the hall, but on this night, we are ready for him!"

And so we did, just before midnight - my friend equipped with the blank manuscript, a pencil and the old fiddle acquired from the pawn shop. He laid pencil and paper on a small hall table that he'd brought over and then sounded a tuning fork to enable him to adjust his violin to proper pitch whilst I poured wine. All preparations being complete, we sat down and waited.

As before, at just after midnight, the presence was signalled by the sounds of wheezing, shuffling and creaking doors. Although nothing was distinctly visible to me I had the impression, at least, that a very dim glow drifted along the passage. This prelude - as Jacques called it - soon being over, there followed a short spell of silence and then the piano struck up that same plaintive melody over sombre chords. Jacques took up the violin and, using his thumb, he plucked a scattering of fingered *staccato* notes in an exploratory fashion. His face creased with the effort of concentration as he searched out a scale sympathetic to the music coming from the study. Then, looking quickly to me, in a low voice he said:

"*D minor*, key is *D minor.*"

He reached for the bow and produced a haunting improvisation that was a fine counter to the piano melody, but when that air subsided to leave only the pounding chords, he laid the bow down and plucked again. This time he produced little flurries of notes, *arpeggios*, that insinuated and wove themselves into the fabric of the ghostly music. He jotted and plucked again, then frowned and scribbled some more, and scratched his brow. As he worked he muttered - more to himself than to me.

"The coda........*G sharp diminished seventh*.......*D minor* ......and *A seventh.* No wait….................Not *A seventh* but *C sharp diminished seventh* leading to.........."

and, as the final chord decayed into the night,

"Yes.....ah yes.....*Tierce de Picardie*.......... Finish on D *major.*"

The piano sounded again, repeating the same piece and, once more, my companion joined with the phantasmal performance. He picked up the melody and this time followed it much more closely; after two more repetitions the thing was mastered. With a final scribble and flourish of the paper he smiled with triumph and announced:

"I have it down. I have it down!"

I watched him with an admixture of amusement and reverence. His efforts had appeared frenetic, indeed, almost comical, but that belied the skill required to produce an accurate transcription of the recital so quickly. I returned his smile and asked him what was to be done, and while the clamour of the dark music insisted upon our ears, he rejoined:

"What's to be done? Why, we go in of course."

We moved to the study; holding the lamp in one hand and grasping the door handle with the other I drew a deep breath and pushed. Jacques, by my side, clutched his sheaf of manuscript and we stepped in. The moment the door opened - before we gained proper entry into the room even - the odour of aniseed assailed us and much stronger than which we had perceived earlier that day. As I swung the door wide, the booming music grew loud to our ears and I wondered if the windows might rattle. Our eyes turned immediately to the piano and there we saw the weird and glowing cause of disquiet - a dim and translucent violet radiance. It was indistinct and cast no light upon the instrument nor on any of the surrounding furnishings. Nothing about the eerie phenomenon in any way resembled a human form. Rather, it was as if caused by a type of visible magnetical force - if there can be such a thing - or by some strange local excitation of the atmosphere from within the very particles of air itself.

I stood in the doorway for a moment, struck rigid and immobile by the apparition. But I had enough wit to note that the keys of the piano remained at perfect rest while it gave out its unearthly music. Just then, very suddenly, I felt compelled to back out of the room. Jacques did likewise and I closed the door. We stood in the hall for a moment and I could see an intense look of

169

contemplation cross his countenance before he asked:

"I was prevented from moving fully into the room, were you?" I nodded and he said, "Let us go now and sleep," adding enigmatically, "We must wait until tomorrow before any restoration of peace and well-being can be brought."

A sudden and pressing business engagement required me to leave New Orleans the following morning, and I was not, therefore, at liberty to remain in the house to assist Jacques in effecting the hoped-for cure, though I did not have long to wait for his report of subsequent events and the outcome. I attended his concert in Baton Rouge just ten days after I had left New Orleans and met him for lunch the following day. He was in high spirits and no wonder, thought I; the previous evening had been a great success throughout, ending magnificently with a standing ovation for the quartet's premier performance of his newly completed Sonata.

Of course, after congratulating him on the recital, my next words were to question him on what had occurred in the house on *Rue Royale* after I had taken my leave. He smiled and answered my inquiry thus:

"I stayed on for two nights after you left. You see, I wanted to make certain that the troubles would truly cease. As soon as you had departed I went to the study to take up the manuscript that had been laid out on the piano rack. It was an unfinished work in D minor - something that I had noticed on our first evening at the house - and, I copied it out and added notation for the final section, exactly as played by the ghost. Having completed the work, I signed it on behalf of Nathaniel Norton, and placed the papers upon the rack. After that I remained in the study and worked; you see I was trying to resolve the third movement of my Sonata though, I confess, I gave it up in vexation long before dinner. That night I took up vigil outside the rooms, just as we had done together, and as I had hoped and expected, silence prevailed!"

He leaned back in his chair, and with an air of great satisfaction, he said:

"The trouble has been laid to rest. All along the old fellow had wanted the last movement of his final work, that Piano

Concerto, completed - written down," he moved his hands in a wide arc, rather in the manner of a conductor who has, at that moment, successfully presented a major and difficult work to a delighted and applauding audience. Then he leaned toward me and said, *"Voilà! C'est fini!"*

I congratulated him again; this time for solving the mystery and laying Nathaniel Norton fully to rest. I told him that he had done the old man's soul, and the two ladies of the house, a great service, but his reply surprised me,

"Perhaps so, but if Nathaniel did owe me any debt of service he has already repaid it," before I could ask his meaning he continued, "You heard my Sonata last evening. Let me say that the trouble I had with the *Allegro* resolved after, how shall I say? After a peculiar form of..........*Inspiration.*"

I arched an eyebrow and he went on:

"You see *mon ami*, the night after you left, I awoke sometime before dawn and fancied that I was not alone. Then, I thought I saw a dim glow forming not far from me, and the unmistakable aroma of aniseed filled the air - and do you know? I do believe the old fiddle resting on my dresser began to play by itself." he grinned, "All very odd, wouldn't you agree?"

Post script. Three months have passed since the events described above took place and Jacques has sent to me, by mail, a copy of the program for a Grand Concert in Baltimore that is to take place one week before Christmas. I am gratified to find that my diary will allow me to attend, for among the very fine works listed for performance are two of particular interest: 'Sonata in B minor (Elégie pour Nathaniel) by Jacques Moreau.' and later; the premier of 'Piano Concerto No.1 by Nathaniel Norton.'

***

Ivan by the Sea

Marcus Stewart

Marcus Stewart is based in London and has only recently started writing short stories. In between many day-jobs – some of which have involved writing - Marcus has previously written sketches and jokes for online and radio comedy (including the BBC's Newsjack) and plays for fringe theatre.

Judge Clare found *Ivan by the Sea* to possess 'charming characterisation.' In her words, it was a 'poignant and amusing little tale.'

Ivan liked to walk through Mayfair on the way to work whenever he arrived on an early enough train. To him, this was still the part of London that felt most like the London in his mind, especially early in the morning when vans or lorries would struggle through the narrow streets to whichever specialist shop or boutique required their cargo. He would listen to the beep-beep-beeps of vans reversing onto pavements mixed with early morning birdsong and snatches of foreign language chatter from cafe staff setting up for the day. Even if they were part of a chain, the arrangement of shops and cafes and bars in this part of the city seemed somehow accidental, as if blown by the wind.

Any tourist you saw looked pleasingly baffled, as if by walking one block back from the tourist highway of Regent Street they had stepped through the looking glass into another dimension. He liked that it felt a little separate, and if he was honest, a little higher-class than walking with the crowd. He would smirk at the irony of this affection in frequent moments of self-awareness.

He knew its secret history; that in fact a few decades ago parts of it had been quite dilapidated and it had been a focal point for artists who would gather in disused warehouses and squats and endeavour to change the world. As a boy in Norn Iron, he'd seen it in a TV documentary about Yoko Ono and the Indica Gallery on his little black and white bedroom TV. He saw himself escaping into that world, leaving behind his stifling provincial existence to be his real self, the artist he never became. When he first arrived in London, he recognised Mayfair and glimpses of its hidden history subsumed by the passing of time and the gloss of high-end consumerism. Similarly, he kept the boy he had been about his person, in a pocket somewhere, a well-kept secret.

Ivan made particular note to walk past a certain hat shop

where possible, which had a display of the most elaborate hats on one side of the window as if to say "look what we used to be". That part of the one window display was the swinging sixties so far as Ivan was concerned; the spiritual heart of the Mayfair of his imagination. There were feathers and clashing colours and shapes, cut-outs and fabrics and threads strewn across the display in a millinery explosion. It was a work of art in itself, standing out stridently against the greys and browns of the ever so classy hats and accoutrements of the rest of the shop display, and of the rest of the street.

He would sometimes stop to look at the display and time-travel a little, into his own past, and the past of his imagination, musing about the first time he met Yoko at her exhibition, and how they didn't really get on, but how he had felt a certain chemistry with the young man who took his ticket. On one occasion his daydreaming was broken when a trick of light caused a hat to appear superimposed on his own reflection. Sitting in there, among the flamboyant women's hats, was a fedora with a purple band that Ivan thought was his very self. From then on, most mornings he passed this way he would glance at the hat and nod, as if saying good morning to himself.

While such diversionary walks were romantic and gave space for the soul to breathe and the mind to amble, there was a danger that on warm days - or days when his clothing had been overly pessimistic - he would break out into a sweat. As a thin man he had few places to sweat from, so once in the office toilet a quick dab of a paper towel soaked in cold water across his brow and under his armpits would usually stem the flow and mop the excess. It was at these moments that he would audit his imperfections: his pale, gaunt complexion, getting ever paler and gaunter; his red, wavy hair growing ever greyer and wirier; his nostrils sprouting hairs from his thin, beaky nose, where once there were just empty caverns. As he looked blankly at himself in the wall of mirror, the reflecting image merged with those remembered from other mornings over the years - a slideshow of the many faces of Ivan, ever ageing but never changing, a blank expression while dabbing

176

and then eyes open in surprise, as if to say "who are you?"

When he'd arrived in London he had thought much more about where he was running from than where he was running to, and found himself facing troubles that were at least the equal of any that he had left behind. The swinging London he had dreamed of had stopped swinging even before he was born; there was no scene to join without money, no squats to live in, no career waiting for a clever but directionless Northern Irish boy to fall into. After a couple of years of non-jobs and no-jobs - and the incidental lack of a social life that is an under-reported consequence of having no money - he had found himself with an administrative position at the Inland Revenue and clung on for dear life to its security and stability. Many years later he was now a tax specialist, at what was now Her Majesty's Revenue and Customs. He was not particularly numerate, but was by now familiar working with numbers. It was a job which he could do, and which he had done for long enough that people took it for granted. There had been times when dreams were made of such stuff; the lack of an obvious career alternative meant he often had to remind himself of that.

"Hi babe, how was your weekend?" Michelle asked as he exited the toilet. "Oh, fine thanks, and you?" and then he stopped walking, because he remembered she'd been on holiday, and this was likely to be a conversation of some duration. "How was Cyprus?" he asked, "Is that a bit of a tan I see?" But this was not going to be a conversation about a tan. "It was great! Met a guy from Sheffield on the second day and spent the rest of the week in his hotel room! Jess is still a bit annoyed with me to be honest, for leaving her alone." OK, he thought, nothing to see here, on with the daily grind. But then she asked, "so did you go out at the weekend?" He told her of a walk he did along the river and an exhibition he went to. "But you didn't go out with anyone? Or meet anyone?" Ivan enjoyed his own company and liked peace and quiet at the weekend, and yet this was a question that kept coming up. "I was thinking, you know, you always hear about my dates and all that, but you're always, you know..." There was no need to say what he always was. "And I'm going to make it my project. I think

177

it would be really nice if you had a boyfriend". Oh Christ, why did she have to make him her project? "When...when did you last have one? Or a fling even?" Michelle was a very sweet girl, he had enjoyed her company for years and mostly felt relaxed with her, but this felt...this felt like prying, and he was not so comfortable. She noticed. "I don't mean...I mean...not like a pick up, but, you know...there must be a place for English gentlemen types to meet. Maybe a website?" "Ah, well that's no good for me" he said. "Why?", "Because I'm not English". She seemed confused. "I'm Irish". He couldn't quite believe that after ten years she didn't know this. "Like Oscar Wilde" he tried to help. "Oh. Is he?" she answered, blankly.

It had indeed been a long time since Ivan had been with anyone, and he had become used to it, which in effect felt very much similar to it being a choice. He had carved out a life for himself and the thought of having to compromise it for someone else did not appeal. In any case, his past experience had not been good. The five years he spent with his only real ex had been more like a mugging than a relationship, and the other relationship that really stuck in his mind wasn't even a relationship at all, just a colleague he had been painfully, painfully in love with. But nothing happened. Nothing at all. He was happier - and felt less bruised - spending time with friends and their families and keeping culturally active, in what was after all one of the most cultured cities in the world. It was not a bad life. It was a step up from amateur dramatics in Coleraine.

Michelle's final shot had been to suggest he go on holiday, like her, and maybe he'd meet someone. Maybe not a package, maybe a higher class holiday. And maybe he wouldn't meet anyone, but at least he'd have a nice time. Despite its ridiculous origins, over the next few days the idea began to take root. It was perhaps time he did something different. On lunch breaks and coffee breaks he browsed through travel agency websites and was drawn to pictures of infinity pools, beach restaurants and laughing couples skipping along golden sands. He imagined being there, feeling the sand under his feet, talking to a man - a faceless man for now - maybe

178

spending time together...

On Wednesday his colleague Simon came back to work after a few days off sick. They were the two gay men in the office and they sat together, by accident or design. Sometimes, if a call came from an internal number he recognised Simon would answer "gay desk. How can I help you", which made Ivan snort his tea. They were opposite in every way, which made Ivan rather fond of him.

"I think it's a great idea, seriously! You never go on holiday anywhere proper, you should treat yourself" was Simon's verdict. "Why don't you come out with me to the Canneries?" He insisted on pronouncing 'Canaries' as 'Canneries', which after all this time Ivan simply accepted. "Have some fun with me and my friends?" Ivan had long since made clear his opposition to clubbing or being part of any 'scene'. "We don't do the clubs anymore, we just hang out in Martin's apartment, swim in the pool, go to nice restaurants. Have a really chilled time. They're all nice guys, all laid back, and one of them's an artistic director somewhere, you might hit it off. Or, if you don't like any of them, you could...you could just hang out with me if you want". Ivan thought it was a really nice offer, and it was really nice of Simon to offer it, but after weeks of research he knew where he was going to go: he was going to Mauritius.

He had kept returning to images of Mauritius in the brochures, and Chloë in the project team had had her honeymoon there and said it was fantastic. He booked it, and enjoyed the daring of booking it. Duly committed, his work gained new purpose, because to avoid coming back to a nightmare on his return he had to completely finish two cases and a development project before flying out. He worked late, skipped lunches and generally kept himself to himself. Over the next two months task followed task until he was done. Then, although brimming with excitement, more tasks to be completed - to the airport, through check in, security etc. On the plane he enjoyed some complimentary glasses of wine and then forced himself to sleep, so he'd be as awake as possible on the morning he arrived. All was preparation.

It struck him with a jolt when he suddenly found himself looking out of the aeroplane window at a blue ocean, with a little green island down below. He looked down on vistas he barely had the capability to imagine as the plane smoothly descended towards the runway, punctuated only by Ivan's need to repeatedly blow his nose to adjust his ears to the change in air pressure. It was magnificent.

The plane landed and still there was a wait, the casual meandering of the plane to its terminal, the slow shuffling of the passengers along the corridor with their cases, a muttered 'thank you' to the air stewards at the door. Onwards, through passageways and along escalators, into a glass and concrete airport like many others, which had clearly been designed to maintain as much of a neutral, temperate, American / European environment as possible, but from which he could see nothing but brightness outside, and in which he felt only the cold breeze of over-compensating air conditioning, which he was certain was doomed to failure.

He queued eagerly to have his passport stamped alongside families and lovers in hats, sandals and t-shirts (he would change into similar clothes later). "Edwin, get off of that case!" Apparently, children could be called 'Edwin' these days. "I'm so sorry" the mother said to Ivan before he'd even realised it was his case being mounted. "Oh, no problem. Kids like climbing things don't they?" he said, feeling initially that it was better than saying nothing, but then doubting himself somewhat. "I know, but they pick their moments". Ivan had a sudden urge to share his excitement with another human being. "Have you been here before?" he asked. "No" she said, "first time". "We're going to Bel Ombre" said the dad, looking up from his phone momentarily before losing interest again. "Where are you going?" continued the mum. "Grand Baie, in the north-west," Ivan replied, "but I want to see as much as I can. Spend time on the beach definitely, but also have a look at the old churches and see Port Louis..." and then the queue moved forward and it was the family's turn to be checked. "Have fun!" said the mum as she moved forward, bags in one hand, Edwin's neck in the other, and the dad a few steps ahead, leading the expedition.

Ivan continued his itinerary in his head in the form of pictures, little vignettes of himself loosely placed within the images he'd seen online. He imagined the people in these images moving and talking and the sounds of music, laughter and the gentle to-ing and fro-ing of the waves against the golden sand. When he was called forward he smiled broadly at the immigration woman and felt an excited tingle as his passport was stamped. She smiled back, as if she meant it. He had packed everything he needed in his hand luggage, so after a quick pee he was on the airport shuttle bus and away to his resort.

The bus journey was much longer than he'd anticipated and gave him an hour and a half in which to compose further vignettes while collecting more and more information to add to them - the manner and style of dress of the people, the types of vehicles he may see or use, the general condition of buildings, road surfaces and pavements. The motorway was surprisingly high quality and took him between mountain ranges, through shabby little towns and a half-built city with supermarkets and car-showrooms. After about an hour the bus passed through a final set of hills to give him his first full view of the sea. It was the lightest, glassiest blue, only differing from the sky in texture. He had never seen so much absolute blue. His imaginings diminished in intensity and he slipped almost into a kind of trance as he passively stared out at the calm, clear ocean. As the bus found its way around each resort it darted towards the coast and back again several times, teasing him, heightening his anticipation of arrival. And then, the name of his hotel was called. He was actually there.

Ivan stepped off the bus into the wall of heat that makes the atmosphere in such a place and enjoyed the feeling of being enveloped in it. He conceded that he was completely incorrectly dressed, and so checked in and went to his room as quickly as he could to drop his bag and get changed.

He had made one very good decision, to go for a hotel by a beach, and not a 'resort'. He was with locals and not just Europeans, and it was very much in his mind to meet people. He undressed just in front of his balcony, looking out through a gap in the palm trees at the wide blue sea and sky, and downwards and sideways at patches of beach. He saw the little brown figures of young men playing football, heard the French chatter of local men playing cards by the juice stall. He had never travelled so far, been somewhere so definitely different, so luxurious in its weather, its food, its landscape. The men were so healthy and vibrant, the food looked so fresh. And he began to imagine those friendly voices below welcoming him; the man hiring out canoes perhaps, taking an interest in where he was from, idly chatting, and then sitting down together...

He suddenly snapped back into full consciousness, back into the world of his hotel room and the sights and sounds of outside, which were further away than in his imagination. Much further away, really. How was this actually going to happen? It struck him that these handsome young men, so different from him, are out here earning a living. They probably have wives and children to feed. They may well all be straight. Is it even OK to be gay out here? He had no idea. No idea at all. He hadn't done any research on that aspect of the trip. How could he find people without seeming sordid? Would a man approach him, as happened with Michelle? But why would a man approach him here, if not in London? He felt a slight sinking feeling as it occurred to him that his little fantasies may have to stay fantasies, that most likely nothing would happen. That he was not Michelle. He was just Ivan by the sea.

Sensing the beginnings of a dark mood, he summoned up his inner life coach and decided not to be pessimistic nor optimistic, but to leave himself open to possibilities. In the meantime he would just enjoy what the holiday had to offer. It was still thrilling to watch the boys playing football - they were so clearly enjoying themselves - and the whole beach was full of local people enjoying their Sunday. A mother and three children were swimming in among tourist couples with inflatable rings and everyone seemed happy. He would just let go and enjoy it the same way, with no plan, and no expectations. He would go for a swim in the sea. He replaced his pants with swimming trunks and covered them with shorts and t-shirt for decency. Duly attired, he picked up a towel and bounded down the stairs of the hotel and across to the beach.

Barefoot on the tarmac of the road, his feet tensed up in response to the hot sharp jabs of the little stones within it. Hitting the sand, the soles of his feet were softened by contact with the hot grains and his toes and the arches of his feet spread out with every step. He enjoyed the effort of pushing his feet through the sand to propel himself, and only stumbled a little when he lay his towel down at the foot of a welcoming palm tree.

He was struck by the feeling of space and air and the rising joy of being somewhere different. He couldn't remember ever having been on a beach where it wasn't overcast and blowing a gale. He spent a few minutes just standing, taking it all in. He felt the blanket of warm air over him, the sea breeze playing through his leg hairs under his khaki shorts, the hot-plate touch of the sun's rays on his bare polar-white arms. He would need to be careful and apply plenty of sun lotion.

But he could swim first.

He took off his t-shirt and shorts and walked on towards the water, feeling the unusual sense of the sun's heat directly on his chest, smelling the spices of cooking chicken waft across from the stalls at the back of the beach with a sea-salt odour underneath it. This was magnificent. And then the sand became harder as he approached the sea, his hot feet suddenly cooling as he stepped into it, his whole body in a tingling embrace as he dived into the first wave and immersed himself. He was so keen to swim he went straight in, with so little depth that his belly scrubbed along the sand. Within a few strokes he was far enough out that he could flip around in the water onto his back and float aimlessly, looking up at the wide blue sky and the wisps of white streamers that were the clouds. The warm water held him up to the sun as its currents gently caressed his skin, sweeping gently across and under his exposed back and chest, little waves kissing gently his face, arms and legs. He grinned, wildly, like he couldn't remember doing for years. This was actually what he needed. Just water, warmth and the space to be.

After a few minutes he went back to his tree to dry off and put on some lotion. The tree was wonderfully shady, and so, not remembering having had such an opportunity before, he decided just to lie on the towel and dry off naturally. He lay back and closed his eyes for a few minutes, just listening to the sounds, and the absence of sounds - the absence of traffic rumble, of shouting, of working and all the stress that came with it. Just a few minutes of glorious calm. And then he finished drying off and went back to the hotel to cover up.

He already felt a bit hot and tingly when he put the lotion on.; it seemed that he may have a bit of a burn already, but if he was lucky it would turn into a tan. He had started to tan a little around the face and hands in recent years. It may, in any case, be better to look a little pink than ghostly white. He put on his long sleeved t-shirt, and long linen trousers this time, and set off to look for snacks and trinkets along the beach road.

Building up gently, on that first walk he took in the atmosphere and didn't really talk to anyone. When asked if he needed assistance by shopkeepers and stall holders he said "no thank you", unless he'd definitely decided to make a purchase, in which case he'd say the minimum amount required. The next day, when he was settled, he planned to make the same trip again and might then venture to make conversation, but for now he was simply absorbing the sights and sounds.

That evening he decided to eat in the hotel, and maybe there would be some conversation with fellow guests. There wasn't; they were all families, friends, couples. But there was still plenty of time for that. In any case, he was a little distracted by the shirt he had put on, it seemed of a much rougher fabric than he'd realised. As he reached to serve himself at the buffet it tore at his shoulder, and at one point when he stretched it grazed across his chest. Then, on hearing a member of kitchen staff drop a whole serving of fish curry - which received a round of applause - as he swivelled around to look his trousers gouged at the skin on his right shin. He realised the shirt wasn't the problem. It felt as if the skin had been ripped off his shin and blood would trickle down into his sock at any moment. He waited for it to happen, but it didn't.

When he had finished eating he stood up with difficulty as every part of his skin apart from the area around his shorts was now tight, like he had been shrink wrapped. Shrink wrapped and steamed. Ivan *sous-vide*. He had a little flurry of panic - he had burnt several times in his life and peeled frequently, but he didn't recall ever having been so comprehensively cooked. He made it slowly back up to his room like an arthritic old man and spent twenty minutes trying to apply most of a bottle of sunscreen to the affected areas. He took two paracetamol tablets - he always carried some with him - and lay on the bed without the covers on. No sooner had he begun to worry that he wouldn't be able to sleep, he fell asleep.

In the night Ivan woke several times; any movement making the sheets feel like a row of tiny razors. When the sun came up he knew he couldn't sleep again, but he also couldn't move. He didn't know how long it took, but eventually he managed to edge his legs to the side of the bed and lift himself up. "Jesus!" The pain was excruciating. He was sweating and panting and really starting to worry a little. It was when he stood up that he realised his calves and ankles were swollen up to at least twice their normal girth, red and sore atop equally swollen feet.

He managed to shuffle to the bathroom. He took more paracetamol, and rubbed on more lotion, but instead of providing relief it stung enormously. He knew he had to do it, he had to keep the skin moist, and to stop the swelling he had to keep it cool. Soaking a towel in cold water, he wrung it out and laid it over his legs when he got back into bed.

The tough of going to the hospital crossed his mind, but he didn't know if his insurance would cover it. What could they do anyway? Give him wet towels and more lotion? And he didn't fancy spending his holiday in a hospital, especially out here. He would stay where he was. He wouldn't be able to leave the room anyway, he wouldn't be able to put on shoes or trousers. Luckily, they provided room service, and he had brought some books.

If Ivan could do anything, it was endure. After three days, two novels and multiple wet towels the swelling had in his legs had reduced enough such that he felt he could venture out, but only gingerly, and not far beyond the beach and the food stalls. He didn't make it to the churches, or Port Louis, but after a while families coming and going from the hotel would say hello to him, the strangely fully clothed invalid they thought must have come here to die. It was, nonetheless, a magnificent place with lovely food, and very friendly, helpful hotel staff. They formed his company for the most part, serving him food and drink and unobtrusively tidying his room, tip-toeing around his oddly bloated purple body as they picked up wet towels.

Two weeks later, at the airport on the way home, by complete coincidence he found himself checking in next to the same family he'd spoken to on the way out. They had travelled all over the island, eaten at multiple restaurants, been hill walking and seen the volcano, befriended locals and a family from Lewisham. It had been a once in a lifetime experience. Even the father was now animated and engaged and asked Ivan eagerly about his experiences. They seemed a little embarrassed when Ivan told them he'd stayed more or less in the same place. But he insisted he'd had a wonderful time. It had all passed so quickly.

He had started to peel on his neck and shoulders a few days before. On the plane he noticed he was peeling from his chest. When he was back at work he was hardly asked about his holiday, as if everyone knew, or as if he'd never been away at all. The only reminders were occasional pains and the continual peeling. For at least two months the skin peeled from his chest - a part of his body which had never burned before. He would scratch every now and then but otherwise forget about it until he took his shirt off at home when a cloud of skin flakes would billow out like ash. He tried not to worry about it, he was sure it would heal eventually. His freckles were now darker, perhaps now also larger than they had been previously, but otherwise he expected to be back to normal soon. As his skin tone returned, however, he noticed a mole on his belly appeared to have expanded, to be almost leaking into the surrounding skin. A little lump appeared on top of this mole, which had not been there before. While the ash diminished each time he took off his shirt the mole remained, and he couldn't help but to look down and check on it on every occassion.

The doctor was noncommittal - it could indeed be problematic, but there wasn't really any reason yet to think so. He referred Ivan to a specialist, whose first available appointment was in three weeks. Ivan considered this to be ample time for cancer to develop and watched the mole ever more closely. He tried to bury the thoughts, but couldn't help thinking this could be the end. This could be the pathetic end to his life, one trip out to a beach paradise resulting in inoperable skin cancer. An immediate god-given punishment for the tiniest taste of physical pleasure, of enjoyment, of escape. Without really thinking about it at all, it began to seem inevitable.

On the appointed date he waited an hour in a room full of people who may well have felt equally doomed. He tried to enjoy this last hour of not knowing the thing he felt it was inevitable he would come to know. For all of ten seconds he tried to watch the television, but daytime TV was the exact opposite of life affirming. He watched a little girl playing with building blocks in the corner for a few moments, but this too failed to hold his interest. Finally, he opted for staring at a wall and thinking of as little as possible.

Once Ivan was in front of him the specialist looked at the mole, touched it and decided a course of action in seconds. The only way to know if it was cancerous was to conduct a biopsy. Ivan asked if this was something the specialist could do, but unfortunately it was not. Ivan's heart sank at the prospect of another appointment, but to his surprise the specialist told him to wait outside for twenty minutes to half an hour and they would conduct the biopsy right there. Ivan began to perk up - this would be quick and easy and he'd have an answer soon enough. He could soon begin to put his affairs in order.

After just short of 35 minutes a woman called for Ivan from another door and he followed her back through it. To all intents and purposes this new room looked like an operating theatre. "I'm here for my mole" he said, in case there had been a mistake. "Yes, please lie on the bed" the woman said. He tried again - "it's just a biopsy". The woman stopped preparing what she was preparing and walked back over to him. "For a mole of that size we just remove the whole thing and test it. Then if it is cancerous you've no need for an operation, and if it isn't there's not much more of a scar than for a biopsy. It's all painless and it'll be over in minutes. OK?" She seemed sympathetic. He felt he should trust her. So he removed his shirt as instructed and lay on the bed.

He watched her as she prepared. The woman had brown hair, somewhere between wavy and curly, and wore rather large glasses. They looked new, so he concluded this must be fashionable again. She reminded him a bit of his Auntie Maureen, who had worn very similar glasses. Maybe Auntie Maureen looked like this woman when she was young. Thinking it through, it struck him that films from the time when Auntie Maureen was young actually shows women with small pointy glasses, whereas at the time when he remembered her other people had large glasses as well. For the first time in his life he realised Auntie Maureen could not be defined by her glasses. But he couldn't actually remember her face.

He interrupted this musing when he realised the woman was spreading a cold gooey liquid over the area around the mole. With horror he realised she had forgotten to knock him out - "I'm still awake!" he cried. "I know" she responded, calmly, "I'm just cleaning the area, then I'll give you a local anaesthetic". That was the word he'd wanted to hear and he was momentarily reassured. "It'll take a couple minutes to cut out, then I'll stitch you up and you can go home. I'll make another appointment for you later in the week to have the stitches taken out". Stitches? But the mole wasn't very big, he'd thought they'd pretty much scrape it off. Instead, she told him she would cut all the way down through the skin leaving a hole where the mole was, which when stitched would leave a 1cm scar. And he'd be awake.

She began injecting local anaesthetic into his skin. It made the area cold, but didn't appear to take away the feeling. He told her, and she explained this was normal for this type of anaesthetic, that he would feel it but it wouldn't hurt. He struggled to come to terms with the idea and was barely beginning to construct a reasoned argument why it was not a problem when she made the first incision. He would really have appreciated a full description of the weirdness of this procedure before he'd stepped in the room.

He flinched. "Does it hurt?" she asked. "I can feel it" he answered. "But does it actually hurt?" He was trying to remain calm but was sweating profusely through his back. She noticed this when she asked him to shift up the bed a bit. "There's nothing to worry about" she told him, with more incomprehension than sympathy. "I know" he said, which was simultaneously true and irrelevant. Every one of his muscles was clenched tight and he started to pant.

She injected more anaesthetic and pointed out that this was more than she'd ever had to give to anyone else. To reassure him she performed a little test - she would scratch the area where the anaesthetic had been administered and then an area where it hadn't. Indeed, he couldn't feel the first scratch, only the light pressure of something on the skin. "Tell me when you can feel it". He tried to control his breathing and closed his eyes so as not to undermine the test. "I can feel it nai" he said, and opened his eyes. She looked back at him even more uncomprehending than before. "You weren't from Belfast when you came in" she said. He tried to laugh it off, "my accent sometimes comes back for special occasions". Like when terrified and lacking any kind of control.

He felt deeply embarrassed. Even though he knew he was facing no actual risk from the procedure, his body was nonetheless screaming at him that what was happening was happening - that someone was cutting a slice out of his body. He knew it was a routine procedure - and obviously for everyone else she'd ever performed it on it had been a walk in the park - but he simply couldn't help sweating and shaking and regressing to childhood. No longer scared of death, he wanted more than anything just to get out of that room.

As she cut into him, he told himself there was no pain. But he felt it, he felt the blade piercing his skin, he felt the pressure of the downward slice, even the increased resistance when a larger blood vessel was cut - confirmed by glancing up at the work at hand and seeing the woman mopping a spurt of blood. He only really had her word for it that there was a difference between feeling what was happening and feeling pain. Reflecting on it, it was true he had no instinct to say "ow", but he did, however, have an enormous impulse to scream "HELP!".

190

After the cutting had finished and he'd watched a lump of himself being placed in a plastic vial he felt each piercing of the needle and the pull of the thread through his remaining flesh. It made him feel sick, and he had a terrible imagining of vomiting there and then, which would in no way have made the situation better. This fresh calamity averted, he lay there a while as she washed up; exhausted, sweaty, humiliated, traumatised, but alive.

He was back at work the next day and in time to say goodbye to Simon, who had got a job in a bank. In his head all the while Ivan went over his trauma again and again, each line of thought punctuated by the knowledge that he was going to be ok. The biopsy had been almost immediate and he'd received the result later that evening. It was entirely benign.

He joined his colleagues at the leaving drinks and was surprised that Simon spent most of his time talking to him. He was keen to keep in touch, and Ivan said he was sure they would bump into each other again. Simon seemed rather emotional at not working with Ivan anymore. It was funny how people could act after a few drinks. Ivan never drank much, and despite Simon's protestations he excused himself early so as not to be home too late. He had a walk planned for the morning.

As he walked home through Mayfair, he reflected on how much he'd enjoyed working with Simon, and how much he would miss him. Simon had always been very pleasant to be with. He liked him very much. Almost with each step, came the creeping realisation that he was in the process of making a mistake. He started to feel that if he kept on walking he would be walking away from an opportunity that had presented itself to him every day, and yet every day he had passed it by, as a matter of routine. He had cheated death - this time - but the thought of dying made it clear how temporary everything actually was. And now, to further emphasise the finality of everything, Simon was going. He realised what he needed to do, and if there was ever a time to do it, it was now.

Ivan stopped suddenly in the middle of the pavement and turned all the way around on his heels to face the way he had come, forcing a disoriented tourist to take evasive action. He felt no guilt, only a little foolish at having neglected his true desires for so long. With growing exhilaration and a sense of purpose he marched quickly - then ran - back in the direction he had come from, to do what he should have done long ago. When he arrived at his destination, he pushed the door open and stood there, momentarily frozen in anticipation of what he was about to do. He looked directly at the slightly startled man standing in front of him, made his request, and the transaction was completed. After all these years, it was his.

Continuing his walk home, the fedora placed elegantly on his head, Ivan walked with bold strides and his head held high. He felt like a new man.

***

Stayin' Alive
Robert Grossmith

Robert Grossmith is a UK writer, born 1954 and based near Norwich. His stories have been widely published, including in *The Time Out Book of London Short Stories*, *The Best of Best Short Stories* and *The Penguin Book of First World War Stories*. He has also published novels and poems and has a PhD on Vladimir Nabokov. He has lived in Sweden, the US and Scotland, working as a teacher of English as a Foreign Language, translator and lexicographer. Further information is available at https://www.goodreads.com/author/show/2965361.Robert_Gros smith.

'This story etches elderly insecurity in sharp, controlled strokes. There is a stark physicality in this work that is masterfully deployed using measured prose to ease out, real, raw emotions.' says Judge Anisha of Robert's entry to Nivalis 2017.

One of the best things about dying, he thinks as he lies in bed pondering the accumulation of missed opportunities and unforeseen consequences that constitute his life, is that eventually everyone you've ever known will die too and there'll be no one left to remember any of the stupid or thoughtless or embarrassing or shameful things you did while you were alive. It's not easy finding upsides to death but this, he thinks, must surely be one of them.

He spends a lot of time these days, far too much time, thinking about death, his own and other people's, though he keeps these thoughts largely to himself. He certainly doesn't share them with Annie, who's too busy enjoying her retirement and their grandchildren and all the other too-late consolations that are supposed to make up for the stealthy or not-so-stealthy approach of an everlasting oblivion. How does it happen that two people who once used to pride themselves on their almost telepathic ability to read each other's thoughts can now have drifted so far apart that each has become virtually a closed book to the other?

He slides his ample body out of bed as quietly as he can, fumbles for the torch he's placed on top of the bedside cabinet and pads barefoot to the bathroom, anxious not to wake Annie, who looks exhausted after the day's exertions. They got to work early this morning, as soon as the flood siren sounded, first barricading the front and back doors with sandbags supplied by a detachment of troops from Catterick, then shifting whatever items they could lift to the upstairs (pity the poor bungalow-dwellers!). They managed to haul one of the sofas onto the living-room table but the other sofa, the older and shabbier of the two, now stands in a foot or more of freezing filthy water.

Luckily they had completed most of the heavy lifting by the time the water started pouring in but they had left the kitchen alone entirely, which means at the very least that the fridge and the freezer will be a write-off – you'd never get them properly clean again, would you? -- maybe the other appliances too. Well, that's all for later. Right now the main concerns are taken care of - the phones and tablets are fully charged and they have spare batteries for the torch and a plentiful supply of candles and tea lights. There is also an old paraffin heater, consigned to the garden shed years ago, which he has managed to coax into a grudging, sputtering, life. The rain has been endless, relentless, monsoon-like for weeks on end – it is still raining now, he can hear it drumming insistently against the bathroom window -- but at least it's not that cold for the time of year.

Some Boxing Day this is turning out to be. He regrets now that they didn't go to stay with their son in Ireland but decided instead on a no-frills Christmas at home in Yorkshire, just the two of them. Well, no-frills is certainly right.

They were given the option of a lift by rubber dinghy to a sports hall in Wetherby, which is being used as an evacuation centre. But whether from some atavistic urge to defend their property (who from? looters? it hardly seems likely) or just from sheer bloody-mindedness they decided to stay put and wait it out upstairs. According to the latest flood report, water levels are expected to continue rising for another day or so before they finally begin to fall. He thinks of his mum and his gran, hard-headed Eastenders who lived through the Blitz and all manner of perils and privations during the War. A flood like this would have been no more than a minor inconvenience to them.

In the bathroom he points the torch downwards with his free hand so as not to risk missing the bowl. It takes him ages to pee these days, he really ought to get his prostate checked out, though he's afraid of what they might find. The proud parabolic arc of his youth has dwindled to a weak sluggish trickle, repeated several times nightly, more like draining a wound than emptying his bladder. When he is satisfied the operation is complete, he opens the bathroom window and takes a look outside. No street lamps of course, just a pearl-button full moon shining serenely down on the silent flooded road with the slanting rain glinting like tracer fire in the moonlight.

Returning to bed, he feels Annie shifting uneasily beside him. A low guttural moan escapes from her lips.

"Sorry, love, did I wake you?"

196

She raises a hand to her chest, fingers splayed on top of her nightdress. "Touch of heartburn, I think. Feels tight." Her voice sounds tight too, strained, reedy.

"All that lifting this morning. Not surprising at our age, bound to take it out of you." She says nothing. "Can I get you something? Glass of water? We've got some Gaviscon in the bathroom, I think."

"Leave it for now," she answers with difficulty. "Maybe it'll go away."

She breathes in short shallow sips, eyelids fluttering, lips pursed. The darkness conceals any further evidence of her distress.

Could it be heartburn? Or something worse? Their last meal was a hurried makeshift affair, a few bits and pieces salvaged from the fridge before the waters claimed it, slices of turkey with salad and pickles. Maybe the pickles.

He settles back beside her, though he knows that sleep, any kind of sleep, is impossible now. Too much on his mind already, and now the added concern of whether Annie's having a heart attack, which trumps all his other worries. Just a matter of getting through the night, surviving till the morning, then he'll phone the doctor and get her checked out. Then it'll just be a matter of getting through the following days and weeks, with the clean-up and all the hard graft that entails. The thought extends itself, unbidden, in his head. Then it'll just be a matter of getting through the years that remain until first one of them, and then the other, gets sick and dies. Then it won't be a matter of anything at all. Life, it seems, is nothing but a series of assault-course obstacles to be overcome in a race that no one ever finishes.

The dark night of the soul, is that what these gloomy thoughts portend? No, let us not over-dramatise here, let us not over-exaggerate as they redundantly say these days. Not a dark night – a phrase he can't help associating more with Batman than St John of the Cross – rather a dim crepuscular evening, a gloaming of the soul.

He recalls a conversation he had a few weeks ago with his friend Gary, a biology teacher also recently retired, over a lunchtime drink at the village pub. Gary's the only person he ever really opens up to these days. He can be completely honest with Gary in a way that he cannot with Annie who long ago grew weary of his glass-nearly-empty pessimism and refuses to give him an audience any longer. Gary on the other hand has an interest in esoteric subjects and welcomes the opportunity for speculative discourse.

"The way I see it," he recalls Gary saying, "life's a lottery and we're all winners. The chances of any of us being here in the first place are infinitesimally small. Think of all the accidents that might have intervened to prevent your mum from meeting your dad, or that might have prevented them from having sex – sorry to be so indelicate! – on the night you were conceived. Not to mention the chances of your sperm reaching the egg among all those countless others sperm trying to make the journey. Multiply that by the number of accidents that might have prevented your grandparents from meeting, and *their* parents, and so on all the way back to the start of the human race. Then factor in all the events that had to occur to create the Earth in the first place, and then life on Earth, and then human life. It's mind-boggling. Every single one of us is a lottery winner, gazillions-to-one chance. And you don't hear many lottery winners complaining." He paused, then laughed, a short staccato bark. "Though I'm sure you'd find something to whinge about if you ever hit the jackpot."

Was Gary right? Is he naturally predisposed to melancholia? Or is it life that's made him so? He hasn't always been such a doom-merchant, it's only during the last few years, since the dread spectre of Old Age appeared on the horizon with its carnivalesque retinue of Decline, Decrepitude and Decay. Who wouldn't get depressed at such a ghastly prospect?

Another fragment of his conversation with Gary returns to him. "Everything's a bonus," Gary said, "everything's a gift. That beer you're enjoying, that's a gift. That full stomach you've got after that delicious pie and chips you just had, that's a gift. The smile on your grandson's face when you lift him high in the air, that's a gift."

"I can't lift him like that anymore. My back."

"Well it *was* a gift when you *could* lift him like that. People wonder what the point of life is," he continued, "as if there should be a purpose to it, a reason for it, a hidden meaning. But isn't it enough that we're alive, this miracle of consciousness, this being here now? Why does everything have to have a point?"

"Fair enough," he said. "But then it's all suddenly snatched away – bam! Gone – as though none of it ever happened. We're here for such a short time."

"Well, I guess that's true. But isn't it easier to lose something you've been given as a free gift, something you had no right to ever expect, than it is to lose something you think you're entitled to?"

Beside him Annie stirs again. The bed springs groan rheumatically as if echoing her discomfort.

"How is it? Feeling any better?"

"Worse," she manages to say. "So tight. My chest. Like a giant hand pressing down on me." And he can see, despite the darkness, that her face bears a glassy sheen of sweat.

"Should I call someone? The doctor? An ambulance?"

She opens her eyes and for the briefest of moments that telepathic connection is back between them again. "Who is there to call?" the disembodied voice says. "The house is flooded, the road's flooded, the village is flooded, half the county's flooded. It's the middle of the night. It's Boxing Day. What are they gonna do, winch me up to a rescue helicopter though an open window? Or load me onto a stretcher and ferry me to dry land in a rubber dinghy? We don't have many options here." All this without a single word being spoken.

"Let me get the Gaviscon," he says finally. "That might help."

He returns to the bathroom and gropes around in the cabinet until he finds the box of pills. He shines the torch on the back of the box – it isn't easy to make out the small print without his reading glasses -- checks to see if there are any warnings or hazard notices. Annie, like many of us, has allergies and dietary constraints. Satisfied, he stumbles back to the bedroom, noticing for the first time as he crosses the landing the distinctly putrescent reek of stagnant dirty water wafting up the stairs from down below.

"Here, take these, love. Chew them, don't swallow." He holds two of the rubbery discs out for her to take. "Says on the box they're suitable for pregnant women and breast-feeding mothers, so they won't do you any harm."

Normally she would find some wisecracking reply to a remark like that but not tonight. She raises her head with effort to take the pills, then lowers it slowly back down. He takes her hand and gives it a gentle squeeze. "Let me know if it gets really bad. If we need to get you to a doctor we will, somehow." An easy promise to make, not so easy to deliver on, but she returns his squeeze all the same.

A jumble of possible scenarios flashes through his mind like a series of alternative endings to a movie. In the scariest of them he's kneeling astride her on the bed, administering CPR or trying to. But he doesn't know CPR, all he can remember about it is a public information film from way back that said you should press down on the heart attack victim's chest using the same rhythm as the chorus to the Bee Gees' 'Stayin' Alive'. He can't see himself doing that. He was never a fan of the Bee Gees.

And once the scenarios have begun, it's impossible to stop them. Fragments from a post-Annie existence like kaleidoscopic shards of coloured glass reflecting him back to himself. A hospital doctor resting a sympathetic hand on his shoulder as he breaks the unbearable news. A well-attended funeral in the village church, his son and daughter returning from their respective foreign outposts (Dublin, Paris) to hold up their grief-stricken dad like a stumblebum drunk. An empty silent house, as if the house itself is in mourning. Bereaving, bereft.

Have to pull myself out of this, he thinks. He needs the loo again, which doesn't make sense because he has drunk nothing since the last time he peed less than an hour ago, so where is it all coming from? Just as well he taught languages. The sciences were never his forte.

Returning to bed, he tries to shift his position as little as possible so as to give Annie the best chance of sleep, but his body is as restless as his mind and he finds it impossible to get comfortable. It reminds him of how he used to feel coming down from amphetamines – the body shattered, the mind still spinning like a top – which he occasionally took as a student when the deadline approached for an essay he would otherwise have been unable to finish. He wrote poorly on speed but at least he wrote fast. He used to get the stuff from a girl he sometimes slept with, whom he treated abominably.

And with that he is off again, interrogating his past, his student self, quizzing him, indicting him, accusing him of all sorts of crimes and misdemeanours, petty and not so petty, like someone kicking up the dust of a building abandoned long ago. Who else but him remembers these things? No one, probably. So why beat yourself up about them? But he does, there's no why or wherefore. Spending all his time either fretting over the vanished past or fearing an ever-receding future.

At some point he eventually does drop off — a fitful sleep but thankfully dreamless — because the next time he opens his eyes it's beginning to grow light. For a moment he's not sure where he is, then full consciousness returns. He swings his head to look at Annie. She's breathing quietly, still alive. Alerted by his movement, she opens her eyes.

"Feeling any better?"

She nods. "I'm fine. It must have just been heartburn."

Relief floods through him like a, well, like a flood.

He gets out of bed, crosses to the window, draws the curtains, looks out. Against all expectations it seems to have stopped raining. There's even a hint of pale blue sky in the far west, a ragged scrap of colour struggling to free itself from the brooding grey clouds. The water level looks to be about the same, the car in the driveway -- which he didn't have time to move -- still submerged up to its wheel arches.

"It's stopped raining." he says.

"Good." She sits up in bed. She looks her old self again, though of course appearances can deceive. "The sooner we can start the clean-up the better."

"You won't be doing any cleaning up. Not till we get you checked out by a doctor."

She doesn't protest.

Perhaps, after all, it makes sense for them to go to the

evacuation centre until things are more certain. He will discuss it with Annie once they are both up; she can be seen by a medic there.

He turns back to the window and the panorama of inundated fields spread out before him, the landscape magically transformed into a fairyland archipelago, the surrounding hillocks and hummocks become temporary islets. Nothing to do now except wait till the floodwaters drop and the clean-up can begin. He's already drawing up a mental list of all the things he needs to do, at the top of which is a call to their insurers to arrange for a loss adjuster to visit. No, at the top of which is making sure Annie's all right. Last night was too close for comfort.

He sits down on the edge of the bed, pats the bedclothes above her knees. "Well, love, this'll be a Christmas we won't forget in a hurry, eh?"

She yawns and taps the flat of her hand against her open mouth the way he's seen her do for over forty years. "I'm starving, aren't you?" she says. "What are we going to do about food?"

And just to see her restored like this is enough, just to have the old Annie back again with all her little habits and idiosyncrasies, all her quirks and foibles, just this is enough. Yes, the coming days will be difficult, that goes without saying. But they won't be – and he is surprised at the sudden joy he feels at the recognition of something so simple – they won't be a time of inconsolable loss. Not yet anyway. Perhaps not ever, if he goes first. This at least is something to be grateful for. What should he call it? A temporary reprieve? A stay of execution?

Or perhaps, as Gary would say, a gift.

***

The Dark Dealer in Opposites

Jonah Jones

Jonah Jones was born in Oxford, graduated from Cardiff and worked as a tutor, and audio engineer. Now retired, he lives in Llantwit Major, South Wales. He has had both stage and radio plays produced and a few short stories broadcast and published. He has also had cartoons published and is currently editing a short film he wrote and directed.

He blogs at www.thelonelieststory.com.

Jonah's entry to Nivalis 2017 *The Dark Dealer in Opposites* is a paranormal, philosophical piece, and as Judge Clare says, it is "Unusual, uneasy and darkly alluring".

Now it was the mid-Thirties, a time in limbo when so many things seemed possible; when the far-sighted began to see light after the storm that had brought such horror. Growth was to be anticipated, an end to death and destruction. There was genuine warmth after the frenzied heat of the Twenties, overcompensating for the cold of the European mud. A decade previously he had wondered whether he was as dead as the millions of stupid soldiers lying beneath that sad soil. He needed to break out of the cycle of pointless routine; survival, making a living, finding new friends because all the old ones were dead - tentative, lest his new friends become as dead as the old. So he set out to retrieve a sense of purpose by the very act of travelling. Destinations didn't matter. Anywhere that didn't have cold mud.

Somewhere along the way he met the Dark Dealer in Opposites. He'd heard about him from Alphonso, the flop-house handyman.

'Tell me Alphonso – where can a man get a good game of cards around here?'

'You must meet the Dealer.'

'The Dealer? Does he have a name?'

'I heard it said that his given name is Diego. No one knows. They give him the title Santa Muerte.'

'Holy Death?'

'Si. Nombre loco. He does not deal in death but possibilities, changes, new roads.'

'Is he Spanish?'

Alfonso shrugged. 'His eyes seem not Spanish but who can tell? He speaks with different accents. He speaks all languages. When he speaks, everyone understands.'

'Where can I find him?'

'The Hotel Manticore. Behind the market.'

So it was that Tomasz found the hotel and was directed down the uneven stone steps to the badly lit room where the Dealer held court. There was no sense of foreboding because the man was charming and blessed with a beautiful smile; his flawless white teeth framed by olive skin. Although it was hot in the dark room, the Dealer wore a Panama hat embellished by a shot silk headband with warp and weft of green and blue that shifted colour as the angle of the light changed. His jacket was draped over the back of his chair but he still wore a snakeskin waistcoat, fully buttoned over his pale cream shirt. Those around him seemed hot and uncomfortable but not the Dealer. He was cool, alert, quite dapper and slightly alien. A European man in a warmer climate, as if he had stepped off a trading dhow to stroll the narrow merchant-filled streets of Zanzibar; not speaking, simply observing with eyes the colour of wood ash.

He inclined his head slightly towards the newcomer, picked up the silver-tipped cane which was resting against the table leg and pointed it at the empty chair opposite him.

Tomasz bought fifty dollars worth of assorted chips from the sad-looking woman by the door, who took the cigarette from her lipstick-plastered mouth while she scrutinised the bills under the dim light. Apparently satisfied, she reinserted the cigarette, handed him the chips and returned to reading her magazine at a range of six inches from her eyes.

Tomasz sat down opposite the man at the gaming table who studied his face for a time and then indicated that the ante was five dollars by pushing one red chip from his stack to the centre of the table. He waited until Tomasz had done the same, then picked up the pack of grubby cards. As he shuffled them, he said in a soft voice 'The game is draw. Joker's wild.' He allowed Tomasz to cut them, dealt two hands of five and sat back to watch Tomasz's reaction to the cards by which he was constrained, that charming smile lit by the green-shaded banker's lamp. A few spectators moved closer as Tomasz looked down at the cards, clamping his teeth together so as to show nothing by his expression. A three and a seven of spades, four of hearts, six of clubs and the nine of diamonds. As worthless a hand as it was possible to have. He moved them around against each other to give the impression that he had something worth sorting and then put the three and the four down. He was dealt another two cards; five of hearts, seven of diamonds. A pair of sevens and sevens had always been special to him.

The Dealer hadn't even looked at his own cards. He pushed forward two more red chips and grunted. A little probe; a suggestion of intimidation.

To let him know that the intimidation had been ineffectual, Tomasz looked coldly at the man's face and did the same.

He paused, looked down at his cards and then added another chip to the pot. The Dealer grunted again, looked at his own hand, allowed himself a wry smile and threw them in. The Devil had backed down but had perhaps learned something about his opponent, even though he hadn't paid to see the cards. The evening was becoming interesting.

There was no buck to pass; the Dealer remained fixed throughout the proceedings. This was the way they played it out there. If you didn't like it, you could always bow out. Tomasz decided to stay.

Leaning back in his chair, the Dealer snapped his fingers and pointed to the cards. The sad-looking woman brought three new decks and the Dealer showed one to Tomasz who nodded, so the Dealer broke the seal.

'What do they call you?' he asked as he did so.

'Tomasz. What do they call you?'

'Many names. The Dealer will do, for now.'

That was a point lost as far as Tomasz was concerned. The man knew his name while he was no wiser.

The Dealer dealt three hands onto the cloth and called out 'I have dealt a third hand! Will no one join us for a five dollar game?'

Reacting to that, a man with an exaggerated limp and a sweat-bathed face came to join them at the table. He was as expressionless as the Dealer when the cards were in play but directed a short smile of greeting towards Tomasz each time the Dealer collected the cards from the previous game.

After three games, from which the Dealer took two outright and Tomasz bluffed one, a ginger-headed man who looked nervous as a weasel came to the table together with a tall black man with a shaved head that emphasised his gold earring.

'Call me Quail,' the black man told them. Apart from that he spoke only of the number of cards he required, constantly gazing at whomsoever might be in play. Tomasz gathered the impression that Quail was a traveller, like him. He certainly didn't seem to be part of the Dealer's regular entourage. He stacked his chips carefully in neat piles which implied that he was a tight player.

The weasel, on the other hand, quickly revealed himself as a loose player, even at the early stages of the play; long before he'd had any sort of a chance to assess his opponents. He bet on everything with apparently little regard for the relative strength of his hands. Easy to read, he began losing consistently, evidently believing that Lady Luck was about to smile upon him during the next hand, and then the next. She was lulling everyone else into a false sense of security.

On occasion, the door to the dance floor swung open, the light and the music changing the whole aspect of the gaming room. The shadows of the dancers moved across the walls joyfully, like children at play. Some of the Dealer's entourage would smile as they watched the frolicking. Then the door would close again, returning those around the table to sombre concentration.

Individuals came and went but the entourage moved and made noises like one being. They sniggered and smirked until the Dealer showed some annoyance at their sycophancy and they quietened down. Tomasz began to believe that the Dealer had more respect for his opponent than he had for those that supported him.

He shuffled the cards with easy grace as Tomasz focussed upon the ring on the wedding finger. It was a good tactic to wear a flashy ring, distracting the watchers.

'Fire-opal,' the Dealer told him, rocking his hand so that the light could strike it at different angles to bring out the inner colours. 'See how it shimmers and shifts in the light? That is to remind me of what changes, what stays the same and to know the difference.'

The sweaty one, now named Triberg by Tomasz, was working to some stratagem that was all his own. Every card shown was noted down in a brown book. Numbers and odds and chances of breaks, he was working with some form of mathematical structure, trying to see some pattern revealed in the pages of his book, not looking at the others; not judging their styles.

He would be losing soon, Tomasz reckoned. Mathematics only works to a point. Good players are guided, not bound by it.

The Dealer seemed to know what Tomasz was thinking.

'Of course we know that life is a game but is God playing chess or poker?' He indicated the room and its occupants 'Is this a tableau or a play? Should we study the structure or the changes?'

Fortunately Triberg didn't seem to take the hint. Tomasz smiled at the Dealer. Perhaps they were growing to understand each other. Things began to swing the way of the Dealer and the Wanderer.

The heat was rising in the room. Even so, the Panama remained firmly on the Dealer's head. Tomasz began to wonder whether the man had something to hide, apart from the expression in his eyes when he looked at his cards. Maybe he had horns. The hatband seemed to be closer and further away than the rest of the man, like a rainbow or a peacock's tail. A promise of gold, a lure or perhaps merely an expression of ego.

As the evening wore on, other players came and went, emerging from the darkness and blending back into it, like waves on a moonlit beach. Losing, winning, breaking even but throughout it all, the Dealer sat like some potentate, moving the cards, trying the table, commanding the game.

Sequences of cards and tells. The Devil's Hand, the Dead Man's Hand. Ways of reacting noted and acted upon. Lady Luck moved like a wraith from player to player, smiling or pouting for no reason discernable to those that sat around the table.

'Ach! The Devil's in those cards,' the ginger-headed man said as he stood up, pushing the chair violently away from the table. As he walked away into the surrounding darkness The Dealer smiled at Tomasz. They both knew where the Devil truly sat.

At times, Tomasz found that the action on the table took second place to his awareness of the outside world. There were silences when the cicadas could be heard through the muted music next door. A donkey braying in the distance, the sound echoing down the narrow streets. Someone playing gypsy swing style guitar on an instrument that wasn't quite in tune while someone else tapped out the rhythm on a table. Patterns of sixths and sevenths, minor keys and blue notes throughout, testing the formality of the scales. Sometimes a wailing female voice would join in with songs in a corrupted local version of French.

Triberg left in confusion, still trying to wrest some sense from his book of patterns. Another equally sweaty man joined the players. He played with dollar bills, not chips, licking his thumb before counting them out onto the table.

There were frequent power cuts in those parts. The rats and the rot ate through the cables, allowing the current to leak down to the damp earth. Whenever the light went, Tomasz felt a firm hand close around his own, protecting his cards from untoward meddling. The Dealer had lit a cigar and in the dark times the light from the cigar reflected in his eyes. Tomasz focussed hard, hoping to see the Dealer's hand in that reflection but all he could see were the shifting shapes of the smoke. Red light flooded in from the bar whenever the door was opened, picking out different parts of the room, then returning it to hazy blue as the door was shut again. Even when the lights were working, there were occasions when the room was too dark to judge the expressions on the other players' faces. In those moments they all had to guess what the others were thinking.

There are times when you have to go with what you know and leave the chaos to its own indulgence.

Music came and went, styles changed, drunken voices joined in or fell silent.

Intervals, resonances. Every decision is the death of a possibility.

There was something approaching pandemonium all around them and yet Tomasz was able to remain focussed, save for one factor; a half-caste woman of distracting beauty who moved around behind the Dealer's chair, like a moth around the flame.

Tomasz knew that this place wasn't the same level of reality that past places had been, as if it were the reflection of a reflection. He wasn't trapped and yet how could he leave?

He and the Dealer were holding their own against all the others, so it seemed that the Dealer was interested in moving things forward. 'How is it that you are still alive?' he asked Tomasz while he was shuffling the cards.

Tomasz shrugged. 'Maybe I have a guardian angel.'

Give nothing away, not even your history. The man already has the advantage over names.

The Dealer looked up above Tomasz's head, as if to search for this creature. 'Maybe you have.' He returned to looking at Tomasz's eyes, then the sweat on his brow, the way poker players do, assessing, theorising, wondering how to test the theories. Giving nothing in return.

'Would you say that you were a lucky man, Tomasz?' he asked shuffling the cards, maintaining eye contact as he did so.

'In some matters, not in others.'

'Unlucky in love, perhaps?'

'Perhaps.'

'So – lucky with the cards, therefore.'

Tomasz didn't react to that and so the Dealer continued on his philosophical pathway, addressing the assembly with more than a little pomposity.

'Luck is the ability to react instinctively to circumstance.

211

Intelligence without intellect.'

He was probing, trying to discover more about Tomasz, who held his council in order to keep some advantage. Now he had been made aware of a fundamental difference between them. Luck to him was purely the belief that he was lucky.

The Dealer realised that he was achieving nothing with that topic of conversation but for some reason wished to hold the initiative. He rotated his hand in the light to better show the fire-opal's shimmering colours.

'Change,' he said as he dealt three cards to Tomasz alone. 'We must all learn to deal with change. Look at your cards Tomasz.'

Tomasz did so and then looked back at the Dealer with a quizzical expression.

'Place them on the table, face down.' Again, Tomasz complied.

'Now look at them again.'

He picked up the cards. They were entirely different from the ones he had just seen.

'So now we play with these new rules,' the Dealer informed all those at the table. 'The cards may change as soon as you look away from them.'

Tomasz shook his head and began to collect his chips. This was too rich a game for him.

The Dealer seemed disappointed. 'Surely not too strong for a man who was at Mons.'

Tomasz couldn't move his hands, arms, legs. Prickling coldness swirled through him. How did this man know?

He looked down at the remaining chips in the middle of the playing cloth until he was able to speak, then he stared as calmly as he could at the Dealer. 'I was never at Mons.'

The Dealer knew a liar when he saw one. 'I see. It must have been another Tomasz with a scar on the back of his hand and three moles on his face.' He smiled humourlessly, then pressed the point. 'Another Tomasz who claimed he had seen angels protecting the

British. Another Tomasz who lost all his friends to those angels.'

Unable to move or to avoid that gaze, Tomasz sat back in the chair.

'Angels seem to follow you, Tomasz. Perhaps this time they are on your side.'

Another deal lay in front of him and mindlessly he pushed forward the chips as he looked at his hand without seeing the cards. All he could see was the swirling changes around him and all he could hear was the Dealer speaking with soft sympathy.

'Such demons, your angels must be.'

Now he was playing mechanically and winning although never knowing why.

The Dealer tried to lighten his mood by saying 'You shouldn't spend too much of your time thinking about the past or the dead. They can not be changed,' and sitting back in his chair, the cards ignored for a time. 'I never understood people who study dead things. What can you learn? A stuffed animal is not an animal, it cannot react to changes.'

He followed Tomasz's eye-line to the beautiful half-caste who was swaying to the music.

'Yes, Tomasz, look at her,' he said. 'See how she changes as the things around her change. She is looking upon you with interest Tomasz, even though she belongs to me.'

The woman stopped swaying and looked at the Dealer with a sullen expression as he continued. 'She sees the power in you - don't you my dear? She sees the power flowing from me to you. She is excited by power.'

The woman turned away from the Dealer and walked haughtily away, her beautiful buttocks moulding the tight dress which caused the Dealer to smile even more broadly as he enjoyed the spectacle.

He turned back to Tomasz. 'Women, eh? They suck the power out of you so that they can make babies and then complain that all they have left is your shell. Women are spiders, mosquitoes, leeches, vampires, and we love them as they steal our strength.'

A strange rhyme came unbidden into Tomaz's mind

Good or ill, on God rely

Win or lose, it soon rolls by.

Someone was speaking to him; telling him that he wasn't alone against the Dealer. Maybe it was an angel, maybe one of his dead friends that the Dealer had dismissed as no longer having any relevance.

From that point on, Tomasz began winning,

There was a moment when he saw the woman again. She was standing back behind one of the pillars, half-hidden, looking exclusively at him; his eyes, his hands, his shoulders as he played. He was pleased that she found him so interesting but he kept his pleasure to himself as he returned his attention to the game.

Something had changed as he looked at the Dealer. The eyes were somehow duller, the shadows around them were darker, the face was looking tired. Age seemed to be gaining on him. The Dealer knew that Tomasz could see the weakness creeping into his body.

'I am getting tired,' he told those remaining at the table. Then he turned specifically to Tomasz.

'You have played an excellent game – might I suggest a little change of the wager? One last hand. If you win, I will give you this silver cane and you will never see me again. If you lose, you will become one of these,' he indicated his zombie like henchmen, 'and work for your living until the debt is paid.'

Tomasz nodded and the ten cards were dealt. Two hands. Every other person relegated to the status of observer. Tomasz and the Dealer alone. Tomasz looked at his cards. A pair of kings. He took three and one of those was also a king. He had the three wise men.

The Dealer took two cards and smiled. The bet had already been laid and so the two hands were laid down. The Dealer held a pair of eights. He smiled again as he looked at Tomasz's cards.

'Thank you Tomasz, the lonely one,' he said and then sighed. 'I shall sleep well tonight.'

With a flourish he handed Tomasz the cane as if it were a sceptre and then looked around the women standing behind him.

'You must show Tomasz back to his hotel,' he told the blonde who smiled coquettishly at Tomasz.

'I'll show him there,' said the half caste as she pushed her way forward into the line.

The Dealer smiled at her. 'I thought you'd gone back to your room.'

The smile she returned was sweet as a saw. 'You aren't always right.'

He nodded in acceptance. The woman looked at Tomasz with a questioning look.

'Fine by me,' he said.

He thanked the Dealer and shook his hand.

'You are a good player,' the Dealer told him unnecessarily, 'but you still have some demons to conquer. One day you might be as good as I am. Farewell.'

She took him back to his hotel by streets and squares that made no sense but he was a stranger in her town and so decided to trust her. Once they were together in his room, she opened a drawer in the cabinet and produced a pack of cards, giving Tomasz an uneasy feeling. How had she known they were there?

'Shall I tell your fortune?' she asked him.

'No – I'd rather let things come as a surprise.'

She shrugged and then sat on the bed, dealt two hands face up and asked him to explain to her why he was so good at cards. Another voice whispered 'Don't tell her' and so he fudged the issue. Inspiration, luck, judging by the expression of the hands, not the face.

Seeing that she was not going to get anywhere in that direction, she put the cards to one side and smiled at him. Since she showed no sign of continuing the conversation or of leaving, he moved closer to her and touched her neck, sending her breathing sweetly out of control. She arched her back and gasped as he kissed her collar bone, then stood up to let her dress fall to the floor.

In that passion they had no separate existence. She was part of him. She was his driving force and its dissipation.

Afterwards she became separate as they lay together smiling, she curled alongside him, he watching the ceiling fan circling and sucking the smoke from his cigarette.

In the morning there was no sign that she had ever been there, save for her musk lingering on the sheets. He looked at himself in the dirty mirror. The moles on his face had changed their position, offering a new pattern for interpretation.

Even I am not a constant. How does this construction know that it must maintain itself while all the material of its construction changes? Why should this thing be the same as it was yesterday?

He was looking at the mould into which his substance might be poured and out of which that substance might flow. Now he could live with demons and angels.

In the streets outside, the harsh daylight was both revealing and dazzling. Tomasz needed to assure himself that the previous evening hadn't been a fantasy, so he walked through the market to find the Hotel Manticore again. The exterior looked the same but as soon as he went inside it was as if it was a different place. Nothing was familiar. The steps down to the gaming room were no longer there.

Members of the hotel staff were moving the tables around. He sat at one which they had finished shifting and ordered a café cortado.

When the waiter brought it to him he asked him why they were shifting the furniture.

'There is to be dancing tonight Señor.'

'Did you serve me yesterday?'

'I don't think so Señor – I am new here.'

After lunch he found himself confused but strongly set as he walked the narrow streets shaded by the jacarandas. Just once in a while, he longed for the sound of rain on trees but mostly he was able to accept the bleak, dreary heat. Homeland continued to hold too many horrors for him.

A lively funeral passed by as he sat next to the fountains and on the coffin rested a Panama hat with a shot silk hatband that shimmered and shifted as the angle of the light changed, like the carapace of a scarab, set in such a way as to confuse attacking predators. A peacock's tail. A rainbow.

He smiled as he realised that he still didn't know whether the Dark Dealer had horns. Maybe he wasn't even dead, maybe he wasn't in the box.

Thunder clouds were forming across the strait and a capricious gust of wind blew the Panama from the coffin and into the watching crowd. A boy picked it up and laughed as he tried it on his head. The hat was too big and he couldn't see until one of his friends knocked it into the air.

Innocent laughter. A scramble. Another child is wearing the hat, another gust, flying hat, hat falls, a third child takes up the prize and runs with it for a while until he is also dispossessed. A fourth and a fifth. Now begins a squealing tune from a reeded pipe somewhere on the roof tops above them to draw the chase into a dance. The wailing reed is joined by the ringing thump of a drum, doubled and trebled by the resounding walls. A new heartbeat for the one so recently stilled. The sombre faces in the crowd have lightened. Some laugh as they watch the frolicking as they had the night before. All engrossed save one.

One of the cortège wasn't watching the children; he was looking straight at Tomasz. An androgynous face with a slight smile. The figure crossed his arms across his chest and flapped his fingers to resemble little wings attached to his shoulders, then bowed.

He heard the words 'Don't let her know that you know me,' and he knew that his guardian was no angel. It was a demon and it wasn't alone.

The people and the coffin moved on. The thunderstorm broke across the mountains and dusk came down like a roller blind. Following one glorious minute of sunset, the sky was black and shot with sudden stars. Tomasz walked for a while along the harbour wall, watching the ships come and go, then set off to find the game.

There was another hotel where the Hotel Manticore had been. Not a modern building but one that appeared to have been there for centuries. The previous evening it might have done but in his new way of being, the fact didn't surprise him.

'What is the name of this place?' he asked the man at the door.

'The Xanadu,' he was told.

At the gaming table he faced the Lady Dealer. She passed the old pack to one of the people while watching his eyes. Perhaps she could detect the changes. If she could, she didn't show it. As she told him 'If you care not for your future, we must play for your present,' another voice was telling him insistently that she bluffed too often.

'What happened to the other dealer?' he asked her.

'There is no other dealer, Tomasz.' She held forward her hand to show the fire-opal ring on her wedding finger, split open a fresh pack and began to shuffle the cards with a dealer's expertise.

He watched her as she faced him. She seemed so cool and so prim under that dark green blouse under the snakeskin waistcoat but he could recall the soft body beneath those layers. He felt the warmth of her, saw the rounded breasts unconstrained and enjoyed the sight and the smell of her dusky skin in the shifting light reflected from the ceiling fan above the bed. Wave upon wave.

The object of his attention handed the pack to him to cut.

'Now - what stakes shall we offer each other today, Tomasz?' she asked with a menacing smile.

The crowd was gathering, giggling and smirking. He should have felt fear or at least foreboding, but as before, there was no suggestion of either. Unclear though it might appear as yet, there would be a solution to the rising chaos and for the present he had demons on his side.

The game was truly about to begin.

The pack was cut and he handed it back to her. Then he placed the cane on the table.

'My name isn't Tomasz. That was someone else who died last night. I am called,' he thought for a while, 'Enrico. Enrico will do for now.'

***

She

Rahel Saadya

Rahel Saadya holds an MFA from Goddard College and doctorate from Columbia University. Sara Pritchard selected one of her short stories as finalist for the New Letters Alexander Capon Prize in fiction. She is finalist for First Publication with Soundings Review, Honorable Mention with Glimmer Train, and three-time semi finalist for the Pirate Alley Faulkner Fiction Award. She is recipient of an Arts Fellowship from the Drisha Institute.

"Effective and touching, dealing with its subject matter in a refreshing and individual way" says Judge Clare about *She*.

She likes how he laughs. Sissy like, a little maudlin. "Whatever *she* wants today," he says, twirling a piece of her hair.

"Wow. My hair is a special person," Ellen says, her first day on the job in a beauty salon in downtown Phoenix, arriving only yesterday from Boston where she lived her entire life. She looks at what's left of her dirty blonde hair. Glad that it's going. Such a cliché. *She* deserves better.

"She is, you know. Gotta respect her," Horatio says.

Ellen looks in the mirror, uncrosses her legs, stares at Horatio. She was raped two years ago, her sophomore year in college, a fact that never escapes her. Yet here she is letting this unknown man flit around her, creating a silver mess of her hair, foil concealing gold hair dye. He looks like an angel, a little pudgy, deliberate in how he talks, a pool of light around him. She sees how he's left the tips of her hair out of the foil for a different colour.

"Tell me your life story," Horatio says.

"Yours first," says Ellen.

"Well, this is my third salon. I started in Austin where I learned everything—"

"More than that," Ellen says.

"Well, there's Grandma from Cuba, Grandpapa from Puerto Rico. You know, Grandpapa hit Grandma, and Grandma hit my Ma."

Ellen pulls her head away. "Not you. You didn't get socked up? Did you?"

"No, little tiger. I stay safe. Only sweet love for me," he says, hands on her shoulders. "Now relax that neck."

Horatio moves behind her. He flashes his palms two times. Ellen knows that means a 20 minute wait for colour and highlights to process. Horatio throws her a kiss.

Ellen stares into the mirror. She opens her eyes wide. She misses her parents. They don't live together anymore. Not after

223

what happened. Her father is overly emotional; that's what her mother says. Her mother is too controlling, says her father. Ellen likes how he checked in on her, coming over the house when her mother wasn't home. But he can't do that anymore. He'll have to count her Girl Scout badges all by himself. Of course, he'll keep telling her how much life owes her back. She thinks that's total crap. Of course, she can't tell him.

"Time," says Horatio. He bends over her. She sees a bald spot at the top of his head. "I'm a reinvention of myself," he says, peeking into a few of the foils. "That's why I can reinvent you."

Ellen blinks at him. She wonders how much of a renovation he can do on her with most of her life gone already.

Horatio motions her to sit and bend her head back into the sink. She feels him peel back the foils, rinse the hair, soak each strand, press in his thumbs to melt her forehead, scratch the dings out of her skull one by one. He floats a towel over her head, hand on top, escorting her back to the seat.

He twirls her around in the chair. She can't see. She feels tugs, the sound of him clipping away. She closes her eyes, imagining scissors dangling in the air. The ends are the important thing.

Horatio turns her back to the mirror. Cuts through her hair on one side making some sort of triangle. He picks up a razor. Sizzles everything off above the opposite ear. Applies paint of the earth at the tips, bright green in quick blots. Repetitively applied. He moves away. Ellen stares at the new asymmetrical *she*.

"What do you think, fellow hairstylist?" he asks. "Did I get all the edges?"

"Do I get to do you next?" Ellen squirms in her seat.

"Got a client coming in. We need pastries. Don't you think?"

"Think about what you want me to do when I favour you back," Ellen says.

"I wanna be loved," Horatio says. "Doesn't everybody?"

He spins her around, gives her a mirror to look at the back. His hands lay heavy on her shoulders. Too close. But he doesn't know. This is how it started, before she was chased, pinned down.

Horatio doesn't know she was chased from behind.

"I do a great haircut and wax," she says.

"Ouch. Not today, beautiful one," Horatio says. "She doesn't need another haircut so soon," he says, holding out a piece of his hair.

"Can I help with the client? I mean, what else can I do?" She was hoping for tips to pay back her mother for sending her here. Besides, sanity comes from keeping busy.

"Wait until afternoon," he says, checking his watch. "You'll be busy as hell. I'll be back."

Ellen paces around. Sits in the waiting area, fingers fake flowers in a vase. Strolls in back, watches two manicurists file their own nails. They say they don't speak English when she tries to talk to them. She retreats into one of the rooms used for waxing and massages. She needs light. She walks back out front and changes the CD player, playing some sombre soul music.

She stops. Goes back to her station and pulls out a pen. A blue pen with well saturated ink. She goes back to the coffee area, pours herself a fresh cup. She takes the pen. Presses down. Finds another spot. *Awe*, that's a spot that burns. She applies greater pressure. Her body offers endless possibilities—her thighs, her stomach, the bottoms of her feet. But it's her wrists that are visible today. White and coy. Turned palm side up. She drives the pen in. The tip splits her skin, blue swelling everywhere. She waits until she sees blue ink under her skin.

Blue squirts everywhere, onto her jeans, onto the floor. Good thing there's napkins close by. She sops up all the blue. She hopes before Horatio comes back. The Styrofoam cups stacked up for customers remain pristine white.

A month ago, Ellen's mother mentioned Pam, a second cousin once removed, who recently moved to Phoenix to be with her veterinarian boyfriend.

"Now that seems like a nice way to get started again," her mother said.

225

"Who's Pam?" Ellen asked.

"She came to your confirmation. Don't you remember?"

All Ellen remembers is how hard the Bishop hit her face. Sister Mary Kathryn said that might happen. Otherwise, how would Ellen know she was an adult? If adulthood began at age 12, she sure made such a mess of it in just one decade. No nun ever struck her. Why were men so violent?

A week later, Ellen's mother presented the idea of her living with Pam. "Isn't that nice she invited you?" her mother said.

"For what, Mom. A three-way? I'm not into that," Ellen said.

"Oh, come on, Ellen. This is just what you need. Get out of here. Start over. Don't you think it's nice of her to offer?"

Ellen knew it was all a lie, all her mother's idea. But why? They were waiting for a court date for her to testify against the second rapist in her case, that preppy asshole, that pig, privileged enough to get everything deferred forever before serving time. Why move to Phoenix when she'd be needed back in no time for a trial in Boston? Or, maybe she wouldn't be needed. Ellen's dream scenario. *That* got her to sign on the dotted line. She was moving to Phoenix, getting away from it all. Her beauty school instructor was a friend of the husband of the owner of the salon in Phoenix. She didn't care what the place looked like, she just wanted to get out. She packed and threw out what wouldn't be needed. She left one winter coat in her mother's downstairs closet.

The plane ride over was choppy and long. The furthest west Ellen had been was to Philadelphia. She missed home. Her mother believed in her after all the things she did, fucking up. Her mother told her to not think about herself like that. But she *was* a victim, Ellen shouted back. And she was to blame for what happened to herself. *No guilt, no guilt,* her mother said, charm bracelets tinkling against her hand.

Ellen looked out the window when the wheels locked into place. There were ridges of sand down below, promising a desert. Ahead was a mirage of a city. *Maybe Phoenix?* Buildings looked scattered, in a couple of places, huddled together, tall and proud. How odd, Ellen thought. There was green on the ground. Where did the water come from in a place like this?

Ellen walked in between terminals. She walked on grass. She touched the blades, letting them hit her hand. That's when she decided she liked the colour green.

Pam picked her up in front. Ellen vaguely remembered her when she saw her. Pam was bronzed all over. Her mother said they graduated from high school together. But Pam looked younger. She was smiley, throwing her arms around Ellen.

"So where does all this grass come from?" Ellen asked.

Pam laughed. "We pipe it in. The water, that is. Weird, right?"

Ellen sat back, watching Phoenix out the car window. Trees in cement canisters stood by every storefront, along every sidewalk. Misty water floated over everything, even entrances to buildings. The irrigation system must be massive, Ellen thought. But how did they get the water to leap up? There must be more water piped into Phoenix than around Boston. Totally unfair. Some brilliant dude must have thought of this, because it was always men who wanted control, however violently, grabbing with their hands, funnelling water from who knows where to make a city in the middle of the desert.

After a wide intersection, the scene changed. It looked more like the suburbs. "Where are we?" Ellen asked.

"Still in Phoenix," Pam said.

Ellen looked around at rows of low houses surrounded by long narrow yards covered with grass, filled with trees, misty water everywhere. Kids ran outside with their mothers, maybe their nannies, jumping into swimming pools, coming out for a second to go to the bathroom or eat something. Ellen imagined what her hand would feel like skimming the top. The sun was hitting her face, heat evaporating into her mind. She closed her eyes, wishing for the mist that rose above the ground.

The car stopped. Ellen opened her eyes. A good-looking dude was at the car door. He opened it like a porter. Only he reached down to kiss Pam, and what porter does that? Ellen figured he must be Mike. Her mother told her Pam dropped her big-time job as an NBC news anchor in Rockefeller Center to be with him after a year of long-distance dating. Ellen decided she couldn't exactly hate Mike living under his roof. Mike looked older than her mother and Pam, even though they all went to high school together. Ellen liked knowing he was a veterinarian. She liked animals, but like her father, neither was allowed to keep pets because her mother forbade it. A man who took care of animals, Ellen decided, must be a nice man, even though he was a man.

"We're here," Pam said. "Are you ready for lunch?"

"If it's not too much trouble," Ellen said. "It's so nice for you to take me in. Tomorrow work starts and I want to pay you back. My mom, too. But she doesn't want anything. You know how she is." Ellen felt Pam's hand on her lap.

Ellen thanked Mike for bringing in two rolling luggage bags and her backpack. He placed them down in the room she would be staying in. He put his arm around Pam as the three of them walked back downstairs. He kissed Pam full on the lips. Ellen sat in the farthest corner of the kitchen, rocking herself back and forth. Pam and Mike stood side by side at the refrigerator, pulling out bread, fruit salad, a platter of assorted sushi like a relay team.

Her mother said Pam was the lucky one, never married, reconnecting with a popular boy from high school at a class reunion, one of the boys who never talked to them. That was two years ago, the same year Ellen started college. Some things last, some things don't, Ellen thought. Like her parents' marriage. Her father turning pathetic, her mother said. Her mother becoming too needy, her father said when she told him her mom took her to see the same therapist she saw.

"Don't want you to be startled," Mike said. "Hope you brought a bathing suit. We eat meals in the pool."

When Ellen comes home to Mike and Pam's after her first day at the salon, she throws her backpack down on the floor. Not enough customers, not enough tips. Horatio told her to wait for the fall when the streets would be filled with tourists.

Ellen blinks at herself in the mirror; her hair frosted gold and green. Not the puke colour, but the colour of grass. She picks up her backpack, straightens the rug.

"Hello?" Ellen says. She hopes Pam and Mike won't say anything. She hopes her mother told them to go easy on her.

Ellen eats dinner sitting on a bar stool in the low section of the pool. Her bare knees keep hitting white cement tiles, her elbows braced up on the sidewalk that runs along the perimeter. Her butt soaks in the blue water, her nose fixed on chlorine from the pool water and garlic from the food.

"So, who's this Horatio?" Mike says, sitting a foot away from her. "How'd he get your hair so gold? Man, you're like a million watts."

"Leave her alone. She's only been here one day," Pam says.

"Two days," Mike says.

Ellen nods, rocking back and forth on the stool. She likes Mike less than she did yesterday. Mike and Pam start feeding each other with their day. Pam's searching for work, which Ellen fears is all in vain, what with Pam's experience and a city like Phoenix. What news station even exists that needs Pam's major network talent? Ellen starts nodding off as Mike goes on about his routine dog and cat neutering. Until he starts talking about some emergency snake that came in with hardening skin.

"Doesn't it just fall off?" Pam asks. "You'd think the owner would know that."

"That's the point," Mike says.

"I'm sure there's skin crème at the shop that can help with that," Ellen offers.

Pam and Mike ignore her. They begin hugging each other, feeding each other food. Ellen stoops to scratch her leg, right where she bled clear through to the bone. Brown-red blob soaking through, green like gangrene, but not that, the doctor said. The fact there's hardly a scar has no bearing, no relevance. Ellen starts to gag.

"Hey, drink this," Mike says, spilling water into her throat.

"My god, are you okay?" Pam wipes Ellen's cheek.

She feels like a baby, all protected. Her cheeks are hot.

Ellen dreams about her children. She has two, a boy and a girl. She wraps her legs together, hiding that part of her where they might come from. Light wakes her up. She's fully clothed. Sheets tucked under her.

She makes her way to her second day of work without breakfast, only coffee. She's rarely hungry. Is breakfast even a required meal? The salon isn't the same place as yesterday. All new faces, scads of women hanging out in the waiting area. A red-headed stylist says it's Horatio's day off. Ellen wonders why he didn't tell her.

Rita, the receptionist, hands her a list of clients and what they are in for.

"They're all mine? Wow. Looks like I won't even have time for lunch."

"Your first is scheduled for two hours. Not here yet. Be sweet about it," Rita says. "Don't let the next one wait. Smush them together." Rita uses her hands to demonstrate. "Like you do with a sandwich. That's how you get big tips and get them both back."

Ellen takes a breath, looks outside. There's heavy mist at the door of the big hotel across the street; a woman comes out, newspaper fanning her head. Ellen sees bra-straps drooping over her shoulder, a tank top halfway tucked into shorts.

"I think that's the woman," Rita says. "Remember what I said."

The woman is in for the works—a haircut, colouring, blow-dry, manicure, pedicure, and bikini wax. A way to retreat, she says, from the heat outside.

Ellen sits the woman down, putters around, looking for wax and nail polish, the colour potions she felt half familiar with, scissors that feel clumsy in her hand. Rita stops her, holding a razor and several pairs of clippers for her to choose from, shows her a closet where all the supplies are, for anything she needs.

At half past 11, Ellen is mixing the woman's colour, nails and wax done. There's a vibration in her pocket, her phone. It's her mother with the lawyer, Mr. Frisk.

"Is this convenient?" he asks Ellen.

"Well—."

"That means *yes*," her mother says.

"I can get an earlier trial date," Mr. Frisk says.

"No way." Ellen hears whispers. She knows Mr. Frisk is twisting his eyebrow, pressing his lips together to avoid all-out protest. "Are you guys alright there?"

"Just explaining to Mr. Frisk where you're coming from, honey," her mother says.

Ellen feels pressured, like someone coming from behind. She doesn't want a pen anymore. She wants a knife.

"I thought you wanted to get this thing done and over with as soon as possible," Mr. Frisk says. "That's not the case anymore?"

"No."

"Ellen, why not? Don't you think this would be better if Mr. Frisk arranged it? The sooner, the better. Isn't that what we discussed?"

"Not anymore. Not now. I got to go. I have a customer."

Ellen presses her phone off. She busies herself, dropping in colour, squirting in fixing solution. She needs this gig to work out. There's no time to fly back to Boston. She wants the whole thing to go away. No way she wants to look at him. Maybe he won't show up, like he did when they set bail. Maybe his lawyer will come in his place, or his father, or a priest. Someone else in his place to listen and plan, make him out as the victim, and she the jerk. Maybe that's why her mother wanted her out here in the first place, a job without her talking to anybody, her looking like someone normal.

She watches the colour congeal.

Ellen feels odd watching Pam and Mike in the pool during

dinner. They're acting like she isn't there, or that she can't be looking. She's never seen anyone, not even her parents, try to fit inside each other's bodies like Pam and Mike do. Ellen moves her quiche and salad around in her plate.

"That's enough," Ellen says. Pam and Mike look at her. Ellen waves. They smile and go back to feeding each other from the same plate.

Ellen pushes herself off her stool and moves to the high end of the pool. The water is up to her elbows; the drain forces her knees away from the sides. This feels safer, staying at a distance.

What is it about them, Ellen wonders. They carry that no-worries-look about them. What are they trying to prove? Ellen can't imagine love like this, wanting to be inside someone else's body.

Lucky Mike. Pam moves all the way from New York City to be with him, giving up a great job, maybe her entire career, never mind an apartment in the greatest city in the world, just to be with him. Ellen knows they'll be off to bed soon, rubbing up against each other in a way she doesn't want to think about. Things are set between them. Really? Isn't Mike there to collect all the dividends of a live-in girlfriend? Sooner or later, Pam will want her old life back, unwilling to risk it long-term with a dude who never stooped so low as to talk to her in high school.

Ellen lifts up the edges of her hair, the part tinted green. She wants to smoke it. But she doesn't know anyone or anywhere to buy grass from. A guy on her floor in college sold it. She should have tried it then. Maybe Mike knows? Maybe Pam? Look at them hanging out in the low section of the pool, the baby side. She doesn't smell any marijuana on them or in the house. What are the rules about smoking pot for veterinarians and unemployed TV news announcers anyways? Would anybody in the state of Arizona care?

Ellen counts out singles, fives and tens at Pam and Mike's dining table, along with towering stacks of quarters, nickels and dimes. Damn the pennies. She throws them in a pile. For two whole weeks, she's worked at the salon, earning more than $900 in tips. She's rich. Maybe she'll go away, go incognito. Avoid the trial, her mother, Mr. Frisk.

She leaves early to start her commute. Three buses to go the 10 miles between Pam and Mike's house and the salon. The heat is suffocating like a sauna at each of the bus stops. Until someone presses a magical silver button at the centre beam of each bus stop. A steady mist of water soaks down on her. She closes her eyes, mouthing 'thank you' to whoever presses the silver button. Because she can't do it herself. She doesn't deserve to.

Her mother and Mr. Fisk call her every day to commit to flying home for the trial. But she can't. She can't face him. She can't do the brave thing, the right thing. Her father asks her why not when he calls on the phone.

By the time she gets to work, she's in a fit. She catches Horatio looking at her, running after her as she ducks into the colour mixing room for a place to cry.

"Stop running," he says, catching up to her. "What's up? Tell me."

"No," she says, refusing his arms, the shoulder he wants her to rest on.

"Yes," he says, his arms hunched over in the air, ready to catch her.

"Can't," she says.

"Can," he says. "You know you're safe with me," he says. "I'm not some straight guy, macho, with some ulterior motive. Come on, Ellen."

She looks up at him. "Can't."

"Let's not start that again." He flicks his hair back. "When you're ready. Find me. We'll talk."

Ellen nods her head. "Do you have a boyfriend?" she asks him.

"Sure do. He's in London. I'm seeing him next week."

"He's coming here?"

"I'm going there."

"Oh."

"Don't look so sad. I'm here now." She watches Horatio start to press toward her. But he stops. "I want to hug you, but you never let me," he says. "He's taking me someplace special. Told me to bring a tux." Even in the dark, Ellen sees him smile.

"A tux?" Ellen says. "Have you had sex yet?"

"Mind your own business," he says. He starts to turn and then looks back. "I'll tell you when you're ready to tell me everything, Ellen." He walks out the door.

Ellen looks for a pen.

Ellen closes the salon that night, sweeping the floor, counting the money, imagining it is her place, her store. Will she ever have enough guts for something like that? Maybe if she wasn't raped. But if she wasn't raped, she'd never be here. She'd be graduating college, going to some fancy job. She wouldn't blink men away.

She feels safer in the salon than anywhere else. Smiling customers, tipping customers. There's Horatio, the receptionist, and others who are becoming friends. She wished the salon stayed open late. She'd never have to leave. No going home to eavesdrop on Mike and Pam in the pool. Maybe she'd creep home at lunchtime, to eat alone with Pam. Take a hit of something naughty together. Vodka straight up. A line of coke. Intergenerational female sex.

Ellen comes home to a package from Mr. Frisk. A synopsis of the case, a photo of the crime scene—blood everywhere. A polite plea for her to cooperate. Ellen calls her mother. Her mother isn't home. Is she out dating? Is she out with Mr. Frisk?

Ellen's on the job five weeks. She has a file deck with contact information for 56 clients—22 in the greater Phoenix area, nine from overseas, two from Mexico, 23 living and working within easy walking distance from the salon. She's banked over $2000 in tips and pay. She's giving none of it away. Not re-paying her mother, or

Pam and Mike. She likes looking at the numbers piling up in the bank. She could disappear, go anywhere she wants, with this kind of cash.

But she likes the salon too much. She likes her gay male clients best. Looking for nails and hair, or a wax. They must know how much she needs them for her to rip off hair from their chests, backs, derrieres. She loves the rugged types with thick red beards, hair hard to yank off. She has to muscle it, fight it off, grinning while she does it to them. They're all sailors, able to take whatever she puts into it. Nothing like the swimmers who ask her to be careful around their tan line.

"How 'bout a wax," Ellen asks Horatio.

"No way. You have a reputation, you know."

Ellen squints at him. "I get great tips."

"Because you're thorough. At a cost."

"You're not into S&M, are you, Horatio?"

"I thought you were my friend, Ellen."

"How did you end up gay? Did some priest or uncle abuse you?"

Horatio's mouth opens. He heads to the staff rest room. Ellen follows, shuts the door, stands close to him, hums in his ear.

"Doesn't make things better," he says. "How can you be so cruel to me?"

Ellen looks down. She sees his hands shaking. She reaches over to him. "I'm sorry," she says. "I didn't mean to."

"I've gotta go," he says, dropping her hand. Ellen grabs his back.

"Gotta think," he says. "Why you do the things you do? You know everything about me. But I don't know anything about you."

Ellen looks at the back of his head, black curly hair coming from somewhere in his family. She thinks about the bully grandpapa, his sisters and mother, his boyfriend thousands of miles away.

"Well, Ellen?" Horatio asks.

"There's nothing to know about me," she says. "You don't want to know."

"Maybe I do," Horatio says.

She gulps. "Tonight I will," Ellen says. She doesn't want to lose her best friend in Phoenix.

They meet after work at a little Mexican place with super-hot food. Horatio's favourite. She'll pay the bill. But what's she going to say? How she feels crazy all the time? Wants to hit people, bump into them while she's walking by, inflict pain to get the anger out?

"I thought a lot about you after that first day, you know. After I messed up your hair for you," Horatio says. "You grew on me."

Ellen laughs to break the silence.

"I knew you liked me, too," Horatio says.

"Well, yeh," Ellen says.

"So, tell me. What's going on with you? No bullshit. Okay?"

"What do you mean?" Ellen watches Horatio nod his head up and down, upper body hunched over, elbows on the table.

Horatio reaches over and picks up Ellen's arm. "I mean this," he says. "What's this?" He points to the blotch of blue just under her skin. He squeezes the part that's red, where she's dug her pen in. She winces. "You can get an infection, you know," he says. "Maybe you already have one. Why are you doing this to yourself?"

Ellen looks down. This isn't what she expected. She searches in her handbag for a pen. Horatio pulls her hand out of her purse.

"Don't do it. Stop it," Horatio says. "I accept your silence. But that doesn't mean I have to go along with you hurting yourself."

Ellen digs in to her sofritas salad with extra guacamole. She scoopes up salsa with her fingers. She hasn't eaten this much in two years. She looks up. Horatio isn't eating. Her stomach rumbles.

Ellen presses a napkin to her mouth. "Excuse me," she says, pushing her chair back. She runs to the bathroom, and reaches the toilet just in time.

There's a knock on the door. "Ellen, I'm sorry. I pushed too hard."

She opens the door wide enough to see Horatio, and then closes it, retching into the toilet bowl. When her stomach finally settles down, Ellen stands, washes her mouth out and walks back to the table. Horatio is there, waiting for her.

"I'll take you home," he says.

They wait for the bus. Ellen hears laughter from behind. Guy laughs. She hears them coming from behind. She smells the alcohol.

"What's wrong?" Horatio leans into her. Ellen shrieks.

Horatio put his arm around her. "Tell me."

It was late at night. She was walking alone on her college campus. Coming back from a late-night party where everyone got drunk and high, except for her. The wind rustled by. She thought she was alone. She remembered sighing out loud so she could hear herself. But there was coughing. Someone was coughing close by. She turned around. She smelt the liquor from them. Two white guys in hoodies. She didn't know them. But then, she recognized them, slowing down, expecting a hello, an escort home.

"I didn't like the look of those guys," Ellen says. "I should have run."

Horatio looks at her the way he did when he first started playing with her hair. "What makes you think you should have run?" he says.

"I can't. I can't do this," she says.

"Why didn't *she* run?" Horatio says. "Try it that way."

Ellen gulps. She closes her eyes. "*She* knew them. She goddamn knew them. She flirted with them. She wanted to date them, maybe not at the same time—." Ellen cries, blows her nose, tries to compose herself. "They followed her. *She* was walking back to her dorm. They lived close by, already graduated." Ellen opens her eyes. "*She* was in college."

"Go ahead."

"They followed her from—who knows where. It was 2 a.m. Nobody else was around. She didn't understand why they were catcalling her. She walked faster. They caught up to her, grabbed her from behind. Said she had it coming."

"She *didn't* have it coming. That's not true. Say it," Horatio says.

"She's a cunt, a whore. They'd string her up." Ellen remembers her head falling hard on the ground, void of green or water. The push down, the pounding, what she wanted from them. If only they'd asked, maybe one of them. Not this way.

"Don't go quiet on me," Horatio says.

"*She* thought rape was something committed from the front, not from behind," she says. "She didn't know they had a knife."

"They cut her?"

"On the butt. On the calves."

"She's in one piece now, Ellen."

Ellen looks up at Horatio. "They let her go."

"Mother fuckers," he says.

"She told the police who they were, where they lived. They made her go through a fucking line-up just to test her."

"Evidence. They wanted the evidence."

"There's a trial coming up. "

"Good. She needs to speak out."

"One of them had a prior. He's already tried and sentenced. Hope he rots in hell. The other one's out on bail."

"Kidding me," Horatio says.

"Said he was forced into it. Not something he wanted to do."

"Can't the other guy testify against him?"

238

"The lawyer hasn't said," Ellen says. "The guy out on bail is from a rich family. He was a basketball player."

"Does it matter?" Horatio says.

Ellen wipes her eyes. "This is the way it goes. You believe me?"

"Of course I do."

"You really think I can do this? I feel like a mess, Horatio."

"Of course, you can."

"I feel crazy all the time. It's my fault—"

"No it's not—"

"No matter what you or anybody says."

"Come on, Ellen. Punch me. Take it out on me," Horatio says.

"I can't do that. I could never hit you."

"What does *she* want, Ellen?"

"Children, sanity. I guess I'd need to be sane to take care of children. I used to think I wanted to go to college. But I'm okay now. I like what I'm doing. I'll stay at the job and maybe own my own salon someday. You won't tell anybody, Horatio?"

"No one's gonna stop you. No matter what you want. You need to do what you want," Horatio says.

"Okay." She starts to breath.

"Meantime, there's Phoenix for you," he said.

"Is this place for real?'

Horatio laughs.

"Thank you," she says. "For loving me." she says.

"It's the god-awful truth. Wish you were a man, Ellen."

Ellen rocks in her seat. She hates the feeling of sweat across her back and under her arms. Cars drive by, mixing their petrol in with the heat.

She needs to cool down, wants to feel clean. She reaches over and presses the silver button at the bus stop. Moist air simmers around her. Horatio pulls her in. Her face settles in where his shirt is open. She tastes the salt on his skin, the desert melting in the air, the bus coming along the road, ready to take off.

***

ABOUT THE JUDGES

CLARE WALLACE

Clare graduated with a BA in Creative Writing and Cultural Studies at Bath Spa University, and went on to gain a distinction on the MA in Creative Writing. Having worked earlier with Luxton Harris Ltd literary agency, she is currently the Head of Rights and Literary Agent with Darley Anderson, and is scouting for new talent in commercial and accessible literary general fiction and all types of women's fiction. Clare is also building the children's list and is looking for new children's authors and illustrators.

At the Agency Clare represents authors both in the UK and the US including Kerry Fisher, Rosie Blake, Martyn Ford, Cesca Major, Kim Slater, Polly Ho-Yen, Dave Rudden, Beth Reekles, Caroline Crowe and Adam Perrott and illustrators Jon Holder, Clare Mackie, Loretta Schauer and Lorna Scobie.

BRETT ALAN SANDERS

Brett is a writer, translator, and recently retired teacher living in Tell City, Indiana. He earned a BA in Spanish (with an English minor) from Indiana University and an MALS at the University of Southern Indiana. He has been a contributing writer at Tertulia Magazine where for 'Tertullian's Blog' he wrote the occasional column 'Arte Retórica,' and a former columnist for the Perry County (IN) News. In addition he served a brief stint as managing editor at New Works Review and has translated for the literary-arts website Suelta. He has published original essays, fiction, and literary translations in a variety of journals including Hunger Mountain, Artful Dodge, The Antigonish Review, *Confluence: The Journal of Graduate Liberal Studies,* and Rosebud. He has also published a YA novella (A Bride Called Freedom, Ediciones Nuevo Espacio, 2003) and two book-length translations from the work of Buenos Aires writer *María Rosa Lojo* (Awaiting the Green Morning, Host Publications, 2008; Passionate Nomads, Aliform Publications, 2011).

www.brettalansanders.wordpress.com

SANDRA SAWICKA

Sandra is a literary agent and foreign rights manager at Marjacq Scripts (a UK based full service literary agency), and had earlier worked for UK publishers and a variety of placements with agencies. Prior to that she completed two Masters' degrees – in American Literature from Warsaw University and in Publishing from Kingston.

Sandra takes care of the worldwide foreign language rights for all authors represented by Marjacq, and as literary agent she is actively building her own client list which includes Katarzyna Bonda, Paul Crilley and Lauren A. Forry. She is currently searching for great historical upmarket fiction, gothic mysteries, pacey, commercial genre titles, road novels and clever book club fiction.

ANISHA BHADURI

Anisha has spent more than a decade in journalism. In 2012, her first published work of fiction featured in the Random House title 'She Writes: A collection of Short Stories'. Following a decade-long stint with *The Statesman* in India, she is currently deputy chief editor at *China Daily* in Hong Kong. The first Indian woman to become a *Konrad Adenauer Stiftung* Fellow, she was a visiting faculty to the Statesman Print Journalism School, Kolkata for nearly five years. In 2009, Anisha won the first prize in a national literary contest for women writers organized by the British Council in India. In December, 2011, she was conferred the Pradyot Bhadra Young Journalist Award for Excellence by Pracheen Kala Kendra. In 2013 Anisha was one of the judges for the Love on The Road short story competition hosted by Malinki Press, and has been on the judging panel of Fabula Press since its inception.

THE EDITORIAL TEAM

Editor

Anirban Ray Choudhury co-founded and was for over a decade the editor of the Quill & Ink, a webzine devoted to the arts. He was also a columnist for the online knowledge portal www.buzzle.com writing on a variety of subjects, ranging from literature to science. A published poet in both online and offline media, he had helped set up Pen Himalaya, one of the first webzines for poets and writers from Nepal. He is actively engaged in several literary projects, and is the guest editor for the Hourglass Literary Magazine from Bosnia.

A finance professional from India, Anirban currently lives with his journalist wife and school going son in Hong Kong, where he prefers to take his breaks from the perpetual monotony of juggling with digits and numbers by delving into football, literature and the arts (though not necessarily in that order).

Associate Editor

Anne Foster has been an illustrator, a decorator for a harpsichord manufacturer, a teacher and now, a writer. She holds a diploma in design from the Salisbury School of Fine Arts in England, and a degree in literature from the prestigious Université Paul Valéry, Montpellier, France. She has authored a book in French "Le Jardin de Sable" (available on Amazon), and before coming on board with Fabula Press, she had twice been published in our contest anthologies.

Anne lives with her family in France, where she is working on her second full length novel.

82674465R00143

Made in the USA
Columbia, SC
05 December 2017